	DATE DUE		

GRAY GHOST

ALSO BY WILLIAM G. TAPPLY

The Stoney Calhoun Novels *Bitch Creek*

The Brady Coyne Novels *Out Cold*
Nervous Water
Shadow of Death
A Fine Line
Past Tense
Scar Tissue
Muscle Memory
Cutter's Run
Close to the Bone
The Seventh Enemy
The Snake Eater
Tight Lines
The Spotted Cats
Client Privilege
Dead Winter
A Void in Hearts
The Vulgar Boatman
Dead Meat
The Marine Corpse
Follow the Sharks
The Dutch Blue Error
Death at Charity's Point

Other Fiction *Second Sight* (with Philip R. Craig)
First Light (with Philip R. Craig)
Thicker Than Water (with Linda Barlow)

Nonfiction *Gone Fishin'*
The Orvis Pocket Guide to Fly Fishing for Bass
Pocket Water
Upland Days
Bass Bug Fishing
A Fly-Fishing Life
The Elements of Mystery Fiction
Sportsman's Legacy
Home Water
Opening Day and Other Neuroses
Those Hours Spent Outdoors

GRAY GHOST

WILLIAM G. TAPPLY

St. Martin's Minotaur ⚏ New York

GRAY GHOST. Copyright © 2007 by William G. Tapply. All rights reserved. Printed in the United States of America. No part of this book may be used or reproduced in any manner whatsoever without written permission except in the case of brief quotations embodied in critical articles or reviews. For information, address St. Martin's Press, 175 Fifth Avenue, New York, N.Y. 10010.

www.minotaurbooks.com

Design by Dylan R. Greif

Library of Congress Cataloging-in-Publication Data

Tapply, William G.
    Gray ghost : a Stoney Calhoun novel . William G. Tapply.—1st ed.
      p. cm.
    ISBN-13: 978-0-312-36303-1
    ISBN-10: 0-312-36303-6
    1. Amnesiacs—Fiction. I. Title.

    PS3570.A568 G73 2007
    813'.54—dc22

                                        2006052301

First Edition: March 2007

10 9 8 7 6 5 4 3 2 1

For Marshall S. Dickman
(not just a fictional character)

ACKNOWLEDGMENTS

Many people contributed directly or indirectly to this book, whether they know it or not. If they don't know it, here's a reminder:

All of the readers and critics who claimed they really liked *Bitch Creek* convinced me to try to write another Stoney Calhoun story.

Striper fishing and sea-duck hunting with Keith Wegener in his duck boat all those times familiarized me with the tides and weather, the birds and fish, and the islands and sand bars of Casco Bay, not to mention the legends and lore of backwoods Maine. We've had some fun, too, haven't we?

Jason Terry did most of the local research for me. He also helped me to bat around ideas and scenarios, some of which went through the meat grinder of my imagination and emerged, inevitably, as important elements of this story.

My editor, Keith Kahla, took a chance, and then gave me his standard—brilliant—editorial criticism.

Fred Morris, my agent, went above and beyond the usual call of duty with this one.

Vicki Stiefel is my anchor, my inspiration, and my true love. She keeps me going.

Thank you all.

... when the lawyer is swallowed up with business and the statesman is preventing or contriving plots, then we sit on cowslipbanks, hear the birds sing, and possess ourselves in as much quietness as these silent silver streams...

—IZAAK WALTON, *The Complete Angler*

Even at the very bottom of the river I didn't stop to say to myself, "Is this a Hearty Joke, or is it the Merest Accident?" I just floated to the surface, and said to myself, "It's wet." If you know what I mean.

—A. A. MILNE, *Winnie-the-Pooh*

GRAY GHOST

CHAPTER ONE

The alarm in Stoney Calhoun's head jangled at two fifty-five, five minutes before the redundant wind-up clock beside his bed was scheduled to go off. Calhoun's internal alarm hadn't failed him yet, but he still didn't quite trust it.

He lay there for a minute, looking out the window at the woods and sky. The stars were bright up there beyond the pines, and clouds shaped like cigars were drifting over the face of the gibbous September moon. It was a few days shy of the full harvest moon.

He focused on the pine boughs. Not a needle was quivering. Not a breath of breeeze. With luck it would stay that way for the next few hours, and the bay would be flat calm, and they'd find fish working the surface. The bluefish and striped bass were on their southward migration. They moved fast and unpredictably, and sometimes the whole damn ocean seemed empty of fish. When you found them, though, they were hungry and violent and happy to crash a fly stripped fast across the surface.

Clear skies and no wind in Dublin, thirty-odd miles west of the sea, didn't mean clear skies and no wind on Casco Bay, of course. Still, it was a hopeful sign.

Calhoun switched on the light beside the bed. Ralph Waldo, his Brittany spaniel, was curled in a ball and pressing hard against Calhoun's hip. He scratched the dog's ribs. "Hey, bud," he said. "You want to go fishin'?"

"Fishin' " was one of those many magic words that got an instant response from Ralph. He jerked up his head, cocked his ears, and peered into Calhoun's eyes to be sure he wasn't making some kind of cruel joke.

"Hop to it, then," said Calhoun. "We don't want to find Mr. Vecchio already waiting at the landing for us. Kate doesn't like it when the client gets there before the guide."

Ralph yawned, slithered off the bed, stretched, and trotted to the door.

Calhoun got up, turned on some more lights, and let Ralph out. He switched on the electric coffeepot, turned on the classical music station from Portland, and went back into the bedroom to get dressed. He liked his music loud. Music wasn't for background. Music deserved to be listened to, even if you had only one useful ear.

Calhoun found himself humming along, but he couldn't place the composer. Sibelius, maybe. The symphony was lush and melodious, the way he liked it, and he was pretty sure that he used to know it.

He pulled on a pair of old jeans, a flannel shirt, and his Topsiders. Then he let Ralph in and gave him his breakfast. While Ralph was eating, Calhoun loaded his cooler with the ham-and-cheese-on-pumpernickel sandwiches he'd made the night before, a couple of Hershey bars, a few apples, and half a dozen bottles of frozen water. The water served two purposes. You could drink it, and meanwhile it would keep the food cool.

A lot of guides packed beer for their clients, but not Calhoun. He didn't see the point. You could drink beer anytime.

He filled a Thermos with coffee, poured himself a mugful for the truck ride, clicked his tongue at Ralph, and lugged the cooler outside. He hefted it into the truck bed, then opened the door for Ralph, who scrambled into the passenger's seat.

Calhoun went back inside to turn off the lights and the music. He stood there on his deck for a minute, looking up at the black starry sky, happy for the isolation of his little house in the woods. Some wispy clouds were gathering over toward the east, which might mean overcast on the coast. The air smelled cool and clean and piney. At the foot of the slope out back, Bitch Creek gurgled over rocks and gravel, another kind of music that Calhoun paid attention to.

A pair of barred owls were talking back and forth in the woods. *Who-who-ha-whoooooo.* One was calling from behind the cabin, and the answer came from up near the road.

Calhoun put his hands around his mouth and gave his own barred-owl call. *Who-who-ha-whoooo.* That shut them up. He smiled, thinking of those owls trying to figure out where this third party, some new interloping barred owl with an attitude, suddenly came from.

He checked the trailer hitch, made sure all the gear was lashed down and the motor was locked up, then climbed in beside Ralph. He turned on the ignition, found the Sibelius on the radio, and cracked Ralph's window open.

"Let's go have some fun," he said.

Ralph didn't say anything. He was ready to go.

Calhoun munched a doughnut and sipped his coffee as he followed his headlights eastward along the empty road. Ralph stood on his seat with his nose poking out his cracked-open window. The Sibelius filled the cab.

Calhoun always felt especially alert and virtuous when he was on the move in the predawn darkness. The roads were empty of other traffic, and no lights glowed from the windows of the scattered houses and gas stations along the roadside. *I'm awake*, thought Calhoun, *and you're still asleep. I've already started living this day. I've got the jump on you.*

Passages from novels and essays, and sometimes entire poems, had a way of sticking in Calhoun's memory, further cluttering his brain. Now he recalled something Thoreau had said. "The morning, which is the most memorable season of the day, is the awakening hour. Then there is least somnolence in us; and for an hour, at least, some part of us awakes which slumbers all the rest of the day and night."

It was still dark when he arrived at the East End boat ramp. Calhoun didn't wear a watch. He usually didn't see any point in knowing what time it was, but when he did want to know, he always could tell, whether it was by the angle of the sun or the moon or just the quality of the light or darkness. Now, according to his internal clock, it was about four fifteen. Mr. Vecchio was supposed to arrive at four thirty. High tide was around seven. A perfect morning tide for stripers. The sun would rise a little after six fifteen. Calhoun liked to be on the water about an hour and a half before sunrise.

There were a couple of trucks with empty trailers already parked in the lot—fishermen even more virtuous than Calhoun, out on the water already. Or maybe they'd been out all night. Some guys did that, mostly chunkers and deep-trollers and eel free-spoolers. Those guys caught a lot of big fish.

He backed his trailered eighteen-foot aluminum boat, a Lund Alaskan, into the water, got out, unhitched it, tied it off, and parked the truck. Then he let Ralph out and lugged the gear down to the boat.

Some lights on tall poles cast the parking lot and the boat landing in a fuzzy orange glow. Beyond the reach of the lights, the darkness was absolute. You couldn't even see the horizon where the sun was supposed to rise in a couple of hours. Here on the coast, the foggy air was moist and dense and smelled like old seaweed, and no moon or stars lit up the sky. Somewhere out there a foghorn honked. Otherwise it was still and dark and silent.

Ralph was staring at some cormorants that were sitting on top of the pilings. When he decided they weren't partridges and were therefore unworthy of his attention, he wandered around the landing, sniffing seaweed and clamshells and seagull shit. He peed on the pilings, then hopped into the boat and lay down on the bottom, trying to be inconspicuous in case Calhoun changed his mind and banished him to the truck.

Calhoun had no intention of leaving Ralph behind. Ralph was good company in a boat, and he loved to go fishing.

Calhoun set up three rods, clamped on reels, strung them up, and tied on flies—a yellow foam Gurgler on the eight-weight floating line for the surface, a tan-and-white Clouser Minnow on a full-sinking nine-weight line for going deep, and a big chartreuse-and-white Deceiver on the nine-weight intermediate line with some wire leader in case they ran into bluefish. He mashed down the barbs with needle-nose pliers and sharpened the hook points with a file. He made sure the foul-weather gear and lifejackets were stowed away in the watertight lockers. He lowered the forty-horse Honda outboard, started it up, listened to its quiet, confident hum, and turned it off. Then he tested the electric trolling motor.

All systems go.

Just about then, headlights swept over the landing. Calhoun figured it was four twenty-five. Mr. Vecchio was right on time.

He climbed out of the boat and walked up to the parking area to meet Mr. Paul Vecchio, with whom he'd be sharing his boat and his dog and his favorite striper holes, rips, and flats for the next six hours. This was an intimate experience, and it mattered a great deal to Calhoun that he liked his client. If he found the man self-important or humorless or bossy, Calhoun became taciturn and sarcastic. He tended to steer clear of his favorite fishing spots with such a client aboard.

Kate kept telling him that he needed to improve his attitude, and Calhoun guessed she was probably right. It went against his grain, though, and he never gave it much effort, so he hoped he was going to like this Paul Vecchio. All Kate had told him about the man was that he was a history professor driving down from Penobscot College in Augusta. He'd written a few books, Kate said, and he was a competent angler, although he hadn't done much saltwater fishing.

Calhoun knew a couple of writers. He found them to be daydreamy and cynical and surprisingly uncommunicative, which suited him just fine. A lot of loud talk didn't go well in Stoney Calhoun's boat.

He didn't much care how skilled his clients were. It was always fun to have a good fisherman aboard, but Calhoun liked teaching anybody who knew he needed it and was receptive to learning, too.

By the time Calhoun had walked up the ramp to the parking

lot, the man was coming toward him. In the fuzzy orange light Calhoun saw that he was tall and rangy with a long creased face and a dark beard peppered with gray. He wore a Red Sox baseball cap, blue jeans, and a green flannel shirt. He had a couple of aluminum fly-rod cases in his hand, and a black gear bag was slung over his shoulder.

"Mr. Calhoun?" the man called.

"You Mr. Vecchio?"

The man waved and came toward him. Calhoun figured he was somewhere in his fifties.

"So do I call you professor?" said Calhoun.

"Call me Paul," he said. "Please. Anyway, I'm not really a professor. Just a lowly adjunct."

"Adjunct," said Calhoun. "What's that?"

Vecchio smiled. "A college teacher who better have another source of income."

"Lowly," said Calhoun. "So what's your other source of income, if you don't mind me asking?"

He shrugged. "I've written a couple books."

"About what?"

"Narrative history. For the mass market. Books that people might actually want to read. I did one about the submarine warfare off the New England coast in the Second World War?" He made a question of it.

Calhoun smiled. He hadn't heard of it.

"They made a PBS movie out of it," said Vecchio, "brought it out in paperback." He waved the back of his hand in the air. "More than you wanted to know. The royalties allow me to be an exploited adjunct professor and go fishing once in a while."

"I'll have to check it out," said Calhoun, who once again was reminded of everything he didn't know, all the stuff he probably used to know before he got zapped by lightning.

Paul Vecchio held out his hand. "I've sure been looking forward to this."

"Yep. Me, too." Calhoun gripped his hand. It was strong and rough. Not what you'd expect from a college professor, even a lowly adjunct. "You should call me Stoney. So you all set to rock and roll?"

"I lay awake all night thinking about it," said Vecchio. "Excited like a kid. I literally didn't sleep a wink. I don't get to go fishing enough."

"Can't promise we'll catch anything," said Calhoun, "but I'm pretty sure we'll have some fun trying."

Vecchio grinned. "That's why they call it fishing, not catching. Suits me fine."

Calhoun decided right then that he liked this man. He knew that snap judgments and first impressions were supposed to be unreliable, but he relied on his, and he was hardly ever wrong. It wasn't just the man's open smile or the way he sort of jangled when he walked or the fact that he liked fishing, though all those things were pluses in Calhoun's book.

No, it was more than that. Stoney Calhoun had a feel for people that sometimes got downright spooky. It was as if he could climb into their heads and know what they were feeling. When somebody was lying or dissembling or withholding some truth, or just being a phony, Calhoun got a jittery, uncomfortable feeling.

"I got some rods all set up," said Calhoun. "If you'd rather use yours, that's okay, but . . ."

"No, that's fine," said Vecchio, "let's use yours. I wasn't sure what I'd need."

"Another thing," said Calhoun. "I got some rules in my boat."

Vecchio shrugged. "I don't mind rules. Hell, it's your boat."

"So what've you got in that bag?"

"This?" Vecchio patted the bag hanging from his shoulder. It was shaped like a miniature duffel bag, and the letters L.L.BEAN were stitched along the side. "I got a windbreaker and a camera, pair of pliers, fish knife, couple boxes of flies. Dry pair of socks. Sunscreen and bug dope." He shrugged. "Is that a problem?"

"Nope. Tie your own flies?"

Vecchio grinned. "I'm not very good at it, but I find it relaxing."

"Me, too," said Calhoun. "We can try some of your flies if you want, once we figure out what they're eating."

"It's always fun to catch fish on your own flies," said Vecchio.

"What about electronics?" said Calhoun. "On my boat, no damn cell phones, no pagers, no laptop computers, no PalmPilots, no GPS."

Vecchio reached into his pants pocket and took out a cellular phone. "I understand about the GPS," he said. "Somebody could mark your secret hot spots." He smiled. "I guess I understand the rest of it, too. Confounded devices. Incompatible with fly-fishing. You mind if I bring along the camera?"

"I got no problem with cameras," said Calhoun. "Leave the damn phone."

Vecchio went back to his car, opened the rear hatch, and shoved his rod cases in back. Then he went around to the front door and leaned in for a moment, putting his cell phone away. He returned to where Calhoun was waiting, and they walked down to the boat.

Vecchio didn't seem surprised to find an orange-and-white Brittany lying on the floor, and Ralph didn't seem surprised when the tall guy hopped in. Vecchio patted Ralph's head, and Ralph sniffed Vecchio's hand, and that was that.

"All set?" said Calhoun.

Vecchio put his little camera in his pocket and stowed his L.L. Bean bag in the watertight compartment under the middle seat. Then he took the front seat and said, "All set, Captain."

Calhoun started up the motor and steered his way slowly through the fog and the dark among the buoys that marked the channel. Here and there the silhouette of a moored sailboat or lobster boat loomed up, and over the soft burble of the motor came the clank of some rigging and the squawk of a gull.

Paul Vecchio sat on the front seat sipping from his coffee mug. He didn't ask a lot of questions or try to make conversation, which was a big relief. Calhoun figured Kate had prepped the man for a morning in his boat. "Stoney hates small talk," she probably said. "Start asking him personal questions, he'll clam right up. And he ain't particularly impressed with credentials, so it don't do any good to brag about your accomplishments. He don't mind talking about fishing and dogs. That's about it."

When they cleared the harbor, Calhoun goosed the motor, the bow of the Lund lifted, then settled, and they were skimming across the flat water. Vecchio turned in his seat and pointed at the islands they passed, and Calhoun named them for him, yelling over the drone of the motor. Great Diamond. Peaks. Long. Little and Great Chebeague. He shrugged at some of the smaller ones. They all had names, he supposed, but he didn't know them.

After five or six minutes, he cut the motor. As the boat drifted on its momentum, he pulled the rod with the sinking line out of its holder and tapped Vecchio on the shoulder with it. "We got a nice rip running up ahead there," he said. "Climb up on the casting platform and throw your Clouser in there a few times, see if anybody's home."

The rip was an area between a couple of little islands where ledges and rocks funneled the currents across a sandbar on an incoming tide. The place was no secret among the Casco Bay regulars, but nobody else was here this morning, and it usually held a few fish. Paul Vecchio handled the heavy sinking line and the lead-eyed Clouser well enough. If a man could cast that rig, he could cast anything. He dropped the fly along the edge of the current, held his rod tip low, and stripped it back.

After five or six casts with no hits, Calhoun said, "Try throwing it all the way across and let the current swing it. Just keep a tight line and follow it along with your rod."

Vecchio did it that way, and on his third cast his line went tight and his rod bowed. "Got one," he grunted, and Calhoun heard the glee in his voice. "Feels big."

After a few minutes, he got the fish alongside, and Calhoun reached down and grabbed it by its lower jaw. A nice striper, twenty-four or twenty-five inches, nothing special. He slid the barbless Clouser out of its mouth and let it slide back into the ocean.

"How big was that fish?" said Vecchio.

"Couple feet. Decent fish."

"I was thinking of getting a picture."

"Sorry," said Calhoun. "Guess we better catch ourselves a bigger one."

They fished the rip for another ten minutes with no more hits, so Vecchio reeled in and Calhoun cranked up the motor.

They worked a rocky point off the back of Great Chebeague with no luck. They found some stripers swirling and sloshing on a grass flat near Cliff Island, and Paul Vecchio took three or four small ones on the surface with the Gurgler before the fish disappeared.

They cruised around for a few minutes, and then half a mile off to the east, where the horizon was growing silvery through the fog, Calhoun spotted a swarm of birds. He gunned the motor. As they got closer, he could see the spurts and sloshes of blitzing fish under the birds. They had corraled a dense school of baitfish. Peanut bunker, probably. The predators were bluefish, Calhoun guessed, though there were likely some stripers mixed in. Big striped bass sometimes lurked a few feet under the schools of bluefish and smaller stripers that slashed the bait at the surface, waiting for some bloody hunks of fish to sink down to them. Easy pickin's for the smart old cows.

Paul Vecchio was standing up in the boat snapping photos with his little digital camera. "Lookit that," he kept saying. "Will you lookit that! Holy shit. This is awesome. What fun!"

"You here to have fun," said Calhoun, "or to fish? Grab a rod and get to work." He handed Vecchio the rod with the wire leader and the Deceiver. "Let her sink a little before you start stripping."

Adrenaline filled the air. Diving, screaming gulls and terns. Panicky, leaping baitfish. Maurauding, slashing blues and stripers. And, of course, the fisherman and his guide, pumped and predatory themselves. Calhoun felt his own pulse racing.

Paul Vecchio began casting. He was sloppy, trying too hard, and his fly kept landing short.

Calhoun didn't say anything, and after a few minutes Vecchio found his timing and winged the Deceiver into the midst of that bloody chaos.

For about half an hour it was a fish on every cast. Calhoun and Vecchio didn't say much. When the fish moved away, Calhoun turned on the trolling motor and caught up with them. Vecchio grunted and laughed and cursed happily. The bluefish ran to a size—ten to twelve pounds, big, strong, toothy gamefish—and there were a couple of two-foot stripers, too.

When Vecchio finally calmed down a little, Calhoun said, "Let your fly sink for a count of ten before you start bringing it back. The big smart girls like to hang out under all that commotion on top, let the little guys do all the work chopping up the bait, and then pick off the hunks that sink down to them."

"That could work as a metaphor," said Vecchio.

"Metaphor?" said Calhoun. "I'm just trying to tell you how to catch a big fish."

"The big ones are girls?" said Vecchio.

"Mostly. All the smart ones are. And that ain't supposed to be metaphor, either."

Vecchio made a long cast, let it sink for a count of ten, began to strip it back. Then something really heavy latched on to it.

Fifteen minutes later Vecchio muscled the big fish alongside, and Calhoun lifted it into the boat. "Big cow striper," he said. He put the tape on her. "Thirty-eight inches. Not quite a keeper, but an awfully nice fish."

"Wouldn't keep her anyway," said Vecchio. "Fish like that, she should keep having babies." He grinned. "That's the biggest fish I ever caught on a fly rod. Thank you, Captain."

Calhoun used Vecchio's digital camera to take a couple of photos of him holding his big fish. Then they let her go.

Vecchio collapsed onto the seat. "You're wearing me out, Stoney," he said. "How about we take a little break? I gotta stretch my legs, take a leak, have some coffee, let my heart get back to normal."

Calhoun shook his head. "Nope. Not now. Those fish ain't going to hang around waiting for us. Stoney's Rule. Never leave feeding fish. God gave you a pecker so you could pee over the side of a boat."

Vecchio smiled.

"Go ahead," said Calhoun. "Ralph won't be offended."

"Come on, man," said Vecchio. "Give me a break."

"You got up with the owls, hired me to bring you all the way out here . . . why? To find you a good place to take a leak?"

Vecchio grinned. "I'll just take a minute. I've got to stretch out these old muscles."

Don't argue argue with the client, Kate was always telling him. *He's paying his money. Give him what he wants.*

Calhoun shrugged. "Okay. We'll go ashore, and you can take your leak. Let's make it quick."

While they'd been following the blitzing fish, the sun had cracked the horizon. Now it filtered through the haze and misty fog. The sea was flat as far as you could see. The rocky islands that peppered the bay were lumpy gray shapes.

Vecchio turned around, lifted the lid on the middle seat, got out his gear bag, and turned around so that he was again facing forward. He sat there with his back to Calhoun and the bag on his lap, rummaged around in it, and finally came out with a bottle of sunscreen. He squirted some into his hands and rubbed it over his face and neck, all the time looking around at the ocean and the islands. He turned around and held up the bottle of sunscreen. "Want some, Stoney?"

Calhoun shook his head.

"You should always wear sunscreen," said Vecchio.

"I know," said Calhoun. "The ozone layer and all. I got some. I use it."

"Okay. Good." Vecchio put away his sunscreen, zipped up his bag, and stowed it back in the waterproof locker under the middle seat. He looked around for a few minutes, then said, "So where we going to go ashore?"

"First place we can land on, I guess," said Calhoun.

"How about that island over there?" Vecchio pointed off to the left at one of the larger lumpy shapes.

"Okay by me." Calhoun started up the motor and putted over to the island. There was a sheltered cove where he spotted a little patch of sand. Otherwise, the shoreline was a jumble of boulders.

"This island got a name?" said Vecchio.

"It's got some Indian name I can't pronounce," said Calhoun. "Folks around here call it Quarantine Island. And me, being a salty Maine guide, I can tell you the story, if you want to hear it."

Vecchio turned around in his seat and grinned. "Of course I want to hear it. Me, being a writer, I love stories."

"It's not a happy story."

"Too late to tell me that," said Vecchio. "I still want to hear it."

Calhoun throttled down the motor so that they were barely moving. "During the influenza epidemic back during the First World War," he said, "the government built a kind of halfway house out on this island. Don't know why they picked this one. I suppose because it's rocky and godforsaken and no good for anything else." He swept his hand around the bay. "They call all these the Calendar Islands. Know why?"

Vecchio smiled and shook his head.

"Someone figured there are as many islands on Casco Bay as there are days in a year. I guess if you count the rocks that stick up on low tide that's pretty close." Calhoun shrugged. "Anyway, they erected this hospital type of place here on Quarantine Island for newly arrived immigrants. They kept 'em here before they'd let them set foot on the mainland. Anybody they thought might have the flu or even might've been exposed to it—or just anybody they didn't like the looks of, probably—was sent here. Men, women, old people, babies. They were mostly Italians. Catholic nuns ran the place. They didn't treat the people with medicine. It wasn't really a hospital. They just kept them here so they wouldn't infect any citizens. Anyway, one night in February of 1918 the place burned to the ground and everybody died. Nuns, children, everybody. A couple hundred people. They had no firefighting equipment, of course. Nothing they could do. Between the fire and the terrible cold, nobody survived."

Vecchio shook his head. "That's awful."

"That ain't the end of the story," said Calhoun. "There was a lot of right-wing patriotic feeling during that war. Powerful anti-immigrant prejudice, plus panic about the flu. And there was that need that ignorant people always feel to have somebody to blame for anything that goes wrong. The suspicion was that some good Maine citizens came in their boats that night with torches and set fire to the place. Nothing was ever proved. Officially it was an accidental fire."

Calhoun paused. "Nowadays, folks hereabouts claim that on a winter's night when the wind's not blowing too hard out here on the bay, if you're on one of the nearby islands or in a boat, you can still hear the screaming and crying and praying to God of all those poor people being incinerated."

Paul Vecchio was staring at Calhoun. "Ghosts," he said.

Calhoun smiled. "If you believe in 'em."

Vecchio nodded. "Sometimes I do."

Calhoun, who'd had some encounters with ghosts, just shrugged. "You still want to go ashore here?"

"I suppose I wouldn't want to do it at night," said Vecchio, "but right now I've got a bladder that won't wait."

"I can't move any faster," said Calhoun, "unless you want a shipwreck." He weaved slowly in and out among the big jagged boulders that were scattered in the cove. Now, on the high tide, they lurked just underwater, waiting to rip open the hull of a boat.

"You know your way around," said Vecchio. "I never would've seen those rocks."

"You can't see 'em until you're right on top of 'em," said Calhoun. "You gotta know they're here." He nosed the boat onto the sand. "Hop out, then," he said. "Pull the boat up a little and go for it. Ralph'll probably want to join you."

At that, Ralph lifted his head, yawned, stood up on the bottom of the boat, and stretched.

"You can go with Mr. Vecchio," Calhoun said to him, "take a leak if you want. Then come right back, before we lose our fish."

Vecchio stretched his arms, bent over at the waist, and flexed his legs a couple of times. Then he said, "C'mon, Ralph. Show me the way."

Calhoun watched his client and his dog climb over the rocks along the shoreline and disappear through some bushes. In a minute they'd come upon what was left of the quarantine building just over the rise. Now it wasn't much more than a big concrete-walled hole with a few charred floor joists still in place. The rest of it had burned into rubble that February night in 1918.

Every time Calhoun thought about it he got the willies.

He poured himself some coffee and sat there in his boat. It had been a good morning so far. They'd found fish and caught a few of them. The sea was calm, the sky overcast, the client competent. Paul Vecchio was good company in a boat, and so was Ralph, and Stoney Calhoun was content.

The tide had turned, and he was trying to decide where they might find fish stacked up on the outgoing when Ralph came scrambling over the rocks. Instead of jumping back into the boat, he stood there on the shore with his ears perked up and started barking.

"What's up?" said Calhoun. "What'd you do with Mr. Vecchio?"

Ralph barked again, looked hard at Calhoun, then turned and trotted back through the bushes.

Calhoun figured he got Ralph's message. *Well, shit,* he thought. *All those fish out there waiting to be caught, and something's happened to my client.*

CHAPTER TWO

Calhoun climbed out of the boat and hauled it farther up on the sand. The tide had already turned, so it wouldn't float away, but he wrapped the bowline around a boulder and tied it off anyway. He sure as hell didn't want to be stranded on Quarantine Island with ghosts and some kind of a problem and no boat.

He pushed through the bushes and climbed up a rocky slope, and then he was looking at the charred skeleton of the old quarantine building. After a minute, he spotted a patch of Ralph's orange-and-white fur through the weeds. He gave a yell, but the damn dog didn't move, and that was unlike him.

As he got closer, he saw that Ralph was sitting beside Paul Vecchio with that alert look he got when he'd spotted a chipmunk in a stone wall. Vecchio was sitting on the ground with his back against a boulder and his arms crossed over his knees and his chin resting on his arms. Calhoun was relieved to see that his client appeared to be all right.

"Hey," Calhoun yelled. "Hey, Paul. Everything okay?"

Vecchio didn't reply. He didn't move. He and Ralph seemed to be mesmerized. They were both staring toward the burned-out cellar hole.

Calhoun went over and squatted beside Paul Vecchio. He looked where the man and the dog were looking.

They were staring at a big black lump that was leaning against the outside wall of the old foundation.

It took Calhoun a minute to recognize what he was seeing.

It was a human body. A black, charred corpse, sitting with its back against the wall facing east, with its hands in its lap and its legs stretched out in front of it and its head bowed.

Vecchio turned his head and looked at Calhoun. "A ghost," he whispered.

"Doubt it," said Calhoun. The faint odor of rotten flesh hung in the damp air. "I don't think ghosts smell like that."

He got up and went for a closer look. The crusty body was seared and blackened and blistered from head to foot. Whatever clothing it might've been wearing had been burned away. You could barely distinguish the black nubs where the ears and a nose would've been. There were no fingers. Just black lumpy paws on the ends of the arms.

Calhoun couldn't tell for sure whether it had been a man or a woman, old or young. By the size of the body, he guessed it was a full-grown man.

Vecchio came over and stood beside Calhoun. He took out his little digital camera and snapped a few pictures. The quick flashes winked in the misty air.

"What do you think happened?" he said.

"Either he set fire to himself," said Calhoun, "or somebody did it to him."

Vecchio nodded as if Calhoun had said something perceptive. "What're we gonna do?"

"We've got to get ahold of the sheriff," said Calhoun. "Don't suppose you lied to me and brought your cell phone with you?"

Vecchio smiled quickly. "I left it in the car like you told me to."

"Then we gotta go back and get it."

"Aren't you supposed have a radio aboard?"

Calhoun shrugged. "Antenna's busted." He didn't bother telling his client that he never brought a radio on board. He couldn't think of a reason why he'd want to talk to somebody while he was fishing, and he certainly didn't want anybody trying to talk to him.

He snapped his fingers at Ralph and headed back to the boat.

With all of the Honda motor's forty horses galloping full speed, it took about twenty minutes to cross the bay to the boat landing in Portland. Judging by the angle of the sun, Calhoun figured it was a little after seven thirty. They'd been on the water about three hours, caught some fish, and now they'd found a dead body. An eventful morning.

He wondered if Paul Vecchio would write a story about it.

There were some other fishermen and a few guides launching their boats, and Calhoun had to wait a few minutes before there was a spot where he could pull up and tie off.

"Go fetch your cell phone for me," Calhoun told Vecchio.

Vecchio nodded, hopped out of the boat, and set off at a jog for the parking lot.

One of the other guides, an older guy they called Beaney, came over and squatted beside Calhoun's boat. "You packin' it in already, Stoney?"

"My sport forgot something in his car," Calhoun said.

"You catch the tide this mornin'?"

Calhoun nodded.

"How was it?"

"Damn good on the incoming. Pretty quiet when she went slack. You're gettin' here kinda late, Beaney, you want to put your clients into some fish."

"I got city folks in my boat today," said Beaney. He smiled conspiratorially, guide to guide, showing Calhoun his stumpy black teeth. "They didn't want to miss out on their beauty sleep. I told 'em no later than five, but you know how it is. So where was you finding 'em?"

Calhoun waved his arm, including the whole of Casco Bay. "Oh, out around them islands, mostly. But I reckon they've moved by now."

Beaney frowned and stood up. "There ain't many secrets out there, Stoney."

That's what you think, thought Calhoun.

Paul Vecchio came trotting back. He handed his cell phone down to Calhoun, who was still sitting in his boat with Ralph.

Calhoun skimmed down through the list of phone numbers in his memory, found Sheriff Dickman's home phone under S, pecked out the numbers, and hit the Send button.

It rang three times and a woman's voice answered.

"Hey, Jane," said Calhoun, "that you?"

"Stoney Calhoun," she said. "Trouble, no doubt."

"Yep. It's me. I got to talk to your old man."

"He's in the john," she said. "Can't it wait?"

"Nope. This is pretty important."

"Okay. If you say so. I'll take you to him. He ain't gonna like it. You doing okay?"

"Doing good," he said. "You?"

"Aside from having to put up with that crabby old husband of mine, I'm just fine. Okay, here we are. Hang on a minute."

Calhoun heard Jane say something, and then the sheriff said, "Jesus Christ, Stoney. What's so damn important you've got to interrupt a man in the middle of an important business transaction?"

Calhoun chuckled and said, "Damn sorry about this." He turned his head away. He didn't want any of the other guides and fishermen who were bustling around on the dock to hear what he had to say. "We got us a dead body, Sheriff," he said softly. "Ralph and my client found it out on Quarantine Island, and it's burned way the hell beyond recognition. It don't look to me like he died of natural causes, though I suppose he could've got zapped by lightning. I think you better come take a look."

Sheriff Dickman was quiet for a moment. Then he said, "You sure about this, Stoney?"

"Hell, yes, I'm sure."

"Sometimes you imagine things, you know. Remember that time when Lyle—"

"I know what I saw, Sheriff."

Dickman sighed. "I suppose you do. You tell anybody else?"

"Just you," said Calhoun.

"Where are you now?"

"The East End boat ramp. Meet me here. I'll run you over there, you can see for yourself."

"A dead body, huh? I s'pose I ought to give the Portland police a heads-up."

"How about you wait on that," said Calhoun. "I don't think this poor soul's gonna be going anywhere for a while."

The sheriff hesitated, then said, "Okay, Stoney. We'll do it your way. Just sit tight. I'll be there in fifteen minutes. Now let me finish what I started here."

Calhoun disconnected with the sheriff and handed the phone back to Paul Vecchio. "I brought sandwiches," he said. "Ham and cheese."

Vecchio shook his head. "I'm not hungry. I could use some more coffee, though."

Calhoun poured each of them a mugful from his Stanley Thermos, and they waited there at the landing sipping coffee and watching the other boats set off.

"So I guess we're done fishing for today, huh?" said Vecchio.

"I don't know," said Calhoun. "Depends on how long it takes with the sheriff. You can hang around if you want. Soon as we're done out there, we can fish some more."

Vecchio shook his head. "It's my own fault for insisting we take a break. If we hadn't stopped at Quarantine Island . . ."

Calhoun shrugged. "We had the best of it. Would've spent the rest of the day workin' hard for 'em. You'd've had to cast your arm off for a few more fish."

"You trying to make me feel better?"

Calhoun shook his head. "Nope. I'd never try to do that. You can go ahead, feel however you want to feel."

Vecchio smiled. "Why don't I pay you now. What do I owe you?" He took his wallet out of his hip pocket.

Calhoun noticed that the man's wallet was thick with bills. He shook his head. "You owe me nothing. We'll go again, have ourselves a full trip. We weren't out there long enough this morning to pay me for anything."

"Hell," said Vecchio, "that was about the best fishing I ever had."

"We'll do it again," said Calhoun. "You can pay me then."

"You sure?"

"I'm sure."

"Well," said Vecchio, "thank you."

Sheriff Dickman's green Ford Explorer with the county sheriff's department logo on the side pulled into the lot about ten minutes later. Calhoun got out of his boat and walked up the ramp to meet him.

The sheriff was a short, solid man with a barrel chest and a bald head and pale blue eyes that always seemed to be laughing at something. He was wearing his tan-colored uniform with his holster on his hip and his flat-brimmed Smokey the Bear hat, and when he came across the parking lot with Ralph trotting along beside him, all the guides and fishermen turned and watched him.

Calhoun shook hands with him.

"Let's keep this quiet, Stoney," said the sheriff. "Last thing we need is everybody with a boat swarming all over Quarantine Island."

"Keeping things quiet comes naturally to me," said Calhoun. He turned, and he and the sheriff went down the ramp to his boat.

He introduced the sheriff to Paul Vecchio, who was sitting on the front seat of the boat sipping his coffee. The sheriff shook Vecchio's hand, then said, "You're in my seat."

Vecchio looked at Calhoun. "I was hoping I could tag along."

Calhoun shrugged. "Up to the sheriff."

Dickman shook his head. "Sorry."

Vecchio smiled at the sheriff. "I'd really like to go. I'll stay out from underfoot, I promise."

"You've got to stay here," Dickman said.

Vecchio arched his eyebrows at Calhoun.

"He's the boss," said Calhoun, nodding at the sheriff.

"Yeah, but you're the captain of the ship." Vecchio was smiling, but he sounded pissed to Calhoun.

"Okay, then," said Calhoun. "Put it this way. The captain orders you to go ashore."

Vecchio shrugged. "Well, shit, anyway." He climbed out of the boat, then held it steady while first the sheriff and then Calhoun climbed in. "We'll go out again, I hope," he said to Calhoun.

"I owe you one," said Calhoun. He started up the motor. "Give me a call." He waved at Vecchio, then backed away from the landing, turned the bow to the bay, and headed for Quarantine Island. When he looked back, Paul Vecchio was standing there with his hands on his hips watching them go. Calhoun lifted his hand, but Vecchio just turned around and trudged up the ramp to the parking lot.

He drove the boat full-bore, following the chart in his head, sticking to the channels between the islands, avoiding the submerged rocks and sandbars.

Ralph sat on the bottom of the boat, his ears perked up and his nose lifted to the wind, and Sheriff Dickman sat up front facing forward. He held his hat in his hand so it wouldn't blow away, and the low-angled morning sun ricocheted off his bald head.

As they cleared Great Chebeague, the sheriff pointed off to the left where a swarm of birds were working a patch of water. Calhoun had taken the sheriff fishing a couple of times, not as guide and client but just as a couple of friends, and he knew that Dickman was a skilled and enthusiastic fisherman, though his bum shoulder made fly casting so painful that he usually used a spinning rod.

When Quarantine Island appeared ahead, Calhoun throttled down so he and the sheriff could hear each other. "That's it, up ahead," he said. "Where that body is."

The sheriff turned and looked at Calhoun. "Go past it," he said, "then circle around, come back."

Calhoun shrugged. "Whatever you say."

"I just want to be sure nobody's following us," he said. "If there's some dead body here—"

"There *is* a body," said Calhoun.

The sheriff smiled. "Right. I meant, since we got this here dead body, I don't want a bunch of nosy people leaving footprints and Big Mac wrappers at our crime scene."

Calhoun scanned the ocean. "I don't see any boats tailing us."

"Just to be safe," said Dickman, "circle around it."

So Calhoun did it the sheriff's way. He putted around the island, watching for other boats, and when he saw none, he nosed the
boat ashore on the same patch of sand where he'd landed with Paul
Vecchio an hour earlier.

The sheriff climbed out and pulled up the boat. Ralph hopped
out and headed for where he remembered the body was.

Calhoun got out, tied the boat onto a rock, and said, "It's over
this way."

They pushed through the underbrush and climbed over the
rocks, and then Calhoun was pointing at the crusty blackened body
leaning against the old concrete foundation.

Dickman went over, bent close to the body, and studied it for a
minute. Then he straightened up, blew out a breath, and went back
to where Calhoun was standing. "Well," he said, "we got ourselves a
dead body, all right."

Calhoun smiled.

"Sorry for doubting you, Stoney."

"I guess you got a right to."

The sheriff shrugged. "I better secure the area and tell the Portland cops what we've got. Assuming we've got a crime and this is
the scene of it."

"Oh, it's a crime scene, all right," said Calhoun. "But you ain't
going to find anything."

The sheriff looked sideways at Calhoun, then took out a cell
phone and made a call.

Calhoun sat on a rock. Ralph came over and lay on the ground
beside him.

When the sheriff was done with his call, he came over and sat
beside Calhoun. "You looked around for evidence already? That
what you're saying?"

Calhoun shrugged. "I wasn't actually looking. I just noticed,
without thinkin' about it. There are no footprints that don't belong
to me or Mr. Vecchio. You're not going to find any cigarette butts, or
shreds of fabric, or paint scrapings on the rocks. Whatever didn't get
burned, the rain washed away. I admit I kind of avoided lookin' too
closely at that body. You observe anything about it?"

The sheriff shook his head. "It's hard to look at, all right. Judging by the smell, it's been dead for quite a few days."

Calhoun nodded. "More like a couple weeks."

"You figure that by the smell?"

Calhoun shrugged.

"This is not a case of self-immolation," said the sheriff. "We got ourselves a murder."

"Looks that way," said Calhoun.

"Because?"

"Because this man didn't come out here alone," said Calhoun. "There's no boat pulled up anywhere, and we'd've heard at the shop if somebody found an empty boat drifting on Casco Bay in the past couple weeks. Quarantine is too far from any other island for a person to swim to, never mind swimming while carrying a five-gallon jug of gasoline with you. No empty gas can lying around, either. So I assume somebody drove him out here, and whoever it was, they at least helped him do this and took the can back with them. More likely, they drove him out here against his will and set the poor soul afire." Calhoun paused. "Which means there were two other people with him."

The sheriff nodded. "Two," he said.

"You see?" said Calhoun.

"I'm listening."

"One to drive the boat," said Calhoun, "and one to keep this poor fella under control."

"Assuming our dead man did not want to be turned into a marshmallow on a stick," said the sheriff.

"Assuming he was murdered, you mean," said Calhoun. "I don't assume it. I know it."

"You know."

"I know."

"That damn sixth sense of yours?"

Calhoun shrugged. "It's the only thing that makes sense, when you think about it. You want to commit suicide, you don't pour gasoline on yourself, light a match, and not even tell anybody or leave a note. People who set themselves on fire, they're making a statement. You want to make some kind of statement, you don't do it on a deserted island. And if all you want to do is just end your life, you shoot yourself or swallow some pills or jump off a bridge."

Now the sheriff was smiling. "What else, Stoney? You know who did it? You got this crime solved for me?"

Calhoun shook his head. "Not me, Sheriff."

"You think like a cop. You know that?"

"I guess I do. I guess I used to be some kind of cop."

"Before . . ."

"You mean before I got hit by lightning and had everything zapped out of my brain?" Calhoun waved the subject away with the back of his hand. "All I can tell you for sure is, I'm not a cop anymore, and I don't want to be. I just want to hang out with my dog, sleep in my cabin in the woods, listen to the birds sing and my brook gurgle, split and stack firewood, and maybe go fishing once in a while."

"So what's it like, Stoney? Having your memory only go back five or six years?"

Calhoun shrugged. "It's all right, I guess. I got nothing to compare it to. I don't feel much like talking about it. It's not very interesting to talk about."

Dickman nodded. "Sorry. I don't mean to get nosy." He stood up. "Let's go down to the boat. The Portland police should be here pretty soon."

Within half an hour, Quarantine Island was swarming with boats and local cops and state cops and photographers and forensics experts. The local medical examiner, a young female doctor wearing chino pants and a blue T-shirt and white sneakers, was there toting an old-fashioned black bag and looking amused by the whole thing. She was tall and gangly with a disorganized tangle of red hair and a cynical smile. Her name was Dr. Surry. Calhoun heard people calling her Sam.

Calhoun made sure Sheriff Dickman had a ride back, and then he and Ralph got in his boat and returned to the landing, where he trailered the boat and then drove over to Kate's shop.

He still thought of the shop as Kate's, even though they had gone fifty-fifty partners a year earlier. They weren't doing much better than breaking even. Calhoun didn't care about making a pile of money, but he wanted the shop to succeed because it was important to Kate.

When he walked in, she was behind the counter talking with a couple of customers, a white-haired man and a younger woman who seemed to be interested in some shirts. Calhoun caught Kate's eye. She looked up, glanced at the clock on the wall, gave him a frown, then resumed her conversation with the customers.

As always happened when he saw Kate, Calhoun felt a tightening in his throat that made it hard to swallow. He guessed Kate Balaban was the most beautiful and desirable and downright sexiest woman he'd ever seen, and he couldn't look at her without feeling a twinge of fear and anxiety. He knew he didn't deserve to have a woman like her love him, and he figured one of these days she was going to tell him that she didn't anymore.

Calhoun went back outside and sat in one of the rockers on the porch. Ralph found a patch of sun, sprawled beside him, and went to sleep.

Pretty soon the customers left carrying plastic bags. A minute later Kate came out. She was wearing shorts and a sleeveless shirt and sandals. Her black hair hung in a braid nearly to her waist. It was tied with a pink ribbon.

Kate Balaban was half Penobscot Indian. She had a square jaw and black eyes and high cheekbones, and by September, her long legs and muscular arms and shoulders and smooth-skinned face were burnished to a deep coppery color.

She just about took his breath away.

She flopped into the rocker beside Calhoun and handed him a can of Coke. She had a Diet Coke for herself. "Didn't know that was a half-day trip you had with Mr. Vecchio this morning," she said. "I thought you planned to fish the whole tide. This another case of you crapping out early because you got sick of spending time in the boat with some client who wasn't quite up to your standards?"

Calhoun took a swig of Coke. "I liked Mr. Vecchio just fine," he said. "He's a nice guy. We had a good time."

Kate turned to look at him. "Well, dammit, anyway, Stoney. You can't just do things like that. How in hell are we gonna stay in business if you aren't nice to the clients?"

"I was pretty nice to him. He wanted to take a break right in the middle of a good blitz. Said he needed to stretch his legs and take a leak, and I hardly argued with him."

"You stopped fishing in the middle of a blitz?"

"Just trying to keep the client happy," said Calhoun.

Kate was shaking her head. "You know, sometimes—"

"Mr. Vecchio caught the biggest striper of his life," he said. "Big old cow, thirty-eight inches on my tape. She was lurking under a bunch of stripers and blues that were blitzing on peanut bunker, and she ate Mr. Vecchio's Clouser when he let it sink down to her. He seemed pretty happy about it, actually."

"And then you quit fishing?"

"You better talk to the sheriff about that," said Calhoun.

She turned and looked at him. "What the hell are you talking about?"

"Mr. Vecchio stumbled on a dead body out on Quarantine Island, honey, and Sheriff Dickman insisted I haul him out there so he could take a look at it."

Kate pulled her head back and looked at Calhoun. "This another one of your stories, Stoney?"

He smiled. "Nope."

"You gonna tell me about it?"

"Not now," he said. "It's a pretty long story, and right now I gotta go hose out my boat. Why don't you come over tonight, I'll grill us a steak and tell you all about it."

"Maybe I will, maybe I won't," she said. "And I told you a million times. Don't call me honey at the shop."

"I'm sorry," he said.

Kate was shaking her head. "You are a hard man to love, Stoney Calhoun."

"Nothing's worth much," he said, "if it comes too easy."

Kate rolled her eyes.

"I'll thaw a couple steaks," said Calhoun, "just in case."

CHAPTER THREE

Darkness had seeped into the piney woods that surrounded Calhoun's cabin. He was sitting on the deck listening to his little trout stream out back gurgle over its gravel bed and swirl and burble against the granite abutments of the old burned-out bridge. A few bats were darting around snatching leftover summer mosquitoes out of the air. The almost-full moon was orange behind some drifting clouds. The barred owls were calling to each other.

Calhoun was slouched in one of his Adirondack chairs with his feet up on the railing, sipping a mug of coffee. He was wearing a fleece jacket against the evening chill. Ralph was sprawled on the deck beside him, snoring softly after another busy day.

Calhoun was waiting for Kate to show up. He hoped she would. Sometimes she did, sometimes she didn't. She never promised, and he knew better than to get his hopes up too high. They had an arrangement that most folks would consider peculiar, if not downright weird.

In the first place, Kate was married to a man named Walter, and in their own way, Kate and Walter loved each other.

Kate was not the kind of woman to cheat, nor was Calhoun the kind of man who'd sneak around with a married woman, no matter how much he loved her.

Walter had multiple sclerosis. He'd been in a wheelchair for several years. Nobody with this disease ever got better. Sometimes they stayed about the same for a long time, but sooner or later they got worse and worse until they died. Walter knew this, and he wasn't particularly philosophical about it.

When Calhoun realized he loved Kate—it happened within an hour of when he first met her—he tried to ignore it. Married was married, and that was that, as far as he was concerned.

To Calhoun's amazement and confusion, though, pretty soon Kate confessed that she loved him right back. Calhoun said they had to just forget it, but Kate said she was going to talk to Walter about it whether Calhoun approved or not.

He didn't approve, but he knew that wouldn't stop Kate. So he insisted that he should be there when she did it.

Walter had been relieved. As embittered and disabled as he was, he loved Kate enough to want her to have a happy and full life, and when he decided that he liked and respected Stoney Calhoun, he encouraged the two of them to go ahead and love each other completely.

Calhoun and Kate said they'd try to keep it private. Walter said you couldn't carry that off forever. Sooner or later, people would get wind of it. His only request was that when they did, they should know that whatever Calhoun and Kate were doing, they were doing it with Walter's knowledge and approval.

So some evenings after she got Walter settled for the night, Kate came to Calhoun's cabin. They ate and talked and laughed and listened to music and made love.

Sometimes she stayed for the whole night, and in the morning they had coffee on the deck and walked in the woods.

Sometimes she could only stay for an hour or two. Calhoun was grateful for every minute.

And sometimes when he was expecting her and feeling like he'd explode if he couldn't touch her skin and smell her hair and taste her mouth, she didn't show up at all.

He tried never to expect her. He tried to be surprised every time her Toyota truck came bumping down his long driveway with its tailgate rattling, and not to be disappointed when it didn't happen. If you had no expectations, you could never be disappointed.

But as far as Stoney Calhoun was concerned, any night that Kate wasn't there was a disappointing night.

He'd rubbed two thick New York strip steaks with kosher salt and fresh-ground pepper and a little rosemary. He'd parboiled a handful of golf-ball-sized red potatoes, slathered them with olive oil, and wrapped them in tinfoil. He'd shredded some lettuce into a wooden bowl, and he'd sliced a cucumber and a tomato and a red onion on top of the lettuce. He'd fired up the grill so the coals could burn down to white embers. He'd found an NPR station that played jazz and blues all night long, and he'd opened the kitchen windows so the music could spill out onto the deck.

And he sat there sipping his coffee and waiting for Kate.

About seven years earlier, Stonewall Jackson Calhoun had been an entirely different man. The present Stoney Calhoun, the man who lived by himself in a two-room house he and his friend Lyle had built in the woods in the township of Dublin, Maine, the man who was a half-and-half partner with Kate Balaban in a struggling fly shop and guide service in Portland, the man who loved exactly one person in the entire world—it used to be two before young Lyle got murdered—this Stoney Calhoun had no memories of the previous Calhoun. They were utter strangers to each other.

The only knowledge Calhoun had of his previous self had been told to him by the therapists in the VA hospital, and he wasn't sure they necessarily told him the truth.

They said he'd been hit by lightning, and he did have a jagged red scar on his left shoulder that seemed to prove it. The lightning had put him into a monthlong coma. It erased his memory, they said, just the way a sudden jolt of electricity would erase everything from the hard drive of a computer. It made him deaf in his left ear, and it messed up his brain's chemistry, leaving him absolutely intolerant of alcohol, neither of which he found to be much of a handicap. He had a perfectly fine right ear, and Coke and coffee gave him as much chemical stimulation as he wanted.

Now and then the Man in the Suit—a grayish, nondescript guy from some government agency who'd been sent to keep an eye on him—came to find out what Calhoun might have remembered from his previous life, and he always seemed relieved, if a bit skeptical, when Calhoun told him that he remembered nothing.

The Man in the Suit liked to bribe and tease Calhoun with fragments of information about where he'd come from and what kind of man he used to be. Calhoun was naturally curious about it, but he tried not to reveal that to the Man in the Suit.

To Stoney Calhoun, his previous self was an abstraction. It interested him, but it was about somebody else.

Calhoun understood that his dreams and nightmares resurrected images from his other life. Mostly they were weirdly distorted and utterly terrifying. And sometimes a word or an aroma or a snatch of music would trigger a familiar image or a remembered emotion so powerful that he would have to sit down, close his eyes, and take a deep breath.

The first time he picked up a fly rod after coming to Maine, Calhoun understood that he used to be a good caster. The timing, the rhythm of it, the feel of the line in his hand and the flex of the rod in his wrist, it was all still there, imbedded in his muscle memory. He discovered he could shoot a shotgun and back a trailered boat down a ramp and repair an outboard motor and sneak up on a deer in the woods and tie a perfect fly and understand the grain on a hunk of firewood so he could split it with one easy whack of his splitting maul.

He could read and write, add and subtract. He could translate French.

He knew how to use tools. He could lay pipe and string wire. He built his own house in the woods. For all he knew he could play the cello or the clarinet. Someday he'd have one in his hands, and then he'd know. He kept learning things like that about himself.

He remembered everything from the time he woke up in that hospital in Virginia. His brain was littered with images. They were vivid and specific, and he could sort through them and find what he was looking for, and then he could study them and see all their details. He could sketch a man's face from the image in his memory, and what he drew would look just like the picture in his head.

He'd also discovered that he knew how to hurt people with his hands, and that it didn't bother him when he had to do it.

When he came to Maine, Stoney Calhoun devoured a thick an-
thology of American literature, in the naive hope that the stories and
poems and essays would help him stitch his past together. In fact he
knew he'd read a lot of it before. Thoreau, Emily Dickinson, Walt
Whitman, Frost, Hemingway, Poe. When he read them, it was as if
he knew what they were going to say before he read it.

Still, it didn't add up. All the stories and all those dream images
and elusive snatches of memory and flashes of déjà vu filled up his
brain, but they didn't give him a past.

Stonewall Jackson Calhoun had been born in that VA hospital
seven years ago. When he left, he was a thirty-two-year-old man
starting all over again.

Now he had just the past seven years of actual memories. He remembered every fish he'd caught, every conversation he'd had, every
face he'd seen, every birdsong he'd heard.

Now he could sit out on his deck waiting for Kate to show up on
a September evening and relive the first time they had made love. He
could spin it out in real time, every word they'd spoken, every murmur and laugh and quick intake of breath, the scent of her hair, the
taste of her skin, the soft scratch of her fingernails on his back, the
nip of her teeth, the power of her legs wrapped around his hips, the
way her tongue outlined the scar on his shoulder.

He could relive not just that first time, but every time since that
first one, too.

Now, as if to make up for those lost thirty-two years, the most
recent seven years filled his brain. He remembered everything and
forgot nothing.

He hadn't yet figured out whether it was a blessing or a curse.

It was close to midnight when Calhoun reached down, scratched
Ralph's ears, and said, "Well, she ain't coming tonight."

He went inside, opened the refrigerator, found one of the ham-
and-cheese sandwiches he'd made for Mr. Vecchio that morning,
and ate it over the sink.

He wrapped the steaks and potatoes in tinfoil, dumped the salad into a plastic bag, and put them into the refrigerator.

He loaded the electric coffeepot for the morning.

He went out onto the deck and peed off the side.

Then he went to bed.

At dawn the next morning, Calhoun and Ralph were sitting on some boulders beside Bitch Creek where it curled out of the woods, flowed under the burned-out bridge, and spread into a curving pool against the slope behind the cabin.

Ralph was staring at a trout that was eating tiny mayflies in the eddy behind a rock right next to where they were sitting. The trout's flanks were orange, and its spots were as crimson as fresh drops of blood. The fish wasn't more than six or seven inches long, but it was full of spunk and aggression, ready and eager to spawn. Calhoun thought it was a treasure, this little native brook trout living and reproducing here in the little stream behind his cabin in the Maine woods. It was descended from the trout that were left behind when the glaciers receded eons ago. It was some kind of miracle.

A little over a year ago Stoney Calhoun had come here with Kate and Ralph bearing the urn that held Lyle McMahan's ashes. Lyle was just twenty-six, a graduate student at the university and a top-notch fishing and hunting guide. It was Lyle who'd told Calhoun about Quarantine Island. One June day he was in the wrong place at the wrong time and a man named Ross shot him dead. He was Calhoun's best friend—except for Kate and Sheriff Dickman, his only friend—and Calhoun still hadn't been able to talk himself out of the guilt he felt for placing Lyle in that wrong place. Lyle had no family, which was why Calhoun got his remains.

At sunrise on a misty June morning they emptied the urn into Bitch Creek, said good-bye and God speed, and watched Lyle's ashes swirl in the currents. Calhoun liked to think that some part of his friend sank to the bottom and remained there in the pool just downstream from the old bridge abutments, living in eternal harmony with the native brook trout, while some of him drifted down the network of streams and rivers all the way to the Atlantic Ocean. These were places that Lyle knew and understood and loved.

Whenever he felt confused or sad or just contemplative, Calhoun would take Ralph down to their creek and sit on a rock and think about Lyle. He supposed it was just his imagination, or wishful thinking, but sometimes he was certain that he heard Lyle's voice forgiving him, and it comforted him.

Calhoun's coffee mug was empty, and he was thinking of heading back to the cabin for a refill when he heard the whine of an engine in low gear coming down his rutted driveway. He sorted through his memory file of sounds and recognized the pitch of that particular engine. It was Sheriff Dickman's green Explorer.

The engine sound got louder, then died, and a minute later the sheriff was standing at the top of the slope shading his eyes with his hand and peering down at Calhoun and Ralph.

Calhoun waved, then stood up. "Pour yourself some coffee," he said. "I'll meet you on the deck."

Ralph went scrambling up the slope. Calhoun trudged along behind him. By the time he got to the house, Sheriff Dickman was lounging in one of the Adirondack chairs with a coffee mug sitting on the arm. He was wearing his tan-colored uniform. His flat-brimmed hat sat on the table, and Ralph was sprawled on the deck beside him.

"Mornin'," Calhoun said.

"Mornin', Stoney," said the sheriff.

"I don't suppose this is a social call."

The sheriff gave his head a small shake. "I'm afraid it's not."

Calhoun nodded. "Be right with you." He went into the kitchen, refilled his mug, took it out to the deck, and sat in the other chair. "Okay," he said. "Let's have it. You identify that body?"

"Nope. He was burned, as they say, beyond recognition." The sheriff blew out a breath. "His face was nothing but charcoal. Didn't have any fingers left to give us prints."

"There must be some missing persons in your files you could match him up with," said Calhoun. "Dental records or something."

"No grown men've been reported missing in the past couple weeks," said the sheriff.

"He could be from somewheres else," said Calhoun, "not local. Or he could've been missing for a year."

"You're right, Stoney. Point is, we don't know who he is." The sheriff took a sip of his coffee. "That new county ME—that's the lady doctor, Dr. Surry, the redhead—she estimates the poor bastard's been dead between a week and ten days."

"When you come up with suspects," said Calhoun, "you're going to have a tough time with their alibis. That's a big difference—anytime between a week and ten days. That's a lot of time to account for."

The sheriff nodded. "First thing is to identify him, and we're kinda stymied there, unless we can come up with some dental records to compare this man's mouth to."

Calhoun watched the sheriff as he talked. He noticed that his friend's knee was jiggling, and he was staring off toward the pine woods behind Calhoun's house, not making eye contact.

"The doctor notice anything else?" said Calhoun.

The sheriff nodded, still gazing off into the distance. He didn't say anything for a minute. Then he turned to Calhoun. "His hands and feet had been bound with duct tape. His throat had been sliced from ear to ear."

"Doesn't sound like somebody setting himself afire to make a political point," said Calhoun.

"Nope," said the sheriff. "Not hardly." He hesitated. "There was something else, too."

Calhoun waited.

The sheriff cleared his throat. "His, um, his penis was cut off, Stoney, and it was stuffed into his mouth."

"Jesus," said Calhoun.

"Yeah."

"Well," said Calhoun, "I'm sure glad you came all the way out here to tell me these things, Sheriff. Cheerful as hell. Gets my day off on the right foot, all right."

The sheriff shrugged. "I figured you'd want to know."

"Why?"

The sheriff shook his head. "Tell me what you make of it, Stoney."

"Well, let's see," said Calhoun. "They take this man out to one of the farthest islands in Casco Bay all bound with duct tape, they execute him, they cut off his pecker and shove it in his mouth, and then they douse him with—what? Gasoline?"

Dickman shrugged. "Not sure. Something like that."

"They soak him so thoroughly with gasoline," Calhoun continued, "that when they touch a match to him, his clothes and face and fingers are burned away, which probably means they don't want you to identify him. They set him up on the east side of the island so the fire can't be seen from the mainland. Or maybe they didn't do it at night. Either way, Quarantine Island is a place nobody has any reason to go to, so they didn't want the body to be found right away." He paused to get his thoughts straight. "Still, they're trying to make some kind of statement."

"His, um, his penis," said the sheriff.

Calhoun nodded. "Sure. That, plus burning him and leaving him there. You could truss up a body with chains and an anchor, drop it over the transom, and let the lobsters have their way with it if you didn't want it ever to be found. These guys want it both ways. They want to make a statement, but they don't want to get caught."

"But what about his penis?" said the sheriff. "Surely that's what this statement is all about. What do you make of that?"

"When you identify the body, figure out who he is, then you'll have a better idea. Maybe he was fooling around with somebody's wife. Maybe he was a homosexual who made a move on the wrong man. Maybe it was a man-hating woman who did this. Or maybe cutting off his penis says more about whoever killed the poor bastard than it does about him. It's too early to theorize about the penis thing at this point. It could set you off in the wrong direction, you see?"

The sheriff was nodding. "That's damn good thinking, Stoney."

"You find a lot of clues at your crime scene?"

The sheriff laughed quickly. "Nope. You were right. It was clean."

Calhoun took a sip of coffee. "Are you anticipating any jurisdiction issues here?"

The sheriff rolled his eyes. "It's a mess already. Local cops, county sheriff, state cops. I'm anticipating more competition than cooperation on this thing."

"What're you doing about the media?"

"The state police called a press conference and gave a statement, which, knowing you, you didn't hear about."

"I hope to hell my name wasn't mentioned," said Calhoun.

The sheriff smiled. "Not hardly. They just said the body was found by some fishermen and left it at that. You aren't part of this story."

"Damn right I'm not."

The sheriff smiled. "They made no mention of the man's penis or the fact that his throat was cut, which makes the story a lot less interesting to the media than it would be otherwise, though the fact that he was burned to a crisp is plenty interesting enough."

"So when the whackos come out of the woodwork to confess—"

"Right," said the sheriff. "Unless they mention slitting his throat and cutting off his penis, we'll know they're lying."

"You're hoping somebody will hear the news and come forward about a missing man, help you figure out who he is."

"That's the idea." He smiled quickly. "'Course, it would help if we could give out his picture to the TV people, but under the circumstances, we decided against doing that." The sheriff put his forearms on the table and leaned toward Calhoun. "You've done this before, Stoney. You understand how it works."

Calhoun shrugged. "It's in the movies, on TV, in every damn mystery novel. Everybody knows how it works."

The sheriff was looking at Calhoun. A little smile was playing around his eyes.

"What?" said Calhoun. "You're lookin' at me funny."

"I think you know."

"You better spit it out, Sheriff."

He nodded. "Okay. Here it is. I need you to help me with this case."

Calhoun shook his head and waved the back of his hand in the air. "Not me, Sheriff."

"Stoney," said the sheriff, "you would not believe the stupidity I've been hearing."

Calhoun smiled. "Of course I'd believe it."

"Islamic terrorists," said the sheriff. "Ku Klux Klanners. Nazi skinheads. Communist revolutionaries." He smiled. "Lesbians, for Christ sake." He shook his head. "That penis appeared to be circumcised, which was all one of our especially brilliant state police detectives needed to decide this was all about anti-Semitism. Anyway, they all seem more interested in promoting their favorite conspiracy theories than analyzing and interpreting the evidence, and it's God damn discouraging." He gripped Calhoun's wrist. "I want you to help me, Stoney. You think straight. You know how to analyze things. You're objective. You notice things, and you remember everything. You're smart as hell, and you're discreet, and most of all, I trust you. I need you. What do you say?"

Calhoun took a long, thoughtful swig from his coffee mug. Then he put it down on the table beside the sheriff's hat. "I don't know what I used to be," he said, "but I know what I am now. I'm a fishing guide. That's what I'm good at, and that's all I want to be. I got a dog who loves me and a woman who loves me. I got my little house in the woods, and I got my trout stream out back. I'm content, Sheriff. I was given a chance to start my life over again, and I figure that's a rare gift. There's a helluva lot I don't know. But one thing I do know is, I like this life of mine. I'm enjoying every minute of it. I've got no worries worth complaining about, and I don't intend to do anything to change that. This life of mine feels fragile to me. Like I'm lucky to have it, and if I do the wrong thing, it'll just shatter in a million pieces. I don't want that to happen. Do you understand?"

Sheriff Dickman fished in his pants pocket, then put a leather folder on the table beside Calhoun's coffee mug. "I want you to take this," he said.

Calhoun shook his head. "I know what that is, and I ain't taking it."

The sheriff flipped open the folder and pushed it toward Calhoun. Inside was a badge. "This is yours," he said. "I want you to be my deputy. Help me on this case. You can keep guiding and living your perfect damn life. I just want to consult with you, maybe ask you to come with me to poke around once in a while."

"I understand you think I should feel honored and flattered," Calhoun said, "but that ain't how I feel. You asking me to do this just makes me all jangly and uncomfortable. I can't exactly tell you why. I'm not saying it's rational, but it feels bad, and I can't ignore that feeling." He reached over, flipped the folder closed, and pushed it away. "You're a good friend," he said to the sheriff, "and I hope to hell you'll continue to be my friend. But I don't want your badge, and I don't want to be your damn deputy sheriff. I don't want to go traipsing around with you on your investigations, and if you decide you've got to be mad at me and stop considering me your friend, I still ain't going to do it. I don't mind you talking to me once in a while, and I don't mind telling you what I think, as long as you don't take it too seriously. Maybe I used to be some kind of cop. I'm pretty sure I was. But I'm not now, and I don't want to be again, and that's that."

The sheriff peered at Calhoun for a minute, then nodded. He reached down and gave Ralph's forehead a scratch. Then he stood up, picked up the deputy badge, and dropped it into his pocket. He twisted his hat onto his head and looked down at Calhoun. "You are a disappointment, Stoney Calhoun."

Calhoun nodded. "I understand."

"I guess I don't know what being friends with you means anymore," said the sheriff. "I asked you to help me, Stoney, and believe me, asking you for a favor isn't the easiest thing in the world for a man to do, and you refused, and while I suppose I've got to respect your reasons, friends help each other. In my book, that's what being friends means."

Calhoun shrugged. "In my book," he said, "friends don't ask their friends to do things that go against their grain."

"They do when they really need them and their friends don't volunteer to give a hand." The sheriff turned, went down the steps, and climbed into his truck.

Calhoun stood at the deck rail and waved as the green Explorer headed out the driveway.

The sheriff did not stick his hand out the window and wave back.

CHAPTER FOUR

They had no guide trips scheduled for that day, which was the second Wednesday in September. Calhoun didn't understand it. September was the best month of all for catching a big striped bass on a fly along the coast of Maine. In August, when the fish were hard to find, either he or Kate had clients every day, but it seemed that most folks gave up on fishing after Labor Day. He figured they had to do a better job of getting the word out. Kate was talking about hiring somebody to set up a Web site, and as little as Calhoun knew about marketing, he guessed it might be good for business.

He and Ralph arrived at the shop around nine, and a little while later a couple of electronics salesmen from Boston came in to pick Calhoun's brain. The Boston guys bought a handful of flies in exchange for some local wisdom, a courtesy that Calhoun wished more fishermen understood. He spread a topo map on the counter and was showing them where they could launch their boat on the Kennebec, and where in the estuary they might have some luck on the afternoon tide, when Kate came in.

Both men turned to look at her. Calhoun found himself smiling. Kate was wearing a pink T-shirt, faded snug-fitting blue jeans, leather sandals, red toenail polish, a touch of pink lipstick. Her black hair hung in two long braids off the front of her shoulders. Calhoun didn't think any man could help but stop whatever he was doing to look at Kate Balaban.

She flashed a big smile at the two customers, said, "Mornin', Stoney," and headed for the office in back. Ralph got up from where he was lying near the front door and followed her.

After the customers left, Calhoun took his mug out back for a refill. Kate was at her desk with her reading glasses perched low on her nose, frowning at the computer. Ralph was curled up beside her.

He sat in the chair next to her. "Everything okay, honey?"

She nodded, still peering at the computer. "If we were making any money it'd be better. But, sure. Everything's fine. Why?"

"You're frowning."

"I guess I've been frowning a lot lately." She took off her glasses and turned to look at him. "I need to talk to you, Stoney."

He leaned back in his chair. "Fire away."

She shook her head. "Not now. Not here. You mentioned something about steaks yesterday. I suppose you ate 'em all, huh?"

"Nope. Still got 'em. Potatoes and salad, too."

"Let's see how things work out tonight, then." She gave him a quick smile, then put her glasses back on and resumed frowning at the computer.

Calhoun knew better than to ask her any questions.

It was a typical Wednesday morning in the shop. The Loomis rep dropped in to talk about their spring line of fly rods and left some samples for Calhoun and Kate to try out. A few customers came in to buy flies and check out the end-of-summer clearance sales. The phone rang several times. A guy from Concord, New Hampshire, wanted to talk about setting up a guide trip, but he wasn't ready to pull the trigger on a date.

Kate spent most of the morning at her desk writing e-mails and paying bills.

Around noontime Calhoun went back and stood beside her.

She poked a couple of keys, plucked her glasses off her nose, looked up, and said, "What's going on, Stoney?"

"Thought I'd run out for sandwiches. What would you like?"

"Nothing. I've gotta head home in a minute. Might not be coming back. You and Ralph can handle the shop for the afternoon, can't you?"

"Sure we can." He hesitated. "You sure everything's okay, Kate?"

"You already asked me that." She shrugged. "Why don't you go get your sandwich. I'll wait till you get back before I leave."

The sun had fallen behind the hill. Calhoun was sitting out on the deck listening to the water music from Bitch Creek and drinking coffee and waiting for Kate. Ralph had a belly full of dinner and was snoozing beside him. Bats and swallows were zooming around the yard. The barred owls were calling to each other. The coals were glowing red in the grill.

All in all, it didn't get much better than this.

Calhoun heard the rumble of Kate's truck before it turned off the road into his driveway half a mile away. He put his coffee mug on the table. Ralph lifted his head, yawned, stood up, and started wagging his stubby tail.

Kate pulled in next to Calhoun's trailered boat. When she stepped out into the floodlit yard, he had to swallow a couple of times. She was wearing a pale orange ankle-length dress that fit tight around her torso and hung loose from her hips. She'd pulled her black hair back into a long ponytail and tied it with a ribbon that matched her dress.

She looked up at the deck. Calhoun stood up and waved. She gave him a big smile full of white teeth. "Hey," she said.

"Hey."

Ralph scampered down the steps and went to her, his whole hind end wagging. She scootched down to rub his ears. Then they both came up onto the deck.

A silver necklace inlaid with turquoise hung from Kate's neck. Her long dangly earrings and heavy bracelet were also silver and turquoise. She walked straight over to Calhoun, put her arms around his neck, kissed the side of his face, and pressed herself against him. "I'm sorry, Stoney," she murmured.

"Sorry for what, honey?"

"I've been pretty bitchy lately. It's not that I don't love you. I hope you know that."

"I'm glad to hear you say it, either way."

She leaned away from him, looked deep into his eyes for a minute, then smiled and covered his mouth with hers. When she broke away from the kiss, she whispered, "How far along are those coals?"

"Gonna have to let 'em burn down a little more," Calhoun said. "They won't be right for at least an hour."

"Good," she said. "Perfect. I don't want to wait anymore." She took his hand and led him into the house and to his bedroom.

They were sitting out on the deck under a starry September sky. They'd made love and then they'd eaten steak and potatoes and salad. Ralph, who'd had his share of steak scraps, was sprawled on his side under the table. The moon had risen over the hill, and Stoney Calhoun couldn't imagine feeling more contented.

Kate was wearing a pair of Calhoun's sweatpants and one of his sweatshirts. Her hair hung loose around her shoulders. He thought she was the most beautiful woman in the world. She was lounging in one of the Adirondack chairs with her feet propped up on the deck rail sipping some Jack Daniel's. Calhoun had a mug of coffee.

"You get enough to eat, honey?" he said.

"Ate too much. I'm stuffed."

A minute later, he said, "Sheriff Dickman came by this morning."

"About that burned-up body you found?"

He nodded. "He wanted to sign me on to be his deputy, help him with the case."

"What'd you tell him?"

"I told him no damn way."

Kate was silent for a minute. Then she said, "How come?"

"Just didn't feel right. Soon as he mentioned it, my stomach got all knotty." He shrugged. "Solving murders is the sheriff's job. It ain't mine. This case, it's got nothing to do with me. I feel like if I stuck my nose into it, everything would fall apart."

"You gotta do what you think is right."

"I like my life," he said. "That's all. I don't want to change any-thing about it."

Kate looked up and seemed to be studying the stars. "Nothing ever stays the same, Stoney."

He nodded. "I know that."

"No matter how hard you try, something always comes along."

"You think I should've taken that damn badge?"

"You should do what feels right to you."

"Well, that's what I did. Now the sheriff's mad at me."

"He'll get over it." She reached across the table and put her hand on top of his. "I told you I needed to talk with you."

He smiled. "I remember you said that. Guess I was hoping it was so unimportant that you forgot all about it."

"It's not unimportant." She took a sip from her glass. "It's about Walter."

Calhoun waited.

"He's never going to get better."

"It's a terrible disease," said Calhoun. "I feel bad for him."

"I took him to a nursing home down in York this afternoon," she said. "Left him there. He'll never come home again. He'll keep getting worse and worse."

He squeezed her hand. "I'm sorry, honey."

She cleared her throat. "I feel as if I let him down. Like, if I loved him more, I wouldn't've done that. Wouldn't've handed him off to strangers."

"You love him plenty," said Calhoun. "Walter knows that."

"He says he does." She looked up at him. Tears glittered in her eyes. "I'm not sure he's right, Stoney. You see what I'm saying?"

"Maybe you better spell it out for me, honey."

"I keep thinking," she said, "that if I didn't . . . didn't love you so damn bad . . ."

"Walter's better off in the nursing home," said Calhoun. "That's got nothing to do with you and me."

"Sure," she said. "Walter was the one who said it was time he went there. But, see, that doesn't make me feel any different."

"It's a hard thing," he said. "You'll get used to it."

"He probably won't . . . won't die for a long time." Kate was crying freely now. Tears ran down her cheeks.

Calhoun, as usual, didn't know what to say. He just looked at her for a minute from across the table, then said, "Come here, honey."

Kate got up from her chair, came around the table, and sat on Calhoun's lap. She put her arms around his neck and buried her face against the side of his neck. "I feel so awful," she murmured.

He held her tight and said nothing.

"So," she said after a minute, "I decided I can't come here and be with you anymore."

Calhoun felt an icicle stab through his heart. He slid his hand under Kate's sweatshirt and stroked the smooth strong muscles of her back. He could feel that she was shaking.

"You understand, Stoney?" she whispered.

He nodded. He wasn't sure how his voice would sound if he tried to speak words.

"It just wouldn't feel right," she said. "Like you taking that deputy's badge. Some things, it really doesn't help to analyze them. You've got to consult your heart."

Calhoun cleared his throat. "You don't have to explain, honey. It's okay."

She turned her face and kissed him hard on the mouth. Then she pushed herself up off his lap. She stood there in his baggy sweatshirt and sweatpants looking down at him. Her face was wet. "I'm gonna leave now, Stoney, before I lose all my courage."

He looked up at her and nodded.

She turned, went halfway down the steps, then stopped and looked up at him. "Is that all you've got to say?" she said.

"What do you mean?"

"About what I just said," she said. "Do you have an opinion?"

"What do you want me to say?"

"You could—you could tell me I'm wrong. You could argue. You could have some emotion. You could . . . fight for what you want." She was still crying. Or maybe she'd stopped and had started all over again. "You think I'm doing the right thing?"

"I'm pretty sure you've given it a lot of thought, honey. Nobody knows what the right thing is. Like you said, you consult your heart and make your best guess."

"Don't you care?"

Calhoun shook his head. "That ain't really a question, is it?"

Kate smiled at him through her tears. "There's nobody like you, Stoney Calhoun," she said. Then she turned and continued down the steps.

Calhoun started to follow her.

At the bottom of the steps she turned and looked up at him. "Don't come down, Stoney. Please. Just stay right there and wave to me when I go."

"Sure," he said. "Okay."

She swiped her wrist across her eyes. "I'll see you at the shop tomorrow."

"I'll be there."

"We're still partners, don't forget," she said.

He nodded. "Partners. You bet."

She got into her truck, backed around, and started up the driveway.

Calhoun lifted his hand, and Kate flicked her headlights.

He stood there on his deck until the sound of the Toyota's engine faded away in the distance. Then he collected the knives and forks and plates and glasses from the table and took them into the kitchen.

Calhoun was back out on the deck sipping coffee and looking at the stars and listening to some blues from the radio in the house. It was about an hour since Kate had left, and already he was feeling lonely and bereft. He wondered how he was going to work beside her, knowing she didn't want them to be anything more than business partners.

Ralph, who had a good sense for Calhoun's moods, had curled up right under his feet, trying to give him comfort.

When he heard the car engine out on the road half a mile away downshifting and turning into his driveway, he hoped it was Kate, coming back to say she'd changed her mind, or that it was the sheriff, saying he'd been wrong to be upset and wanted to be friends again.

But Calhoun's ears told him the engine wasn't Kate's truck or the sheriff's Explorer. It was that damn Audi sedan, which meant the Man in the Suit had come back.

Calhoun went inside, took his Remington twelve-gauge autoloader off the pegs, made sure it was loaded with Number 8 birdshot, and went back out onto the deck.

The Audi pulled into the place next to Calhoun's boat where Kate had parked earlier. Its headlights went off, the driver's door opened, and the Man in the Suit stepped out. He looked up at the deck, shielded his eyes against the glare of the floodlights, and said, "You can put that damn shotgun down, Stoney. I'm not here to rob you."

"Shoot all trespassers," Calhoun said. "You're the one who gave me that advice."

"And damn good advice it is," said the Man in the Suit. "Except I'm not a trespasser. I'm your friend."

"Friend," said Calhoun. "Not hardly. Well, come on up. It ain't even midnight yet. Good time for a visit."

The Man in the Suit was wearing a gray suit with a pale blue shirt and a dark blue necktie and shiny black shoes. He always wore a suit, and it was generally gray, just like the rest of him. Gray, indistinct, utterly forgettable. He'd never mentioned his name to Calhoun, and Calhoun didn't want to suggest he had any interest whatsoever in the man by asking. He just thought of him as the Man in the Suit. He'd been dropping in at odd, unexpected times ever since Calhoun moved to the woods in Maine. His mission was always the same: to try to determine what Calhoun remembered about the time in his life before he'd been zapped by lightning.

Calhoun understood that he'd known things—secrets, he

guessed, information that was important and valuable—and who-ever the Man in the Suit worked for didn't want him to remember them.

Calhoun understood that remembering would be dangerous.

The fact was, he remembered nothing, but the Man in the Suit had made it clear that even if something from before did pop into Calhoun's head, it would be in his best interest to deny it.

So each time the Audi pulled into Calhoun's dooryard, they danced their little dance, the Man in the Suit asking Calhoun what he remembered, and Calhoun saying he remembered nothing, and the Man in the Suit never knowing whether he was lying or telling the truth. As far as Calhoun could tell, the Man in the Suit always assumed that he was lying, but he never pushed it.

When the Man in the Suit first started coming to visit, Calhoun threatened to shoot him, and he was at least half serious. The whole idea of the Man in the Suit scared him and made him mad. Pretty soon the Remington twelve-gauge became a kind of joke between them.

Not that Calhoun trusted him, or especially liked him. The Man in the Suit worked for the government. He knew everything about Calhoun's forgotten life. He used what he knew to bribe and bully Calhoun, who protected himself by pretending it was all irrel-evant to him.

The Man in the Suit came up the steps and sat in the same Adirondack chair that Kate had been sitting in barely an hour ear-lier. "Who's that?" he said.

"Who's who?"

"The music. On the piano."

"That's Oscar Peterson. Everybody knows Oscar Peterson."

The Man in the Suit shrugged. "It's nice." He jerked his chin at Calhoun's coffee mug, sitting on the table. "What're you drinking?"

"Coffee. Want some?"

"No. Got a Coke?"

Calhoun went inside and returned the shotgun to its pegs on the wall. Then he snagged a can of Coke from the refrigerator, took it back out, and put it on the table in front of the Man in the Suit.

"Thanks, Stoney." He cracked it open, took a swig, put it down, and peered at Calhoun. "So—"

"I don't remember anything."

The Man in the Suit nodded. "Okay."

"So you can leave now. I'm going to bed."

"Anything you'd like to know?" said the Man in the Suit. "From before, I mean?"

Calhoun shook his head. "Nope. I'm all set."

The Man in the Suit smiled. "I understand you've had some, um, stress recently."

How the hell did he find out about Kate so quick? Calhoun thought. The son of a bitch had a way of worming into Calhoun's life, of knowing things that were none of his damn business. "What the hell are you talking about?" he said.

"Sheriff Dickman. He needs you, he asked for your help, and you turned him down. Why'd you do that, Stoney?"

"That ain't your affair."

"Sure. You're absolutely right about that. Still, I don't understand. There's that murdered body, throat cut, burned and mutilated, which is pretty damned interesting, and you got a chance to help out, help a friend, help your society, and you refused. That's not being a good citizen."

"I'm not interested in some murdered body," Calhoun said, "whether it's burned and mutilated or not. And I don't care about being a good citizen. And I don't care whether you understand or not. And it pisses me off that you're so damn nosy."

The Man in the Suit shook his head. "Sometimes you disappoint me, Stoney."

"Disappointing you don't bother me one bit." Calhoun gazed up at the stars for a minute, then looked at the Man in the Suit. "You saying I should agree to be the sheriff's deputy? That why you're here? To tell me that?"

"I was a little surprised, that's all. I don't like to be surprised. I kinda thought you'd jump at the chance, and you didn't. It makes me think I don't understand you."

Calhoun shrugged. "That burned-up body ain't my problem, just because I happened to find it."

"No man is an island, Stoney."

"Oh, Christ. You gonna burst into song?"

The Man in the Suit smiled. "The sheriff could use you. It'd be good for you. You've got talents, you know. You shouldn't let them go to waste."

"I got talents, all right," said Calhoun. "I can steer a boat in the fog. I can smell bluefish from a mile away. I can cast a whole fly line with just one backcast. And if you don't get the hell out of here, you'll see how accurate I can be with that twelve-gauge of mine."

The Man in the Suit held up both hands. "You'll do what you want. I know that. I'm just saying, as a friend, you ought to reconsider working with the sheriff. Just give it some thought."

"If I say okay, will you go?"

"Sure."

"Okay. I'll give it some thought."

The Man in the Suit drained his Coke, then stood up. He held out his hand. "Shake on it, then."

Calhoun shook his hand.

"That's smart, Stoney."

"I only said I'd think about it. I didn't say I'd do it."

"But," said the Man in the Suit, "you will think about it, because whatever else you are, you're a man of your word."

"I don't expect to change my mind."

"Oh, I expect you will." The Man in the Suit bent down, patted Ralph, who was snoozing on the deck, then straightened up and went down the steps to his car.

Calhoun didn't bother waving as he turned and drove out the driveway.

Calhoun opened the shop at eight thirty the next morning. He'd left Ralph home to bark at the chipmunks and sleep under the deck. Ralph got restless if he had to spend the whole day cooped up in the shop. Kate was off on a guide trip, so except for a few customers, Calhoun had a quiet day for listening to the radio, tying flies, and thinking about things.

A little after three in the afternoon Kate pulled her truck with her boat trailered behind it into the side lot.

Calhoun went out to help her unload the boat and get the trailer off her truck.

He asked her how it went.

She said good. They caught some fish. The clients seemed to enjoy it. Anything happen in the shop?

Calhoun said nothing special.

Then some customers showed up, and he went back inside to wait on them.

Kate hosed out her boat, then came into the shop. She went to her office and turned on her computer.

At five, Calhoun went back to say he was leaving.

She looked up, smiled, and said have a nice evening.

You, too, he said.

Business partners. It was going to take some getting used to, he could see that.

Something was wrong. He sensed it just about the time he turned into his driveway. He didn't know what it was, and he didn't know where that spooky feeling of unease came from. He'd felt it before, though, and he knew enough to trust it.

So instead of continuing to drive his truck down the rutted driveway to his house, he pulled off the side into the bushes. He got out, pulled his .30-30 Winchester Model 94 lever-action deer rifle out from the floor behind the seat, jacked a cartridge into the chamber, and walked. He went slowly, holding the rifle at port arms, careful not to snap a twig or rustle a branch, and when he knew his house was just around the next bend, he slipped off the roadway into the woods.

He took a curving route that brought him to the rear of his house. He paused there behind the bushes that bordered the yard. He saw no movement except the rustle of leaves in the breeze. He heard nothing except the caw of a distant crow. He smelled nothing except pine needles.

He slipped around through the woods to the front of the cabin, and that's when he saw the strange vehicle parked in the turnaround next to his boat.

It was a small green SUV, a Subaru Forester. Calhoun went to the place in his brain that remembered all the vehicles he'd noticed in the past six years, scanned down through the images, and identified this one. He'd seen it just a few days earlier, in the parking area at the landing in Portland. The area had been dimly lit, and Calhoun hadn't paid any conscious attention to the vehicle, but there it was, vivid and specific in his memory.

This vehicle belonged to Paul Vecchio, the history professor from Penobscot College, the man Calhoun had taken fishing, the man who'd discovered that burned-up body on Quarantine Island.

He held the short-barreled deer rifle like a pistol, the barrel resting on his shoulder, stepped out of the woods into his yard, and called, "Hey. Mr. Vecchio."

Two bad things happened.

First, Mr. Vecchio did not answer.

Second, Ralph did not come scampering down off the deck or in from the woods to greet him, which he normally did without being called when Calhoun came home.

Again Calhoun called. "Mr. Vecchio. Paul. You here?"

Then: "Ralph, where the hell are you?"

No response from either of them.

He crept up the stairs to his deck, moving silently on the balls of his feet, holding his rifle with both hands, ready to shoot.

When he saw Paul Vecchio, he lowered the weapon.

Vecchio was sitting in the same Adirondack chair where Kate, and then the Man in the Suit, had sat the previous evening.

Except Mr. Vecchio's eyes were half-lidded, and he had a shiny red blotch on his chest, and it was pretty obvious that he was dead.

CHAPTER FIVE

Calhoun laid the .30-30 on the table and went over to look at Paul Vecchio. The blood that smeared the front of his pale blue shirt was dark and sticky-looking. There appeared to be three wounds, two high on the right side of his chest, the other lower, in the middle of his belly. The ones in his chest had done most of the bleeding. Calhoun couldn't tell how big the bullet holes were under Vecchio's shirt.

He squatted down on the deck so that he was eye-level with Paul Vecchio. Even in death, the professor looked mild-mannered and friendly. He seemed to be looking at Calhoun out of the sides of his half-closed eyes, and one corner of his mouth was crinkled into half a grin, as if he were sharing some joke, waiting for Calhoun to laugh.

He remembered how Vecchio had whooped and hollered and shouted how much fun he was having when they'd found the blitzing stripers and blues. He was the kind of man who hugged life against his chest, who jumped in up to his ears.

Now he slouched there in Calhoun's Adirondack chair, still as a stone. Those twinkling eyes were cloudy. His grin was frozen on his face.

Son of a bitch.

Calhoun blew out a breath and pushed himself to his feet. If he couldn't save Paul Vecchio's life, maybe he could avenge it.

And if something had happened to his dog . . .

He went to the deck railing and yelled for Ralph.

He waited. Yelled again.

Where was that dog?

Without thinking about what he was doing, Calhoun surveyed the crime scene. He looked around the deck for spent cartridge casings or anything else that might be evidence. All he found that hadn't been there when he'd left in the morning was a purple plastic sunscreen bottle lying beside the chair Vecchio was sitting in. It looked like it might have fallen out of his hand when he was shot. Calhoun remembered that Mr. Vecchio was pretty sold on the importance of sunscreen.

He knew better than to touch anything, even a fallen bottle of sunscreen. He continued looking around the deck for spent cartridges and found nothing, which meant that either the shooter had picked up his empties or he'd been using a revolver.

He climbed down off the deck and looked under it in case one of the cartridge cases had fallen through the cracks between the floorboards. None had. Then he scanned the parking area. He didn't have much hope of finding tire tracks or footprints. There hadn't been any rain for a week, and the ground was hard and dry, and anyway, there had been quite a bit of traffic at Calhoun's house lately. The sheriff, Kate, the Man in the Suit, Calhoun himself with his truck and trailered boat, and now Mr. Vecchio.

Still, Calhoun looked carefully, mentally dividing the area into quadrants and studying each one systematically.

He noticed nothing.

Next he climbed back onto the deck and went into the house. He looked around, touching nothing, comparing what he saw with the memory images of how each room had looked when he'd left that morning.

He was convinced that nobody had been inside.

He thought about looking into Vecchio's Subaru for clues, but decided against it. He figured he'd better leave that to the police.

Judging by the length of the shadows and the color of the sky, he judged it was about ten minutes before seven in the evening. The sheriff was probably home by now, but since he'd refused to become a deputy and help him with his investigation, Calhoun felt funny about calling him at home. You could call a friend at home for any reason, even business. When you were no longer friends, you didn't do that.

So he picked up the portable phone in the kitchen and called the sheriff's office and, as expected, got the answering service. He gave the woman his name and number and assured her that it was an emergency.

She said the sheriff would call him right away.

He took the phone out onto the deck and put it on the table. He went to the railing and yelled for Ralph again. The fact that he had to call him at all was seriously worrisome. Ralph never needed to be called. Whenever Calhoun came home from the shop or after a day of guiding, no matter what time it was, Ralph was always there, trotting out of the woods or down from the deck, wagging his stub tail, wanting a scratch behind the ears and a rub on the belly. Ralph would come to investigate any vehicle that he heard pulling into their yard, and he always came when he was called.

Mr. Paul Vecchio was dead on his deck, and that was an extremely bad thing. But Ralph Waldo had gone missing, and as far as Calhoun was concerned, that was even worse.

He tried to take comfort in the fact that he hadn't found Ralph's body, the way he'd found Paul Vecchio's.

The phone rang about five minutes after Calhoun hung up with the answering service. He picked it up and said, "Sheriff? That you?"

"It's me," said the sheriff, not sounding any too cheerful about it. "What is it?"

"I got a dead man sitting here on my deck. It's that Mr. Vecchio, the guy I took fishing the other morning."

"The man who found the body on Quarantine Island?"

"Yep. Him."

"You sure he's dead?"

"He's got three bullet holes in him. Two in his chest, one in his belly. I'd say he's been dead for a few hours."

The sheriff blew out a breath. "Okay. We'll be right there. You know how it works. Don't touch anything. Try to keep Ralph from messing up my crime scene."

"That's another thing," said Calhoun. "Ralph's gone."

The sheriff hesitated, then said, "Gone? What do you mean?"

"I mean, Ralph ain't here. I left him here in the morning, and now he's gone."

"You sure?"

"I guess I ought to know."

"Right. Sorry. So what do you—"

"I looked around and didn't find a damn thing by way of clues unless you want to count a bottle of sunscreen that ain't mine. Nothing about what happened to Mr. Vecchio, and nothing about where Ralph is at."

"I'm sorry about Ralph," said the sheriff, "but I expect he'll turn up. Ralph's a pretty resourceful dog. He's probably off in the woods chasing partridges."

"I got a bad feeling, Sheriff. I sure hope you're right."

Sheriff Dickman was silent for a minute. Then he said, "You're a hard man to stay mad at, Stoney, but I intend to keep doing it. I truly do hope Ralph's all right, but my plan here is to focus on this dead man you've got for me. You sit right there. I'll be with you shortly." He hung up.

Calhoun started a pot of coffee brewing, then went out onto the deck and yelled for Ralph.

Ralph did not appear.

After a while, Calhoun went into the house and poured himself a mug of coffee. He took it back out onto the deck, sat in the chair beside Mr. Vecchio, thought about the good morning of fishing they'd had just two days earlier, and waited for the sheriff to arrive.

Darkness was seeping out of the woods into the clearing that surrounded Calhoun's house. The stars were winking on one by one. A couple of bats had come flapping out from the trees to chase mosquitoes. The barred owls were calling to each other.

It was past Ralph's suppertime.

Calhoun sat there sipping his coffee, keeping Mr. Vecchio company and trying not to worry about Ralph, and after a little while he heard the sheriff's Explorer turn into the driveway. A minute later, headlights came bouncing out of the woods and cutting through the gathering dusk. Then the sheriff pulled in, parked beside Calhoun's truck, and got out. He was wearing his uniform, flat-brimmed hat and all, and he had a big cop-sized flashlight in his hand.

He came up the steps to the deck, frowned at Paul Vecchio sitting dead in the chair, then turned to Calhoun and said, "Did you shoot him, Stoney?"

Calhoun rolled his eyes. "You feel obligated to ask?"

"That's your truck parked in the bushes out at the end of your driveway, right?"

"Yep."

"Why is it there?"

"That's where I left it."

The sheriff blew out a breath. "I'm trying to be patient, here, Stoney. So why'd you leave it there?"

Calhoun shrugged. "I had a bad feeling."

"A bad feeling."

Calhoun nodded.

"What kind of bad feeling?"

Calhoun shrugged. "The kind of bad feeling you get when you know there's something unpleasant waiting for you but you don't know what it is."

The sheriff smiled quickly. "And as a result of this bad feeling you had, you decided not to drive all the way in, so you got out of your truck and came sneaking back here to your house. You came around through the woods, did you?"

"That's right."

He pointed at Calhoun's .30-30 on the table. "Did you bring that rifle with you?"

"I did."

"You keep it in your truck?"

Calhoun nodded. "Behind the front seat."

"What did you find when you got here?"

Calhoun tilted his head at Mr. Vecchio.

"Nothing else?"

"Just Mr. Vecchio. And that bottle of sunscreen there." He pointed at the purple bottle.

"That's not yours?"

Calhoun shook his head.

"You didn't touch it, did you?"

"'Course not."

"What about Ralph?" said the sheriff. "Has he come back?"

Calhoun shook his head. "Look," he said, "I'm damn sorry I let you down."

The sheriff waved the back of his hand at him. "Don't worry about it."

"The thing is," said Calhoun, "for a man who's mad at me and doesn't want to be my friend, it's a pretty damn friendly thing to ask about my dog before you even take a serious look at this poor man's dead body."

"He's a good dog," said the sheriff. "I like Ralph. Too bad I can't say the same for his master."

"Well," said Calhoun, "he's gone."

"He'll be back."

"He never did this before. It's past his suppertime."

The sheriff shrugged and went over to where Paul Vecchio was sitting. As he gazed down at the dead man, he pulled a pair of latex gloves from his pocket and snapped them onto his hands. Then he turned on his flashlight and shined it on Vecchio. He bent close to the man's body, studying his face, and the wounds on his chest and belly, and his hands, which were resting in his lap.

Without turning around, the sheriff said, "I could use some of that coffee."

Calhoun went inside, poured a mug of coffee, and brought it out. He put it on the table. "There's your coffee, Sheriff."

"Thanks," the sheriff muttered.

Calhoun sat at the table and watched him.

After a couple of minutes the sheriff straightened up, pulled off the gloves, and stuffed them into his pocket. He sat at the table and took a sip of coffee. "What time did you leave the shop this afternoon, Stoney?" he said.

"Little after five."

"Kate there with you?"

"Yup. She was still there when I left."

"So about what time did you get home?"

"Takes an hour, give or take five minutes. Why? How long has Mr. Vecchio been dead?"

The sheriff shrugged. "Not that long. Few hours at the most."

"You think I came home and killed him?"

"Why would you do that?"

"Well," said Calhoun, "I wouldn't."

"I meant," said the sheriff, "have you got anything like a motive I ought to know about?"

Calhoun shook his head. "I just met him that once. We had good fishing. I liked him. I didn't let him pay me, because we had to quit early. On account of that damn body out on Quarantine Island."

"So you had no disagreements or arguments."

Calhoun shook his head. "You think I'm lying to you?"

The sheriff shrugged. "No, I don't. Not me. But I can't speak for the others who'll be coming." He took out his cell phone. "I better call this in." He pecked out a number, talked for a minute, then snapped the phone shut and took another sip of coffee.

"State cops?" said Calhoun.

The sheriff nodded. "The whole shebang. Detectives. Forensics. Medical Examiner. You name it. They'll all be here."

Calhoun nodded at Paul Vecchio's body. "You want to do some brainstorming about this?"

"With you?" The sheriff shook his head. "Why would I want to do that?"

"Look," said Calhoun, "I gave you my reasons for turning you down. It would've been easier just to say yes."

"A gold star for taking the hard way, then," said the sheriff.

"I never knew you to be sarcastic before, Sheriff."

"I never had a friend spit in my face before."

Calhoun nodded. "Some things've changed since we had that talk."

"Finding a man sitting on your deck with three bullet holes in him is a new thing, all right," said the sheriff.

"Other things've changed, too," said Calhoun. "The other day I was telling you how damn perfect my life was, and I guess I cursed myself pretty thoroughly by saying those things, because now my life ain't even close to perfect."

The sheriff squinted at him. "This about Ralph going missing?"

Calhoun shrugged. "It's about Ralph, sure. I guess it's about Kate, too. And it's about you asking for my help and me refusing because I was just thinking about myself instead of considering what it meant to be your friend. Mainly, I suppose it's about this dead body here on my deck. You and I both know it ain't a coincidence. It's connected to that burned-up corpse we found on Quarantine Island." He blew out a long breath. "Anyway, I guess I've been a dumb-ass, and I'm sorry. I don't like not being your friend."

Sheriff Dickman nodded. "You sure can be a dumbass sometimes. You're right about that, at least."

Calhoun held out his hand.

The sheriff gripped it. "I'm happy to be your friend again, Stoney, but I can't hire you on."

"Because I'm a suspect?"

"Whether you're my suspect or not," said the sheriff, "the others are going to look all squinty-eyed at you no matter what I say."

Calhoun shrugged. "I got nothing to lie about, so I ain't worried. Look. I don't want to be your deputy. I got no desire to go sleuthing around with you. That hasn't changed. But I do want to be your friend, so if you want to talk about it . . ."

"Okay. Why not." The sheriff took off his hat and put it on the table. "Let's do that. Let's give some thought to what we've got here." He ran the palm of his hand over his bald head. "We got Mr. Vecchio sitting here in your chair, and it appears to me that this is where he was sitting when he was shot."

"On account of no blood on the steps or the floor."

"Right. So the question is—"

"Why was he here?" said Calhoun.

The sheriff arched his eyebrows. "You tell me," he said. He reached out, picked up his mug, took a sip of coffee, and put the mug down.

"I didn't expect him," said Calhoun. "He never called or said he was coming. I didn't know he even knew where I lived."

"So why would he come here?" said the sheriff.

Calhoun shrugged. "I don't know."

"Suppose he came against his will."

"In that case," said Calhoun, "there had to've been more than one killer. One to drive their car so they could get out of here when they were done, and one in Mr. Vecchio's vehicle, which they left here."

"If Vecchio came to see you, then it could've been just one shooter who followed him. Vecchio came up on your deck to wait for you, and the shooter came up and plugged him."

"If it was that way," said Calhoun, "Vecchio must've known the guy who did it."

The sheriff nodded. "He just sat there and watched the killer walk up to him and shoot him."

"Like he wasn't surprised to see him." Calhoun hesitated. "Like they planned to meet here, maybe."

The sheriff nodded. "Hmm. Interesting." He looked up at the sky for a minute. "The big question is why."

"Why kill Mr. Vecchio, you mean? Or why would they want to meet here?"

The sheriff shrugged. "Both."

"You asking me?"

"I'm asking you to speculate," said the sheriff.

"As far as them planning to meet here," said Calhoun, "that one's got me stumped. I mean, the only reason to do that would be to talk to me, and I don't know why they'd want to do that. Seems more likely that Mr. Vecchio came here to see me, decided to wait here on the deck for me to get home, and the other guy followed him."

The sheriff nodded. "So why would someone want to kill this man?"

"Well," said Calhoun, "he was a writer. He stumbled upon that corpse out on Quarantine Island. Maybe he was researching it and figured something out, and—"

"And the killer got wind of it . . ."

"And followed him here and shot him."

"To shut him up," said the sheriff. "So maybe Vecchio came here to see you, tell you what he'd figured out about that body."

"Why would he do that?" said Calhoun. "I mean, why me? I only met him that once. It's not like we were best friends."

"Well," said the sheriff, "the other possibility is that the shooter—or shooters—brought him here specifically to your place to kill him."

"If that's the case," said Calhoun, "it means they got some issue with me."

The sheriff shrugged. "Or maybe they just figured they could pin it on you."

"As I understand it," said Calhoun, "for me to be a good murder suspect, I'd have to have the means, the motive, and the opportunity to kill the man. All three."

The sheriff shrugged. "I already told you, Stoney. You're not my suspect."

Calhoun got up from the table, went to the deck railing, and looked out over the yard. He was hoping to see Ralph come trotting into the area that was lit by the floodlights.

"He'll be back," said the sheriff.

"I hope to hell you're right."

After a minute, the sheriff said, "One way or the other, Stoney, you are involved in this."

"Because Mr. Vecchio's body is here."

"Yes."

"I ain't all that worried about it."

At that moment Calhoun heard a distant siren. He listened to it grow louder, and then he heard the distinctive sounds of four different vehicles approaching on the paved road, then slowing down, and then one by one turning into his driveway.

"Here come the troops," he said.

"Gonna be a damn zoo," said the sheriff. "Try to behave your-self."

Headlights came dancing through the trees, and then four vehi-cles pulled into the yard and parked at cockeyed angles. There were three dark SUVs and one state police cruiser. A radio crackled from inside at least one of the vehicles.

Calhoun stood there at the deck railing and watched the various homicide officials get out. He recognized the tall redheaded medical examiner, Dr. Surry, who they called Sam. She was lugging an old-fashioned black bag, as she had when she showed up on Quarantine Island. One of the state police detectives and a couple of the foren-sics people from the other body on Quarantine Island were there, too. Three of them—an Asian man with three cameras hanging from his neck, a bearded man wearing a necktie and a sport coat, and a uniformed state police trooper—he had never seen before.

Calhoun never forgot a face.

The sheriff said, "You better come with me."

Calhoun followed the sheriff down the steps to the parking area.

The others gathered in a kind of semicircle around them. "This is Mr. Calhoun," said the sheriff. "This is his place. He's the one who found the body, which is up there." He jerked his thumb over his shoulder at the deck.

The trooper came over to Calhoun. "Come with me, please, sir."

Calhoun looked at the sheriff, who gave him a little nod. So he followed the trooper over to his cruiser.

The trooper opened the back door. "Get in, please."

"My dog's gone missing," said Calhoun. "I'd rather stay outside so he can find me. I ain't going to run away on you."

"Get in," said the trooper.

"At least open the damn window so I can talk to my dog if he comes looking for me."

The trooper nodded. He had a smooth-shaved face, sharp blue eyes, a square jaw, and perfect teeth. Calhoun wondered if they re-cruited state police troopers based on how well they looked the part.

Calhoun climbed into the backseat of the cruiser. It was separated from the front by steel mesh. The trooper got in behind the wheel and rolled the rear windows halfway down. When he got out, the doors locked with a click.

The trooper leaned against the side of the cruiser. All the others had gathered around the sheriff. He seemed to be doing most of the talking. Calhoun couldn't hear what any of them was saying. It occurred to him that they were all speaking quietly on his account.

After a few minutes, the medical examiner, Dr. Surry, went up onto the deck with her black bag. The young Asian man with three cameras strapped around his neck followed behind her. The sheriff and one of the others went over to Vecchio's Subaru. There were a couple of other vehicles parked between the cruiser and the Subaru, so Calhoun couldn't see what they were doing, but he assumed they were searching it for clues.

The rest of them remained in the parking area, talking among themselves and smoking cigarettes and cigars and shuffling their feet.

Fifteen or twenty minutes passed. Camera flashes kept blinking from up on the deck. Dr. Surry and the Asian man came down. They spoke with the others for a few minutes. Then the doctor came over to the cruiser. "Let him out," she said to the trooper. "I want to talk to him."

The trooper unlocked the doors with the remote on his keychain. Then he came around to Calhoun's door and opened it.

Calhoun got out and looked all around, hoping to spot Ralph, but Ralph was nowhere to be seen.

The sheriff was leading two of the police officials up the steps onto the deck. A couple of others were prowling around the house with flashlights.

The doctor came over and held out her hand. "Mr. Calhoun," she said, "I'm Samantha Surry, the medical examiner. They call me Sam."

Calhoun took her hand. Her grip was firm like a man's. "Glad to meet you, Doctor."

Freckles were spattered across the bridge of her nose. She wore a little subtle eye makeup, which looked good on her. She had a shy smile, as if she and Calhoun shared a private secret.

"Let's go sit," she said. She turned and went to the edge of the parking area, where Calhoun and Lyle had moved some big boulders out of the way back when they cleared the land for the house, and sat on one of them. She placed her black bag on the ground beside her. She was wearing black pants and a gray hooded sweatshirt. Her tangly red hair was tied back with something that looked like a shoelace. She was wearing no jewelry.

Calhoun sat beside her.

She looked up at the state trooper, who had followed them and was standing there at parade rest watching them. "Give us some space, Officer, would you?"

He shrugged and wandered back to his cruiser.

She turned to Calhoun. "Your dog's gone missing, huh?"

He nodded. "It ain't like him."

"I hope he turns up," she said. "I love dogs. I've got a dog myself. Little springer named Quincy. After the old doctor show on TV. He's pretty good on woodcock."

"You hunt?" said Calhoun.

She nodded. "A little. When I can find the time. Birds, mostly. Grouse, woodcock, ducks. Quincy loves to retrieve ducks. What kind of dog you got?"

"Ralph's a Brittany," said Calhoun. It occurred to him that Dr. Surry was trying to put him at ease so he'd be off guard when she asked him clever questions, but he didn't really care. He liked talking with her, and he was pretty sure that he'd never been off guard in his life. "Pointing dog. Damn good hunter. It's what he lives for. Bird smells and food. I don't take him out enough."

She touched his arm. "He'll show up." She cleared her throat. "I got a couple questions for you."

Calhoun nodded.

"Did you touch that man's body?"

"Nope."

"You didn't even touch his skin or the blood?"

"No. I know better than to do that."

"You didn't go through his pockets?"

" 'Course not."

She nodded. "You knew him, though, right?"

"I took him fishing a couple days ago."

"When you found that body out on Quarantine Island."

"That's right."

"Any idea what he was carrying in his pockets that day?"

Calhoun thought for a minute. "He had a cell phone and a camera and car keys and a wallet. It looked like he was carrying a lot of money with him, judging by the thickness of his wallet."

"That purple bottle of sunscreen belong to you?"

"No. Mr. Vecchio used sunscreen. I guess it was his."

Dr. Surry was writing in a little notebook. "The cell and the camera," she said. "Was it your impression that he generally carried them with him?"

"The phone," he said. "He kept that in his pants. Not the camera. I wouldn't let him bring the damn phone on my boat. Why? He doesn't have them on him now?"

She cocked her head and looked at him. "Detective Gilsum thinks you did it, you know."

"Gilsum?"

"He's the state homicide detective."

"Well," said Calhoun, "I didn't."

"The sheriff vouches for you. I trust his judgment, which is more than I can say about Gilsum. He's always looking for the easy way out. I'm only trying to explain why I probably shouldn't answer any of your questions."

"It don't really matter to me, Doctor. I was just curious."

She smiled. When she smiled her eyes went crinkly, as if she were truly amused by something. "Call me Sam, for Christ's sake."

Calhoun nodded. "Okay."

"I'm just the local on-call ME," she said. "I show up, figure out if a dead body is truly dead, give it a preliminary examination, and write up my report. I'm not a cop. I don't do autopsies or anything like that. I don't participate in police investigations. I just do reports. In my real life, I work at a clinic in Portland." She smiled. "So, really, I don't care one way or the other whether they think you and I ought not to have an actual conversation."

Calhoun smiled, too. "So Mr. Vecchio doesn't have his phone or his camera on him, huh?"

"No. Nor his wallet or his keys."

"His car is right over there," said Calhoun. "He must've had keys with him."

"They're not in his pockets," she said, "and they're not in the car."

"Killer took 'em," he said. "And the other stuff, too, no doubt."

"He had a lot of money on him, huh?"

Calhoun nodded. "He did the other day when I was with him. You're not thinking this was a robbery, are you?"

"Not really," she said. "It doesn't make much sense."

"You figure he was shot right there where he's sitting?"

She nodded. "The way the blood was pooled. The lividity."

"You got a look at the bullet holes in him?"

She smiled again. "That is a big part of my job. Looking at bullet holes and smashed-in skulls and knife wounds. I've come up with this wild hypothesis that one of those three bullets is what killed him."

"Could you tell what sort of weapon shot him?"

"It wasn't that .30-30 I saw up there. I'm pretty sure of that. Small caliber. I'd surmise it was a .22." She arched her eyebrows at him. "You own a .22, Stoney?"

"Sure. I got a Colt Woodsman."

"I'm going to need it."

"It's in the drawer beside the kitchen sink," he said. "I imagine all those experts up there have come upon it by now. So you can take the bullets out of Mr. Vecchio and compare them to the bullets that come out of my pistol, and you'll see I didn't shoot him."

"Not me," she said. "But the ballistics experts up in Augusta can do that, and I expect they will. And for that they'll need your gun."

"They'll find it ain't been fired recently."

She nodded. "You'll get it back. Eventually." She closed her notebook and stuck it into her shirt pocket. "I may need to talk to you again."

"Okay. I don't mind."

She gave him one of her quick shy smiles. "You're a fishing guide, I understand."

"That's right."

"Out of Kate Balaban's fly shop."

"Ayuh."

"And you live here"—she swept her hand around the area, taking in the house and the yard and all of the woods—"by yourself?"

He nodded. "Me and my dog."

She smiled. "It's really nice."

"Except Ralph's not here."

"I bet he'll be back as soon as all the commotion dies down." She touched his arm. "I might need to know how to find you, is why I'm asking."

"If I ain't here or at the shop, I'll be messing around in my boat. That's about it."

"Maybe someday you'll take me out," she said. "I'm not much good with the fly rod, but I love fishing."

"We could do that."

"I'm serious," she said.

"Me, too."

"Good." She stood up, reached down, and picked up her bag.

"You actually carry a black bag," said Calhoun.

"I do, yes."

"I didn't know doctors had black bags anymore."

"Doctors don't generally make house calls anymore," she said. "You don't need to lug your instruments around if you only see patients in your office."

"You make house calls?"

She smiled. "Only when there are dead bodies. The bag was my dad's. He was a country doctor up in Presque Isle. Drove all around in his Oldsmobile, visiting sick people who were too poor to come to him. He retired a few years ago, gave me his bag. I got his stethoscope in here. Also the mallet he used for testing your reflexes."

Calhoun looked past her and saw two of the men coming toward them. One of them was the state detective named Gilsum.

Dr. Surry glanced back, then said to Calhoun, "I'll be in touch. About fishing." She reached over and gave his shoulder a squeeze. "Well," she said in a loud voice meant to be heard by the two approaching men, "I'm about done here for now. It was nice to meet you, Mr. Calhoun. Don't let these sons of bitches give you a hard time."

"I'm not all that worried," he said.

She held out her hand. "I hope your dog comes back."

Calhoun took her hand. "Thanks. Me, too."

He watched Dr. Sam Surry intercept the two men who were approaching him. She spoke to them, cutting the air with the side of her hand, making some point, and the two guys shifted their weight back and forth, looking uncomfortable.

He could still feel the burning imprint of her fingers where she had given his shoulder a squeeze.

CHAPTER SIX

As Dr. Surry walked over to her vehicle, the two men turned and watched her. Then the bearded guy said something to the guy in the windbreaker, and they both smiled.

The two of them came over to where Calhoun was sitting on the rock and stood there looking down at him. The man wearing the blue windbreaker and chino pants said, "Mr. Calhoun, I'm Lieutenant Gilsum. I'm a homicide detective with the state police."

Gilsum was a beefy guy with a round face and round glasses and a small, mean mouth. He looked more like a banker than a cop. "This," he said, jerking his head toward the bearded man, "is Mr. Enfield. He's the county DA."

Neither man showed any inclination to shake hands, never mind use their first names, so Calhoun just sat there.

"We've got some questions for you," said Gilsum. He sat on the boulder next to the one Calhoun was sitting on, the same one where Dr. Sam Surry had been sitting. Enfield remained standing.

Gilsum fished a notebook out of his pocket, flipped it open, and studied it for a minute. "There's a .30-30 up there on the deck," he said. "It's yours?"

Calhoun nodded.

"Deer rifle?"

"Guess it could be, if I wanted to go deer hunting."

"You don't hunt?"

"Not deer. They're all over the place around here. I could shoot 'em from my deck. But if I started doing that, they'd stop coming around."

"You like having them around."

Calhoun shrugged.

"So what's the rifle doing there on the table, then?" said Gilsum.

"That's where I put it when I was done with it."

"Done with it."

"Turned out I didn't need it," said Calhoun.

Gilsum glanced at Enfield, then turned back to Calhoun. "Why'd you think you might need it?"

"When I came home from work and turned into my driveway tonight, I thought I might have company."

"What made you think that?"

Calhoun shrugged. "Just a feeling."

"A feeling."

Calhoun was thinking that Gilsum was the kind of guy who'd been fat and unathletic as a kid, probably been bullied on the playground by the other third graders, and that's why he decided to become a cop. "That's right," he said. "A feeling."

"What kind of feeling?" said Gilsum.

"I don't know. Sometimes I get feelings about things. Mostly they're on target."

"You mean you noticed something? Picked up on some kind of clue? Maybe you smelled burnt gunpowder or something?"

"Nope," Calhoun said. "Just had a feeling."

"Do you always greet visitors with a deer rifle?"

"If I'm in the house, I got a Remington twelve-gauge."

"That's not very hospitable."

Calhoun shrugged. "So far I haven't had to shoot anybody."

Gilsum and Enfield exchanged glances. "Maybe," said Gilsum, "you better just tell me what happened when you came home today."

"Not much to tell. When I pulled into my driveway, I got a feeling, like I said. So I took out my rifle and snuck back here and found Mr. Vecchio dead in my chair."

"Your rifle was in your truck?"

Calhoun nodded. "Behind the front seat."

"You travel with a loaded deer rifle?"

"I keep the chamber empty. There's some bullets in the magazine."

"That's your truck," Gilsum said, "parked in the bushes off your driveway?"

"I tried to pull way over. You were able to get by okay, weren't you?"

Gilsum smiled quickly. "I'm interested in this . . . feeling of yours, Mr. Calhoun. You sure you didn't have some kind of information that led you to believe that somebody might be waiting for you, or that you might find a dead body at your house?"

"I'm sure," said Calhoun.

"You have feelings like this often?"

Calhoun nodded. "Now and then."

"How would you describe them?"

"Describe my feelings?" He hesitated. "I don't know. Feelings, that's all. You start feeling jangly and tense, and you know something's going on. You never had a feeling like that?"

Gilsum shrugged.

"You've got to pay attention to those feelings," said Calhoun.

"So," said Gilsum, "on the basis of this—this feeling—you took out your rifle, jacked a cartridge into the chamber, and sneaked up on your own house."

"That's right."

"And what did you see?"

"Just Mr. Vecchio's vehicle and him sitting there with bullet holes in him."

"You saw nothing else. No other person or vehicle."

"Nope. Just Mr. Vecchio and his vehicle."

"Did you happen to pick up any spent cartridge cases?"

"I looked," said Calhoun. "Didn't see anything except Mr. Vecchio's sunscreen, which I didn't touch. I wouldn't've picked up any cartridge cases."

"Of course you wouldn't."

Calhoun narrowed his eyes at Gilsum. "You think I plugged Mr. Vecchio?"

"Why would you do that?"

Calhoun shook his head. "I wouldn't. Didn't."

"Tell us about that argument you and he had."

"Huh?" Calhoun frowned. "I didn't have any argument with Mr. Vecchio. We got along pretty good."

"At the dock the other morning," said Gilsum. "You wouldn't let him go on your boat out to Quarantine Island. He didn't like that."

"That was the sheriff, not me. He's the one who said he couldn't come with us."

"That's not exactly how we heard it, Mr. Calhoun."

"You think he came here because we wouldn't let him ride in the boat with us, and he made me so mad I shot him?"

"That is a plausible scenario," said Gilsum.

"No, it ain't," said Calhoun. "That's plain stupid. Anyway, we didn't have any argument. It wasn't like that."

Gilsum smiled quickly. "Did you go through his pockets?"

"Dr. Surry, she asked me that. I told her no."

"Do you have any idea what he might've had in his pockets?"

Calhoun shrugged. "Wallet. Cell phone. Car keys. The usual stuff, I guess."

"You know this how?"

"I don't know it," said Calhoun. "I know it's what he had in his pockets the morning I took him fishing, that's all."

"How well did you know Paul Vecchio?" said Enfield, the DA. It was the first thing he'd said.

"I spent a couple hours with him in a boat," said Calhoun. "That's about it. He seemed like a nice guy."

Enfield was stocky and strong-looking. He had a sharp nose and suspicious eyes. "Catch some fish, did you?" he said.

"It wasn't bad."

"Mr. Vecchio, was he a good angler?"

"He got better after a while."

"You gave him some pointers, did you?"

"Only when he asked."

"How did you happen to hook up with Mr. Vecchio?" said Enfield.

"He called the shop, talked to Kate, said he wanted to go fishing. It was my turn, so I took him."

"He didn't ask for you?"

"I don't think so. But you should ask Kate. She's the one who talked to him."

Enfield nodded. "Did Mr. Vecchio mention anything about problems he might be having? Troubles with other people?"

Calhoun shook his head. "We just talked about fishing."

"So," said Enfield, "how did you happen to stop off at Quarantine Island that morning?"

"I already explained all that the other day. When we found that burned-up body out there."

Enfield nodded. "Explain it again, please."

Calhoun shrugged. "Mr. Vecchio had to take a leak, wanted to stretch his legs. We'd been into stripers pretty good. I guess he got kind of cramped up."

"Yes," said Enfield, "but why that particular island?"

"It was there, I guess."

"There are several islands in that area."

"Well," said Calhoun, "you're right. As I recall, Mr. Vecchio pointed to that one, Quarantine, and asked about it. I told him the stories, and he said that's the one he wanted to stop off at. He was a writer. I suppose he was interested in things like that."

Enfield nodded as if he'd heard something significant. Then he turned to Gilsum. "I don't have any more questions for him right now."

Gilsum nodded. "Me, neither." He stood up, then looked down at Calhoun. "We might need to talk to you again. You're not planning to go anywhere?"

"Just to the shop. Probably have another guide trip or two coming up. I'll be around."

"I understand your dog ran away."

"Ralph would never run away," said Calhoun.

"I meant, he's missing."

Calhoun nodded.

"Well," said Gilsum, "I hope nothing happened to him."

"That's what's got me worried," said Calhoun.

The two started to walk away. Then they stopped and Gilsum came back to where Calhoun was sitting. "We're trying to keep a lid on this," he said.

"This?" Calhoun waved his hand around indicating his property.

"What happened tonight."

"Good," said Calhoun.

"So don't talk to any reporters," said Gilsum.

"Don't worry about me," said Calhoun.

After a while, an emergency wagon pulled into the yard, and a couple of men went up onto the deck. A few minutes later, they came bumping back down the steps with a big plastic bag strapped on a gurney. Calhoun was pretty certain the bag contained Paul Vecchio's body. The men rolled the gurney over to the wagon, collapsed it, slid it into the back, slammed the doors shut, and drove off.

Calhoun sat there on his boulder while the forensic techs hustled into and out of his house. The uniformed state trooper leaned against the side of his cruiser more or less watching him, but he didn't insist that Calhoun get back into the backseat. Dr. Surry had left after she finished talking with Calhoun. Gilsum and Enfield and Sheriff Dickman hung around the yard talking with each other. Once in a while one of them would talk on his cell phone. A couple of times a tech came out of the house and spoke to them.

They all ignored Calhoun, which was fine by him.

Calhoun guessed it was a few minutes before midnight when they all started climbing back into their various vehicles and driving away.

Gilsum came over to where Calhoun was sitting and said, "You can go inside now."

"I expected you'd have that yellow crime-scene tape draped around my house for a week."

"You've been watching too much TV."

"I don't watch TV at all, actually," said Calhoun. "If you looked around in there, you'd see I don't own one."

"Well, whatever," said Gilsum. "We're all done, anyway."

Then he got into the cruiser, and the trooper slid behind the wheel, and they drove off.

The sheriff was the last one to leave. He seemed pretty anxious to get going. He didn't have much to say, and Calhoun wondered whether he'd changed his mind and decided that Calhoun might've shot Paul Vecchio after all.

He just said he hoped Ralph showed up, and they'd be in touch.

Then he left, and Calhoun was alone.

He went up to the deck. The floodlights lit the area like daylight, and Calhoun noticed that some black blood had seeped into the wooden seat of the Adirondack chair where Paul Vecchio had been sitting. He wondered how long it would take for the weather to wash away the stain.

His .30-30 was lying there on the table where he'd left it.

He stood at the railing and yelled for Ralph.

After a while he picked up the Winchester and went inside. The forensics people had moved around some chairs and left several drawers and cabinet doors open. Otherwise there was no evidence that people had been prowling around in there.

He closed the drawers and doors and pushed the chairs back to where they belonged. Then he found an apple in the refrigerator and a box of raisins in one of the cabinets. He poured himself a glass of water, went out on the deck, and had supper at the table.

Still no Ralph.

He went back inside and got the automatic coffeemaker ready for the morning. Then he made Ralph's supper and filled his water dish and put them out on the deck under the table where Ralph liked to eat.

According to Calhoun's internal clock, it was about quarter past one in the morning. He was supposed to be at the shop before nine to open up. He didn't figure he'd sleep much, but he knew he should give it a try. So he went to the closet in his bedroom, got down his sleeping bag, grabbed a pillow off his bed, picked up his .30-30, and took them out to his pickup. He slid the rifle behind the front seat, then opened the sleeping bag on the truck bed and crawled in, leaving the tailgate down.

He stared up at the September night sky. He knew he should feel bad about Paul Vecchio. He had seemed like a nice guy, smart and mild-mannered and friendly, hardly the sort of man you'd expect to be murdered. Hell, he was a college professor and he liked fishing.

Well, that was all Calhoun knew about the man. Maybe he'd been a drug dealer or a pedophile. You never knew about people.

He would've felt worse about Vecchio, he understood, if it hadn't been for Ralph. Ralph was a hard knot of worry in his stomach. The only thing he could figure was that whoever had shot Vecchio had snatched Ralph, although he couldn't really figure out why they'd want to do that, or how they could manage it. The previous summer an enemy of Calhoun had kicked Ralph and hit him with the butt of a rifle, and ever since then, Ralph had been skittish around strangers.

Maybe they shot him like they shot Mr. Vecchio. But if they did, why didn't they just leave his body there where he fell, the way they'd left Paul Vecchio where he'd been sitting?

Most likely Ralph had slinked away into the woods when Mr. Vecchio and whoever killed him showed up. Calhoun hoped that was it.

He tried to sort through things, to analyze what he knew about Paul Vecchio and his murder, to deduce the connection between him and the burned body on Quarantine Island, but the evening's adrenaline and caffeine had drained out of him, and his brain was too fuzzy to think straight. Scenarios drifted around, and there seemed to be one thought in particular that he wanted to pin down, but he couldn't conjure up the energy to focus on it any more than he could focus his eyes on a single star up there in the sky.

So he let his mind go wherever it wanted to go. There were images of making love with Kate, how she tasted and smelled and felt. It had only been the previous night, but when he remembered that it wasn't going to happen again, at least not for a while, not for as long as Walter was in the nursing home, or maybe forever, it seemed like something that had happened a long time ago.

Calhoun's thoughts kept flipping back to Ralph. He was so full of regrets that he felt like screaming, or crying, or smashing a hammer down on his fingers. Why in hell hadn't he brought Ralph to the shop with him? If he had, it wouldn't change what happened to Paul Vecchio, but Ralph would be here with him, at least.

Eventually his mind went all fluffy, and thoughts mingled with dreams, and after a while there were only dreams.

When he woke up, the sky was still dark and the owls were calling to each other. His leg was cramped, and when he tried to move it, he felt a weight on it. He reached down and touched the fur on Ralph's back. He rubbed it, and Ralph squirmed against him. Calhoun mumbled, "Hey, bud," and he felt the dog's wet tongue give his hand a couple of licks, and pretty soon he went back to sleep.

Calhoun woke up from a dream about having a big tree fall on the back of his legs, pinning him to the ground. He was trapped, immobilized, and some big wolflike animal was breathing into his face and showing his snarly wet teeth. Calhoun tried to yell at the creature, but his words got stuck in his throat.

He forced himself to wake up. He was lying on his stomach inside his sleeping bag hugging his pillow. The chilly September air around him was filled with morning birdsong, hundreds of birds, dozens of different species, all calling to each other. There was no rhythm or tune to it. It was a chaos of noise.

Ralph was curled up on top of the sleeping bag in the V of Calhoun's legs. When he tried to roll over, Ralph groaned and refused to move.

Finally Calhoun slid his legs out from around Ralph and crawled out of the sleeping bag. The sky was turning from purple to pewter. Most of the stars had winked out. Five thirty, according to

Calhoun's mental clock. It was a good thing he didn't require much sleep.

He slid out of the truck, went up to the house, got the coffeepot going, and pulled on a sweatshirt. When he came back out onto the deck and saw that Ralph's food dish was empty, he took it inside, rinsed it out, put more dog food in it, and put it back on the deck.

He poured some coffee and took it down the hill to Bitch Creek. He sat on a boulder beside the pool downstream from the old burned-out bridge and watched a trout feeding on mayfly spinners and listened to the water music and sipped his coffee and thought about Lyle. Calhoun was the one who'd found Lyle's dead body. Now he'd found Paul Vecchio's. It felt like some kind of curse. Whether it was rational or not, he felt responsible in both cases.

After a while, Ralph wandered down and sat beside him.

Calhoun held down his coffee mug, and Ralph took a lick.

"Where the hell did you go?" he said.

Ralph lifted his head and looked up at him.

"Well," said Calhoun, "don't ever do that again."

He wondered if any apparitions would drift down the stream or come ghosting out of the woods this morning. Sometimes that happened, and when it did, Calhoun took them seriously and tried to understand their messages.

There were no apparitions this morning, so when the coffee mug was empty, he and Ralph went back up to the house. Ralph went onto the deck to eat his breakfast, and Calhoun backed his truck down to his boat trailer and hitched it up.

When he went back to the house, he noticed that his Colt Woodsman .22 pistol was missing from the kitchen drawer, but the Remington twelve-gauge still hung on its pegs by the back door.

He showered, got dressed, refilled his coffee mug, and snapped his fingers at Ralph. They piled into the truck, Calhoun behind the wheel and Ralph riding shotgun, and headed for the shop, dragging the boat behind them.

It was a Friday in the middle of September. The summer tourists who swarmed into the shop between Memorial Day and Labor Day to pore over the clothing and books and souvenirs were pretty much gone. Most of the autumn customers were hard-core fishermen hoping to catch the tail end of the striper migration, and they were more interested in information and opinion than in buying equipment. Mostly they gave themselves their best chance of receiving sound advice by buying a handful of flies. Not many of them wanted or needed a guide. It was coming up on the end of the season, and Kate had already switched over to winter hours—closed on Monday, open nine to four Tuesday through Saturday, noon to four on Sunday.

Once Calhoun had tried to talk to her about doing some winter guiding on the bay for sea ducks. He could make some sets of decoys, paint his boat camouflage, and rig up some netting. He could build blinds on a few of the uninhabited islands where he knew the eiders and scoters and old squaw flew. He thought it would be fun, and they could expand their business.

Kate had shrugged. He realized that she was distracted because of Walter, so he dropped the subject for the time being.

They got to the shop around nine thirty, and he parked his truck and boat in the side lot. Kate would be coming in later on. Until then, Calhoun and Ralph were in charge. He opened up, got the coffee started, checked the phone for messages and the computer for e-mails, tuned the radio to the NPR classical music station, and went around straightening out the displays and checking the fly bins. His regular morning routine.

He didn't expect to see many customers, so he decided to spend the morning at the fly-tying bench. They had a standing order from some Massachusetts guys for a batch of landlocked salmon flies. Every spring at ice-out these men spent three or four weeks trolling for salmon on Sebago and Moosehead, and at the end of every spring season they ordered twenty-five dozen streamers. They were retired doctors and lawyers and bankers who had formed their own private fishing club. Their rules required them to fish for salmon the old-fashioned way. They rowed wooden boats. No outboard motors. They trolled with bamboo fly rods and floating lines, and they fished with nothing but old-time Maine feather-wing and bucktail streamers, flies such as the Chief Needahbah, the Edson Dark Tiger, the Golden Witch, the Hurricane, the Magog Smelt, the Nine-Three, the Supervisor, the Warden's Worry.

Calhoun's job was to keep them supplied. They left it up to him to decide which patterns to make. Considering the time it took and the cost of materials, they didn't make much money by selling three hundred flies—even though they charged double what flies imported from Taiwan or Sri Lanka were selling for at retail—but Kate figured it was a start. Authentic Maine streamers tied by an authentic Maine guide might give them a nice niche in the complicated fly market. The Massachusetts fellows loved Calhoun's flies. They said they were spreading the word.

Calhoun decided to tie a batch of Gray Ghosts. The Gray Ghost was perhaps the most famous of all the Maine salmon streamers. It was invented in 1924 by Carrie Stevens, the legendary Maine fly tier, to imitate a smelt, the most important baitfish in her Rangeley lakes system. A lot of new fly-tying materials had come along since 1924, and a lot of new flies had been invented, but Gray Ghosts still took fish, and Calhoun enjoyed the feeling of tradition that went along with tying them according to Mrs. Stevens's original pattern.

Kate showed up a little after noon. She came over to Calhoun's bench, put her hand on his shoulder, and bent over him. He could smell the familiar soapy scent of her. She peered at the Gray Ghosts he'd completed and said, "Real nice flies, Stoney."

He looked up at her. He hoped she was smiling at him, but she wasn't. "Thanks," he said.

Her hand moved off his shoulder and she straightened up. "Well," she said, "I've got to finish doing the inventory and get at the winter orders. I'll be out back if you need me." She headed for her office in the back of the shop.

Her scent lingered in the air after she left, and his shoulder felt warm where she'd touched him. It reminded him of the lingering feeling on the same shoulder when Dr. Surry had given it a squeeze.

Kate was acting awkward around him, a combination of shy and intimate and embarrassed and pissed-off. He guessed she was feeling uncomfortable about what was happening with Walter and how she'd decided to pull back from Calhoun.

He intended to let her call the shots. If she wanted to talk, he'd be happy to talk. If she wanted to have supper together sometime, he'd do that. If she changed her mind and wanted to make love with him, he wouldn't make a fuss about it. He didn't like what had happened. It left a hole in his heart. But Kate was the one with the problem, not him, and he couldn't justify feeling unhappy or angry about it. He'd just have to wait her out.

He spent the afternoon tying flies and listening to music and talking with the few customers who came into the shop, and around four thirty, Kate came out from her office and said, "I see you've got your boat with you."

Calhoun shrugged. "Thought I might go out for a few hours, catch the evening tide, see if I can clear my head."

She smiled. "You need to clear your head?"

He realized he hadn't told her about finding Paul Vecchio shot dead at his house. "Had a little excitement last night," he said.

She was frowning at him. "I can see trouble in your face, Stoney. What happened?"

So he told her. He kept it simple, just finding Mr. Vecchio's body with bullet holes in it and the police and various other official people coming to his house. He didn't mention how Ralph had run off or how worried he'd been or that he'd slept in his truck.

When he finished his story, Kate looked at him for a minute. Then she said, "What are you going to do?"

He shrugged. "I guess I'll go fishing."

"Well," she said, "tight lines."

CHAPTER SEVEN

By the time Calhoun launched his boat at the East End ramp, the tide was close to full flood and the sun hung low and red in the western sky. The afternoon breeze had settled down, and Casco Bay lay flat and impenetrable.

He weaved slowly among the buoys and moored watercraft, and when he cleared the harbor, he gunned the motor. He wanted to put some distance between himself and the mainland. He had no particular destination, and even though he had his rods and other gear with him, it didn't matter much whether he found fish to cast to or not. He just needed to get away from everything, and the best way he knew to do that was to go out on the ocean alone in a boat.

Well, Ralph was with him, but dogs, even a dog like Ralph, didn't count. Dogs didn't make demands or pursue agendas or get hurt feelings or use their love like a weapon. It was people and their complicated, self-centered affairs he wanted to get away from.

He took the same route he'd taken with Paul Vecchio, cutting between Peaks and Great Diamond islands and then out past Long Island and Great Chebeague to where the bay opened into the ocean. He saw only a couple of distant sailboats out there, which was about as solitary as anybody could reasonably expect.

When he felt like he could take a deep breath, he throttled back the motor and putted along, barely moving, more or less headed out toward the area near Quarantine Island where he and Mr. Vecchio had found the fish blitzing a few days earlier.

Now the sun had sunk behind the mainland and the western horizon was fading from orange to yellow. The eastern horizon was purply-black. A soft mist was rising from the dark glassy water. Overhead, a few bright stars had winked on.

Ralph was sitting up on the front seat, alert for flocking birds and blitzing fish, but there were none to be seen from horizon to horizon. The ocean had fallen dead.

Calhoun slipped on a fleece jacket against the September evening damp and chill.

When he figured he wasn't going to spot any birds or fish, Ralph slipped off the seat and lay down in the bottom of the boat.

They putted along while the sky turned from purple to black and the mist turned into fog and obscured the stars, and pretty soon the jumbled rocks of Quarantine Island lay silhouetted ahead of them.

Calhoun shut off the motor. The sudden silence rang in his ears for a minute. Then he heard the doleful clang of a distant bell buoy echoing in the fog. Sound travels forever over foggy water.

A dog barked from one of the islands. Ralph raised his head, perked up his ears, and lifted his nose for a minute. Then he kind of shrugged and went back to sleep.

All Calhoun wanted was a little peace. He tried to keep his mind clear, but regretful thoughts about Kate and Paul Vecchio and the sheriff kept intruding, and he couldn't shake that awful feeling he'd had in his stomach when he thought Ralph was never coming back. He remembered falling asleep in the bed of his truck, his disturbing thoughts becoming jumbled with disturbing dreams, and he remembered how amidst that mental chaos there had been another kind of thought, something analytical and objective, that he hadn't quite been able to get a handle on.

Now that same thought began buzzing around on the outskirts of his brain again. He tried to bring it into focus, to pin it down and see it clearly, but it was elusive, like a speck of dirt on the corner of your eyeball, so that no matter how you moved your eyes around, it was always on the periphery of your vision and you could never look at it straight on.

After a few minutes, Calhoun let the thought slink away into his unconscious. He figured it would be back, and maybe next time he'd nail it down.

As they sat there on the water, surrounded by the misty fog, Calhoun became aware of a new sound. It began as a soft mournful moan, rose into a keening wail, faded, died. Then the same sound rose again, answering, it seemed, from a different direction. It was a human sound, not words, just pure, raw emotion, an infinitely tragic sound that made Calhoun's throat tight.

He closed his eyes and let the rise and fall of the wailing cries wash over him, and in his mind's eye an image began to materialize the way a photograph takes form in a darkroom tray. He saw a fig-ure, a woman, standing atop a boulder with her arms raised and her gray robe flowing around her. It was, he realized, a nun in her gray habit. A hood covered her head, and her face was lifted to the sky, and she was moaning and wailing, a gray ghost calling to Stoney Calhoun.

In his mind he saw the hospital on Quarantine Island ablaze, sooty orange flames burning holes in the black wintry night, and he saw the faces of a hundred souls crowded together inside, men, women, children, trapped, their eyes wide, their hands lifted in helpless horrified disbelief, and he saw the nuns in their gray habits, kneeling in prayer, their heads bowed, their palms pressed together under their chins, and he watched as the flames engulfed them all . . .

When he opened his eyes, the mournful cries had faded away, and then he wondered if he'd really heard them or if they had just been another sputtering short-circuit in an undependable brain that had been zapped with lightning seven years ago.

Ralph was curled up in the bottom of the boat. "Did you hear that, bud?" said Calhoun.

Ralph opened his eyes, looked at Calhoun, let out a deep sigh, and went back to sleep.

He continued to drift out there in the dark, silent fog, but the gray ghosts did not call to him again.

After a while he started the motor, turned the boat around, and headed back to the harbor. He wasn't sure if he'd interpreted the gray nuns' message accurately, but now, at least, he thought he knew what he was supposed to do.

It was close to eleven by the time Calhoun backed his trailer into its slot beside the house, got it unhitched, hosed out the boat, and gave Ralph his dinner. He figured he should wait until morning to call the sheriff at his office.

Then he remembered that they were friends again, so he guessed it would be all right to wake him up.

Jane answered after four or five rings. "Mm," she mumbled. "Who in the world could be calling at this hour?"

"It's Stoney Calhoun, ma'am," he said, "and I'm awfully sorry to wake you up."

"Stoney Calhoun," she said. "I should have known."

"Yes, ma'am. I got to speak to your old man for a minute if you don't mind."

"You got another dead body for him, Stoney?"

"No, ma'am."

"Please don't call me ma'am."

"Sorry. Can I talk to him?"

"It's okay by me. Hang on."

Calhoun waited.

"Jesus, Stoney," said the sheriff when he came onto the line. "I was asleep. I didn't get much sleep last night."

"Me neither. I slept in my truck."

"Ralph?"

"He came back."

"I'm glad."

"Thank you. Me, too. Look, Sheriff. I'm ready to take that deputy's badge if you still want to give it to me."

"You are, huh?"

"Yup."

"What changed your mind?"

Calhoun hesitated. He didn't think the sheriff would understand about hearing the gray nuns calling to him out on Quarantine Island. "I've just been doing some thinking about it, that's all."

"Well," said the sheriff, "good. That's good. I can use you, for sure. I'll drop by in the morning. You gonna be around?"

"I don't have to be at the shop till the afternoon. I'll be right here."

"Get some sleep, Stoney."

"I'll try. You, too."

"I was doing pretty good," said the sheriff, "before you called."

Calhoun was around back splitting firewood when he heard the Explorer pull into the yard. Ralph, who'd been sprawled beside him watching him sweat, pushed himself to his feet and went out to greet the sheriff.

A minute later Ralph returned, and then the sheriff appeared. He was out of uniform. He was wearing blue jeans and a plaid shirt and a Red Sox cap to cover his bald head. He stood there with his arms folded across his chest and a bemused smile on his face while Calhoun balanced a hunk of cordwood on the big oak stump he used for a chopping block and whacked it with his maul, sending two equal halves flying in opposite directions.

Calhoun's T-shirt was hanging from his hip pocket. He used it to wipe the sweat off his face and chest.

"Splitting firewood," said the sheriff. "Good exercise. What is it they say? Warms you many times over. Cutting it, then splitting it, then stacking it, then lugging it. All that before you even burn it."

Calhoun nodded. "It's true."

"That kind of work helps a man think."

"Helps me not think," said Calhoun. "Let's get some coffee."

They climbed up onto the deck. The sheriff sat at the table. Calhoun went into the kitchen and came out a minute later with two mugs of coffee. He put one beside the sheriff's elbow, then sat down across from him.

The sheriff picked up the mug, took a swig, then said, "Let's do this." He fished the leather case that held the deputy badge from his pants pocket and put it on the table beside Calhoun's elbow. "I've got to swear you in."

"Go for it," said Calhoun.

The sheriff smiled. "I forgot to bring the paper. It's been so long since I did it, I can't remember what I'm supposed to say."

"I, Stonewall Jackson Calhoun, do solemnly swear I'll uphold all the laws of the state of Maine that make reasonable sense," Calhoun said. "I swear I'll do whatever you want me to do provided it ain't too dumb. I swear any time you want me to quit I'll go ahead and quit without a fuss. I swear I'll tell you the truth about most things. I swear to disagree with you when I think you're being stupid. I swear if you ask for my opinion about something, I'll give it to you even when I think it'll hurt your feelings." He shrugged. "That about cover it?"

"I should've copied that down," said the sheriff. "It's a way better oath than the regular one. You are hereby and therefore and whereas my deputy, God help us both. Okay?"

"Sure," said Calhoun. "Okay."

"Let's get to work, then." The sheriff took a folded sheet of paper from his shirt pocket and peered at it. "Here's what I know about Mr. Paul Vecchio so far," he said. "He'd been an adjunct professor of history at Penobscot College up in Augusta for the past twelve years. Taught American studies and a course on the New Deal. Wrote a couple of books that kept him in royalty checks. He grew up in Rhode Island, went to U. Maine in Orono, got his doctorate at Michigan. Lived in the town of Sheepscot."

"That's just west of Augusta, ain't it?" said Calhoun.

The sheriff nodded. "Two towns over, to the southwest. Vecchio's divorced, one kid, a teenage daughter who lives with her mother, his ex-wife, in California. A few speeding tickets on the Maine Pike. That's it." He handed the piece of paper to Calhoun. "You take it, Stoney. It's got his address on it."

Calhoun took the paper and glanced at it, which imprinted a photograph of it in his brain that he could look at any time he wanted to consult it. He didn't need the paper, but he folded it and stuffed it into his shirt pocket anyway. He didn't want to seem like was showing off. "We don't really know anything about Mr. Vecchio, then," he said.

The sheriff shook his head. "Nowhere near enough."

"What about that state cop, Gilsum?" said Calhoun. "He's on the case, ain't he?"

"Well," said the sheriff, "Gilsum sees himself as more of an administrator than a policeman. He thinks he's too important to actually go around interrogating suspects and looking for evidence. He's pretty big on delegating and appointing and coordinating and in general letting other people do the real work. Gilsum's a politician. He's angling to be a police commissioner somewhere."

"This is your case, then?"

"It's our case, Stoney. This one and the Quarantine Island case. I've got to report to Gilsum, and that DA, Enfield, he's keeping his nose up my butt. But we got both cases. You and me."

"Just us?"

The sheriff rolled his eyes. "Not hardly. These are big cases, Stoney. There are lots of people on these cases, and I suspect that once we make some headway, maybe come up with a good suspect, Gilsum will take over. In the meantime, he wants us working on them, and that, by Jesus, is what we're going to do."

Calhoun grinned. "Well, let's hope all those others don't get in our way. So where do you want to start? Tell me what you want me to do."

"According to that oath you just administered to yourself," said the sheriff, "I'm not inclined to give you orders. But I'm thinking that we need to know more about Mr. Vecchio, and if you agree . . ."

Calhoun nodded. "I agree. Why don't I head on up to Sheepscot, poke around, see what there is to be seen."

"That's what I was thinking." The sheriff found another folded-up piece of paper in his pocket and gave it to Calhoun. "Directions to Vecchio's house. From my computer."

Calhoun stuffed the paper into his pocket without looking at it. "So what're you gonna be doing, while I'm up there investigating?"

"Me?" said the sheriff. "Hell, Stoney. What do you think I need a deputy for? It's Saturday. This is my day off."

"You're joking, right?"

The sheriff shrugged. "Unfortunately, I am. I've got to hold down the office today. If things are quiet, I'll play around on the computer, see what I can dig up. You can learn a helluva lot about a case these days just sitting at your desk." He tipped up his coffee mug, drained it, put it down on the table, and stood up. "Soon as you finish up in Sheepscot, let me know what you find out."

"You want a report in writing?"

"That's how it's usually done, Stoney."

"We haven't talked about salary," said Calhoun. "How much you paying me?"

"You're a volunteer deputy. Didn't I mention that?"

"I didn't volunteer to do paperwork."

The sheriff smiled. "You can submit your reports orally, if you prefer." He reached into his pocket and placed a little cellular telephone on the table in front of Calhoun. "Just call me."

Calhoun pushed the phone away. "I hate these things."

The sheriff nodded. "I understand. But you've got to take it. I set it so it'd vibrate rather than ring. Keep it in your pocket. If you feel it buzz against your leg, it means I need to talk to you. Nobody else has the number, so it'll always be me. Look." The sheriff picked up the phone and pointed at a little green button. "If it buzzes, just press this button and say hello, and I'll talk to you. Understand?"

"It ain't that complicated," said Calhoun. "It's just offensive."

"Now," said the sheriff, "if you need to talk to me, all you gotta do is press this button here, on the side of it, and hold it up to your mouth and say 'Dickman.' Then put it to your ear and you'll hear me say, 'Hello, Stoney, what's up?' When you're done talking, just poke that little red button. You got all that?"

"Jesus Christ," muttered Calhoun.

"And if you want to call Kate or somebody, all you got to do is hit the numbers and then press that same green button."

"I doubt I could've figured that out for myself."

"So after you finish up there in Sheepscot," said the sheriff, who was making a point of ignoring Calhoun's sarcasm, "give me a call, tell me what you found out."

Calhoun picked up the phone and hefted it in his hand. It didn't weigh as much as the little folding knife he kept in his pants pocket. "Okay," he said. "We'll try it out."

The sheriff reached into his shirt pocket and took out a little stack of business cards. "You might need these," he said. "They got my name on 'em, not yours. In case there's somebody who might need to call us."

Calhoun stuck the cards in his wallet. "You got any other gear for me? Billy club? Handcuffs?"

The sheriff smiled. "That's about it for now."

"I ain't going to wear a uniform, you know."

"I figured."

"You wouldn't catch me dead in a hat like yours."

"My hat looks way better on me than it would on you anyway." He held out his hand. "Thanks, Stoney."

Calhoun shrugged and shook his hand.

The sheriff turned, went down off the deck, and got into his vehicle.

Calhoun watched him drive away. Then he took the coffee mugs into the house.

With Ralph riding shotgun, Calhoun followed the back roads north, avoiding the turnpike as he always tried to do. The countryside southwest of Augusta, the state capital, was laced with lakes with Indian names like Annabessacook and Maranacook and Sabattus and Androscoggin. They were long and skinny, as if some giant or god or great spirit had dragged his fingernails across the top of the earth. The implacable movement of glaciers, Calhoun remembered, speaking of history. Today, on this breezy, sun-drenched Saturday morning in September, the ripply lake surfaces glittered through the trees.

The township of Sheepscot lay on the Sheepscot River, twenty-odd miles southwest of Augusta. It took a little over an hour to drive there from Dublin, following the sheriff's printout of computer directions.

The sheriff's directions took them through the center of town directly to Paul Vecchio's house. It was a little green clapboarded bungalow, old and shabby but well cared for, set back from the two-lane state highway in a grove of tall pines.

Calhoun pulled his truck up to the doorway, told Ralph to sit tight, took a flashlight from the glove compartment, and got out. The pine trees towered over the house and kept it shady. The yard was a cushiony bed of pine needles, nice for a man who objected to tending and mowing a lawn. A woodshed beside the house was filled with cut-and-split firewood. Next to the shed, an aluminum canoe and a kayak rested upside down on sawhorses.

Calhoun tried the front door and found it locked. The back door was locked, too, but he found an unlatched cellar window that pulled open wide enough to slide through feet first.

He turned on the flashlight. The cellar had fieldstone walls and a dirt floor and a low, cobwebby ceiling. It smelled of damp earth and mildew. In one corner, a dozen cardboard boxes were stacked up on a platform of cinder blocks and two-by-sixes. There was a hot-water tank and an oil burner, also mounted on cinder blocks.

Since he was down there, Calhoun opened up the cardboard boxes. Three of them were filled with old college textbooks that were warping and threatening to fall apart from the damp. He figured he could learn something about Paul Vecchio by studying the kinds of books he stored in his basement, compared, on the one hand, to those he gave away and, on the other hand, to those he kept on his bookshelves. But he didn't see how that information would help them figure out who had shot him three times in the chest.

The other boxes held the usual stuff—a set of dinnerware, kitchen appliances, old clothes. Calhoun poked around in all of them and came up with nothing that interested him.

A set of narrow wooden steps led up to the first floor. The door opened into the kitchen. Yellow linoleum floor, white refrigerator, matching electric stove, cheap pine table and chairs in front of a window looking out the back of the house into the pine woods. There were two mugs, one dirty saucepan full of scummy old water, and some knives and forks in the sink. In the refrigerator was a six-pack of Samuel Adams lager missing two cans, two half-empty bottles of white wine, a carton of eggs, half a loaf of twelve-grain bread, some leftovers in plastic containers, and the usual mustard, mayonnaise, ketchup, and pickles.

In other words, nothing that would tell Calhoun who had killed Paul Vecchio, or why.

Nor did the kitchen cabinets yield anything.

There was a small living room with a TV and a stereo system and, as expected, walls lined with books—English and Russian and American novels, art, history, politics. Calhoun opened a few of them at random and saw notes and underlines on almost every page. They were the books of an intellectually curious man.

Off the living room was a small office. It, too, was dominated by bookshelves, more of the same kinds of books Calhoun had found in the living room. A big oak desk was pushed up to a window that overlooked some bird feeders hanging from a wire that was strung between two trees. On the desk were a telephone and a lamp plugged into a surge supressor. The rest of the desktop was bare except for a wire basket that held some slit-open envelopes. Unpaid bills and bank statements. Calhoun scanned the statements. No deposits or withdrawals or checks that caught his attention.

He riffled through the files in the pair of steel two-drawer file cabinets that flanked the desk. Insurance policies. IRA statements. Letters and contracts from publishers and editors. Photocopies of tax returns. Old bank statements and bills marked paid. All neatly organized, what there was of it. Calhoun surmised that Paul Vecchio cleaned out his files periodically. He was a neat man who didn't mind throwing things away.

The bed in the back bedroom was unmade but not messy. The clothes hung neatly in the closet. The bureau drawers were organized. A novel by Steven King, Vecchio's fellow Downeast writer, sat on the bedside table with a bookmark indicating he'd just started reading it. A small framed photo sat beside the novel. It showed Vecchio—Calhoun guessed he was five or six years younger—standing with his arm around a slim, dark-eyed girl, a young teenager. The man's daughter, most likely. In the photo she was looking up at him and laughing.

That was the only family-type photo Calhoun had seen in the entire house.

All he learned from the bathroom was that Vecchio was taking medication for high cholesterol.

A trapdoor in the hallway outside the bedroom opened up to the attic. Calhoun hoisted himself up and shone his flashlight around. There was no floor—just beams and joists and insulation and wires—and nothing was stored up there.

He went through the house a second time, looking harder. He poked through all the kitchen cabinets and drawers; he looked into the freezer compartment; he took off the toilet lid. He got down on his knees and shone his light under the bed, where he saw nothing but a dusty pair of bedroom slippers. He rummaged around among the socks and underpants in the bureau. He opened all the shoe boxes in the closet. He scanned every sheet of paper in the file cabinets.

All the time he was inside Paul Vecchio's house, Calhoun kept an ear tuned to outside. He could handle it if somebody—a relative, say, or a friend, or a local cop—showed up. He'd flash his shiny new deputy sheriff badge at them. He hoped he wouldn't have to.

He spent almost three hours searching the house for clues, and he didn't come up with a single thing that he was tempted to take back and show to the sheriff.

That, he figured, was pretty significant.

He made sure the doors were locked when he went outside. He went over to the truck and let out Ralph, who proceeded to sniff the bushes and pee on those that smelled right.

Something was buzzing against his leg. It felt like a pissed-off bumble bee had gotten itself stuck in his pocket.

Then he remembered the damn cell phone. He fished it out, poked the green button, put it to his ear, and said, "That you, Sheriff?"

"Who else would it be, Stoney? How'd you make out at Vecchio's place?"

"I just finished up."

"And?"

"And you better find out if that Gilsum or some other cops've been here and made off with all the evidence, because there ain't anything here."

"Nothing?"

"Nope. A lot of stuff, but no evidence. And just in case you're feeling dubious, you can be assured that I was trained to search a house for clues. I don't remember it happening, but I can tell. I knew what I was doing in there."

"So what are you saying?"

"I'm saying," said Calhoun, "that somebody beat me to it. Mr. Vecchio was a writer, right? There's a surge supressor on his desk, but no computer. No laptop anywhere to be seen. No printer. No floppy disks, no CDs, no modems, no external hard drives. No research notes, no notebooks full of ideas, no tapes or tape recorders. Nothing."

"Hm," said the sheriff. "I'll talk to Gilsum."

"Mr. Vecchio didn't have his car keys on him, right? When we found him dead, I mean."

"That's right. No keys."

"So whoever plugged him could've taken his keys and gone to his house and cleaned him out."

The sheriff was silent for a minute. "That's good thinking, Stoney. Like the dog that didn't bark. Clues that aren't where they're supposed to be are clues all by themselves." He hesitated. "So maybe Vecchio was working on something about that burned-up body. Maybe he had information, and they found out about it, so they killed him to shut him up, and then they went to his house with his keys to get anything he might've written down. Computer stuff, notebooks, whatever. That what you're thinking?"

"Pretty much," said Calhoun.

"I'll check with Gilsum," said the sheriff. "Listen, Stoney. Reason I called. Something's come up here and I need you."

"I'm supposed to be at the shop this afternoon, Sheriff. I can't leave Kate hanging. This deputy business ain't paying me enough to quit my day job, you know."

"It isn't paying you anything, actually," said the sheriff. "I took the liberty of talking to Kate. Told her I needed you this afternoon, and she said she didn't care, I could have you."

"Can't say I like the sound of that," said Calhoun.

"I see what you mean," said the sheriff. "She said she'd get that college kid over to help out."

"Adrian," said Calhoun. "Got his degree from some university down in Massachusetts, and now he can't find a real job."

"That's the one," said the sheriff. "So let's meet there at the shop. You can check in with Kate, and we can leave your truck there."

"I got Ralph with me."

"Bring him. Or leave him at the shop."

"I'll bring him," said Calhoun. "I ain't ready to leave him anywhere. You want to tell me what's up?"

"Probably nothing," said the sheriff. "But I've got to check it out, and if it turns out to be something, I don't want to be there all by myself. Does that make any sense?"

"You saying you're scared?"

"No," said the sheriff. "I'm saying I don't want to mess up a crime scene."

CHAPTER EIGHT

The sheriff's Explorer was parked in the side lot when Calhoun got to the shop. He parked beside it, and he and Ralph went in.

Adrian, the college kid, was behind the counter talking to a couple of young women who Calhoun figured had come into the shop to flirt, not to buy flies or waders. Adrian gave Calhoun a goofy grin, which pretty much confirmed it.

The sheriff and Kate were in Kate's office in back. Kate was behind her desk, leaning on her forearms talking to the sheriff, who was sitting in the wooden chair across from her sipping from a can of Coke.

They looked up when Calhoun went in.

"Talking about me?" said Calhoun.

"You nailed us red-handed," said the sheriff.

"Must be pretty boring," said Calhoun.

"You got that right," said Kate.

Ralph went over to her, and she reached down to give his ears a scratch. The sheriff pushed himself up from his chair. "Ready to go, Stoney?"

"You're the boss." He turned to Kate. "You gonna be all right here, honey?"

He'd done it again. Even when things were good between them, Kate didn't like him calling her "honey" in the shop. It just slipped out, and he regretted that it made her uncomfortable.

But she nodded and gave him a quick smile, forgiving him his little trespass. "I got Adrian," she said. "You boys go ahead, catch some bad guys."

Calhoun hesitated, then turned and walked out of the shop.

The sheriff and Ralph followed him.

"Let's take your vehicle," said the sheriff, "if you don't mind."

"Gonna sneak up on 'em, huh?"

"That's right."

They piled into Calhoun's truck. Ralph crawled into the narrow area behind the seats and positioned himself so he could poke his nose out of the passenger-side window over the sheriff's shoulder.

The sheriff said to get onto Route 1 heading down to South Portland.

"Any information on Mr. Vecchio?" said Calhoun.

"He got shot dead with a .22, just the way it looked. They didn't find anything by way of useful clues at your place. No tire tracks, no footprints, no empty cartridge cases. That bottle of sunscreen was half full of sunscreen. Vecchio's were the only prints on it. What we need is somebody with a motive to kill him."

"Don't look at me," said Calhoun.

The sheriff turned and looked at him, then shook his head and smiled.

They rode without talking for a while. Then the sheriff said, "Kate seems kinda depressed."

"Hard to blame her," said Calhoun. "Walter's in bad shape."

"She feels bad about how she's been treating you."

"So do I," said Calhoun. He hoped he wouldn't have to talk about it anymore.

The sheriff apparently got the message, because they went the rest of the way without saying much, just the sheriff giving occasional directions.

They crossed the Veterans Memorial Bridge and went through several stoplights, and then the sheriff said, "Hook that left up there after the liquor store."

Calhoun turned onto the narrow side road. It was lined with small ranch houses that featured concrete birdbaths on the lawns and children's riding toys in the driveways. There was a sandy cul-de-sac at the end with some even smaller ranch houses.

The sheriff pointed to one of the houses. "That's the one."

The white shingled siding was streaked with rust, and a complicated television antenna sprouted from the roof. A pair of big propane tanks stood beside the front door. There was a black mailbox in front with no name on it.

Calhoun pulled into the dirt ruts that passed for a driveway and told Ralph to stay put. He and the sheriff got out.

They stood there looking around. "I got a call from the dog officer this morning," said the sheriff. "Somebody reported that this big dog, a shepherd, I think he said, was going around knocking over their trash barrels looking for pizza crusts and growling at the children. The dog belongs to the guy who lives here in this house. The officer wanted to give a citation to the owner, but he wasn't home, and the neighbors said they hadn't seen him around for a while."

A rusted-out Dodge pickup was pulled up beside the house. A charcoal grill and a lawn mower and a few bald automobile tires were half buried in the shin-high grass and droopy weeds on what passed for a front yard.

"What happened to the dog?" said Calhoun.

"The officer finally caught him," the sheriff said. "Took him to the pound, I guess."

They walked slowly around the little lot of land where the house stood. Out back was a wooden doghouse and some plastic trash barrels and a motorcycle covered by a tarp.

Suddenly the sheriff stopped. "Listen," he said.

Calhoun listened. He didn't hear anything. "What?" he said. "I only got one good ear."

"Inside," said the sheriff. "Voices."

Calhoun moved closer to the wall of the house, and then he heard it. He listened for a minute, then said, "It's the TV. There was some music, and then they applauded."

The sheriff nodded. "Let's see who's at home."

They went around to the front. Some stacked-up cinder blocks served as the front stoop. The sheriff stepped up on them and banged his knuckles on the aluminum screen door. "Anybody home?" he called. "This is the sheriff. Open up, please."

Nobody opened up. The sheriff knocked again, yelled louder. Then he turned to Calhoun, shrugged, opened the screen door, and tried the front door latch.

The door pushed open. The sheriff poked his head inside, then yanked it back out again. "Jesus," he muttered. "It's nine hundred degrees in there. Smells like a garbage dump."

They went in. To Calhoun's nose, the odor was a stew of rotten food, sour milk, unflushed toilet, and uncirculated air.

"No dead body in here," he said, "if that's what you're thinking."

"I kinda was," said the sheriff. "You know what a body that's been dead for a while smells like, do you?"

Calhoun shrugged. "I guess I do. I don't specifically remember doing it, but I know I've been in houses where there were old dead bodies, and I'd remember that smell. This ain't it."

"Don't touch anything," said the sheriff.

"Hell, I know that."

The front door opened directly into the living room. On a coffee table in front of a dirty old sofa were an empty beer bottle and an aluminum tray of half-eaten food—one of those microwave dinners, looked like mashed potato and gravy and sliced carrots and some kind of gray meat, pot roast would be a good guess, all of it now covered in fuzzy green mold. The sofa faced the television, which was playing a quiz show.

A folded-open newspaper lay on the floor beside the sofa. Calhoun bent to look at it. It was dated two weeks ago the previous Wednesday.

"Stoney," said the sheriff, "this place isn't big enough for the two of us. Why don't you go ahead and wait for me outside. I won't be a minute."

"I don't mind," said Calhoun. "It's hard to breathe in here."

"If I should come up with something—"

"I understand," said Calhoun. "Better if you don't have some amateur like me bangin' around in there contaminating the evidence."

When Calhoun went out, he saw a chunky woman in cutoff jeans and a tight T-shirt standing by his truck talking to Ralph through the half-open window. A roll of fat bulged out between the bottom of her T-shirt and the top of her shorts.

"Watch out he don't bite you," said Calhoun.

When she whirled around, he saw that she was just a girl, a young teenager, fourteen or fifteen, he guessed. She had a helmet of short, curly blond hair, wide-spaced blue eyes, and a little rosebud mouth. "He seems friendly," she said.

Calhoun smiled. "He is. I was kidding. His name is Ralph."

"Ralph," she said. "That's a pretty funny name for a dog." She turned to the truck window. "Hi, Ralph."

"He was named after Ralph Waldo Emerson," said Calhoun.

"Who's that?"

"He was a philosopher."

She shrugged. "Never heard of him."

Calhoun gave her a smile. "I'm Stoney."

She held out her hand to him. "I'm Mattie. I live over there." She pointed at a little green ranch house across the cul-de-sac. "You looking for Errol?"

"That who lives here?" said Calhoun, jerking his head back at the trailer. "Errol? Errol who?"

"Errol Watson, that's who," she said. "He hasn't been home in quite a while. The dog catcher come and took away Grunt."

"Grunt?"

"His dog. My mom finally called about him. He was gittin' into our trash and scratchin' at the door and howlin' all night long."

"Where's Errol now?" said Calhoun. "Do you know?"

She shook her head. "Errol and me, we ain't exactly best friends. My mom tells me I'm s'pose to steer clear of him."

"Why's that?"

She shrugged. "I don't know. She don't like men very much."

"Is your mom home?"

"Nope. She's at work. She cleans rooms over at the Ramada."

The sheriff came out of the house. He stood there looking at it for a minute, then wandered over to the truck.

Calhoun introduced him to Mattie.

"What's your last name, Mattie?" said the sheriff.

"Perkins," she said. "You're a sheriff?"

"That's right. And this here is my deputy."

"Mattie says the man who lives here is named Errol Watson and he hasn't been home for some time," said Calhoun. "It was her mother who phoned in about Watson's dog. Grunt."

The sheriff smiled. "Grunt?"

"That's the dog's name," said Calhoun.

"What do you know about Mr. Watson?" said the sheriff to Mattie.

"Nothin'. My mom tole me not to be friendly to him."

"Do you always obey your mom?"

She rolled her eyes. "Mostly I do, sure. Errol's okay, but my mom really means it about him. She says it all the time. Don't you go near that man, she says, or I'll take the strap to you." Mattie rolled her eyes and smiled to make it clear that she wasn't afraid of her mother.

The sheriff nodded. "Did she ever tell you why she's so emphatic about it?"

She shrugged. "Not really. I was over there one day watchin' him work on his motorcycle, and she seen us and started yellin' at me. Next thing I know, my mom calls up my daddy and he's over there yellin' at Errol. My daddy's a pretty good yeller. You could hear him all over the neighborhood. After that, Errol and me, we steer clear of each other."

"What was your daddy saying?" said Calhoun.

Mattie shrugged. "Mostly swears. You want me to repeat them?"

"Nope," said Calhoun. "That's okay."

"What's your daddy's name?"

"Lawrence. Everybody calls him Perk, though."

"Where is he now?" said the sheriff.

"He lives in Kittery," said Mattie. "Works at the boatyard. He and my mom got divorced."

"What do you know about Errol?" said Calhoun.

"Not that much," she said. "He just stays home most of the time. Watchin' TV and drinkin' beer, I guess, or else he's out back workin' on his bike. Only time you ever see him, he's comin' in or goin' out. I think he works at a lumberyard."

"Does he drive that truck?" The sheriff waved his hand at the Dodge pickup in the driveway.

She nodded.

"What about the motorcycle?"

"I never saw him take it out," she said. "I think he just likes to tinker with it."

"The pickup," said the sheriff. "Has it been moved lately?"

Mattie shook her head. "Been sittin' right there for a week, at least."

The sheriff nodded. "What did you and Errol talk about that time he was working on his motorcycle?"

"Not much. I asked him some questions, but he just pretty much ignored me."

"Does he have friends?" said the sheriff. "People coming to visit?"

"I don't recall ever seeing anybody."

"How long have you lived here, Mattie?"

"Since the end of June," she said. "Me and my mom moved down from Madrid after school was out."

Calhoun noticed that she pronounced the town of Madrid with the emphasis on the first syllable, Mad-rid, which reminded him that his own Maine accent and manner of speaking was acquired, not inherent. Otherwise, he probably wouldn't have noticed.

"Was Mr. Watson living here then?" said the sheriff.

She nodded.

"What's your mother's name?"

"Allison," said Mattie.

"She keep her married name?"

Mattie nodded. "Allison Perkins. People mostly call her Allie."

The sheriff took out his wallet, removed a couple of business cards, and handed them to Mattie. "Please give one to your mom when she gets home," he said. "Tell her we're interested in what might've happened to Mr. Watson and have her give me a call. And keep one for yourself. Call if you think of anything else. Okay?"

"Sure," she said.

"And when you talk to your daddy, tell him the same thing."

Mattie shrugged. "I'll try to remember."

He smiled at her. "Thank you." He turned to Calhoun and said, "Let's get going."

They started for the truck.

"Wait a minute," said Mattie. "I thought of something. You asked about Errol having friends?"

They turned around. "That's right," said the sheriff.

"I don't know if it was an actual friend," she said, "but one man did come to see him. It was like a month ago, maybe more, maybe five or six weeks. I'm sorry. I just remembered."

"What do you remember?"

"Just," she said with a little wave of her hand, "this nice car driving up, man wearing a suit going up to his door. This was, oh, after suppertime, it was getting dark. My mom was working."

"Did you get a good look at this man?"

She shook her head. "Just his clothes, like he just came from an office."

"What about his car?" said the sheriff. "What kind of car was it?"

"I don't know cars that well. It looked new, with a sunroof. A sedan. Dark red." She shrugged.

"Dark red," repeated the sheriff.

"Like . . . burgundy? You know what I mean?"

The sheriff nodded. "A big sedan? Medium-sized? Compact?"

Mattie rocked her hand. "Medium, I guess. Not big like those old Cadillacs and Lincolns you see on TV. Not real tiny, either."

"Why did you say you didn't think this man was a friend?"

Mattie smiled. "That nice car? All dressed up? Not what you'd expect for a friend of Errol, that's all. Maybe I was wrong about that."

"How long did the man stay?"

She shook her head. "I don't know. I was in the house. I just noticed the car drive up and the man get out."

"Did he go inside? Did he and Errol talk?"

She shook her head. "I wasn't like snooping, honestly. I just happened to glance out the window and notice that car pulling up in front of his house. Only reason I even paid any attention was, we don't have cars like that coming to this neighborhood that much. Next time I looked out, it was gone."

"How much later was that?"

She shrugged. "Couple hours, I guess. But it could've been gone for a long time before that."

"This is helpful," said the sheriff. "Thank you, Mattie. If you think of anything else, you be sure to give me a call. You've got my card."

"Sure," she said. "I will."

They got into Calhoun's truck and waved at Mattie, and the sheriff told him to head back to the shop.

"You didn't want to talk to some of the other neighbors?" said Calhoun after they'd pulled back onto Route One.

"Nope."

"You find anything interesting inside?"

The sheriff shrugged.

"It would appear that Watson was interrupted," said Calhoun. "Left the TV running, his dinner half eaten."

"It'd take some kind of man to eat even half of that shit," said the sheriff.

Calhoun smiled. "You gonna tell me what you're thinking?"

"Not yet."

"I'm your deputy," said Calhoun. "You're supposed to share."

The sheriff shook his head. "If I'm wrong," he said, "I don't want you to think I'm stupid."

When they got back to the shop, the three of them went inside. Ralph curled up on his old sweatshirt in the corner next to the door. Adrian was still behind the counter, and Kate was talking with a customer at the rack of fly rods. The sheriff went over and spoke to her, then crooked his finger at Calhoun.

Calhoun followed the sheriff back to Kate's office. "What're we doing?" he said.

The sheriff sat in Kate's chair and hitched himself up to her computer. "Watch and learn," he said.

"I ain't interested in learning any of that computer mumbo-jumbo," said Calhoun. "My head's too full already."

"Well, sit there and keep me company, at least."

Calhoun took the wooden chair across from him.

The sheriff was pecking away at the computer, mumbling, "Hm," and then, "Ha," and after a few minutes, "I thought so." He looked up. "Come here, Stoney. Take a look at this."

Calhoun got up and went around to the sheriff's side of the desk. On the computer screen was a colored photograph of a thin-faced man with a balding head and round glasses. He looked about forty, and then Calhoun saw his birthday, which was 7/17/62. His place of residence was Portland 04101. No street address.

"Errol Watson?" said Calhoun.

"Himself."

"Looks like a banker."

The sheriff snorted a quick laugh. "Take a look."

The sheriff scrolled down the screen, and Calhoun saw a list headed "Convictions." Errol Watson had five convictions—two for Title 17A, section 253, "Gross Sexual Assault," two for 17A, section 254, "Sexual Abuse of Minors," and one for 17A, section 255A, "Unlawful Sexual Contact."

"Not a nice man," said Calhoun.

"No. I'm prepared to bet my pension that as we speak, Mr. Watson is in a drawer in the refrigerator room in the morgue in Augusta, all burned beyond recognition."

Calhoun found himself nodding. "I wouldn't bet against you. How'd you do that, anyway?"

"I told you to watch and learn."

"Just give me the condensed version."

The sheriff smiled and waved his hand. "I had a hunch, that's all."

"More than a hunch, I bet."

"Well, sure," said the sheriff. "A couple of things struck me, as they probably struck you. First off, our corpse having his pecker cut off and jammed into his mouth, suggesting he might be a sex offender of some kind. Second, Mattie there, her mother being so emphatic, telling her to stay away from Errol Watson. Third, the fact that Watson left suddenly, his dinner half eaten, his dog on the loose, the TV still running. And fourth, just the way he was living. Solitary. Disorganized. Aimless. A man having trouble finding a place in society, no friends or family coming to visit, and who didn't care very much one way or the other." He looked at Calhoun and shook his head. "So anyway, putting all that together, I wondered if Mr. Errol Watson himself might be a convicted sex offender. If so, I knew we'd find him on the sex offender registry. So I just went there on the Internet and typed in his name, and that's how I got what you're looking at."

"Simple as that," said Calhoun.

"Yep. Simple as that. Here. Take a look."

The sheriff typed something, and up on the screen came a page titled "Maine Sex Offender Registry Search." "Okay," he said. "When I went here before, I typed in Watson's name, but you can type in a town instead. Let's look at Portland." He pressed a key, and another page appeared on the screen. He scrolled down a list and clicked on "Portland." Almost instantly an alphabetical list of names with telephone numbers appeared. "Here you are," said the sheriff. "All the convicted sex criminals who live or work in Portland. They update it on a regular basis." He scrolled down the numbered list.

Calhoun read the names as they appeared on the computer monitor. The last one on the list was number 129. "That's a lot perverts for one little city," he said.

"Those are just the ones who've been tried and convicted," said the sheriff. "The tip of the proverbial iceberg."

"Only three women."

The sheriff nodded. "That's the usual percentage. Women don't get accused much, and they get convicted less often. Doesn't mean there aren't plenty of female perverts out there."

Calhoun was nodding. "So these people," he said, "these sex offenders, anybody can see who they are, what they look like, what they've done, where they're living and working. All you need is a computer."

"That's right," said the sheriff. "It's all public information, and they try to make it as easy as possible for the public to get at it. The whole point is for everybody to know who these predatory sons of bitches are." He pushed himself to his feet. "So now I'm going to hustle back to my office and see what else I can find out about Mr. Errol Watson. And I'm going to inform Detective Gilsum and the ME's office up in Augusta that we have a possible ID on our corpse. They can get the dental records of anybody who's spent time in prison."

The sheriff went to the front of the shop and waved at Kate, who was on the phone at the counter. She waved back at the sheriff and gave Calhoun a quick little smile that was pretty convincing around her mouth but didn't make it all the way up to her eyes.

"I'll be in tomorrow," Calhoun said to her.

"If the sheriff needs you . . ."

"Hell," he said, "I'm just a volunteer deputy. I got a responsibility. I'll be here to open up at noon and I'll close at four, and you should stay home and take it easy for once."

"I might just do that," Kate said. "I sure could use a break."

"I'll be here," said Calhoun. "Don't even think about it." He gave her a smile and a nod and got out of there quick before Kate felt obligated to try to smile again.

The sheriff was in the parking lot leaning against the side of his Explorer. When Calhoun caught up to him, he said, "We did some good work today, Stoney. I think we make a pretty good partnership, don't you?"

"It ain't a partnership," said Calhoun. "You're the boss and I'm your deputy."

"I don't really think of it that way."

"I do," said Calhoun. "It's the way I want it to be."

The sheriff shrugged. "Whatever. Either way."

"Those records," said Calhoun. "Watson's, I mean. They should tell you who his victim was, right?"

"Victim or victims, plural. Yes." The sheriff smiled. "You're thinking about somebody with a motive to slice his throat and cut off his dick and set him afire."

"Well," said Calhoun, "if some man had unlawful sexual contact with my minor daughter, say, and sexually abused her, and committed gross sexual assault on her, if I'm even close to imagining what those crimes actually amount to, I can't think of anything I wouldn't want to do to him."

"Or," said the sheriff, "if you just suspected he might've had unlawful sexual contact with your daughter. Or even if you suspected he might've just thought about it."

Calhoun nodded. "You're thinking about Mattie."

"Mattie's daddy. Lawrence Perkins from Kittery."

"Or even Mattie's mom."

The sheriff shrugged. "Anybody who knew what Mr. Errol Watson was makes a pretty good suspect when you think about it." He climbed into his Explorer, started it up, and rolled down the window. "We've still got to find the Paul Vecchio connection," he said.

"If there is one."

"Oh," said the sheriff, "I'm sure there is."

"I'm working at the shop in the afternoon tomorrow."

"I'll find you if I need you."

Calhoun heated up a can of beans and a leftover piece of steak for dinner. He and Ralph ate out on the deck while the sky turned from blue to pewter to purple to black and Bitch Creek bubbled around the rocks out back and the bats flapped around in the yard.

He was in the kitchen washing the dishes when he saw headlights cutting through the woods and pulling into his yard.

He took the Remington twelve-gauge off its pegs and went out onto the deck in time to see the Man in the Suit step out of his Audi. He made a visor of his hand, looked up, then waved and started up the steps.

Calhoun stood there at the top with the barrel of his shotgun resting on his shoulder.

"Put that damn thing away, Stoney," said the Man in the Suit. "I come in peace."

"You never go anywhere in peace," said Calhoun. But he turned and leaned the shotgun against the wall.

The Man in the Suit went over and sat in one of the Adirondack chairs. "You got some coffee heated up?"

Calhoun shrugged, went inside, poured two mugs full, and took them outside. He put one on the table next to the Man in the Suit and held the other in both hands. He remained standing. He figured if he sat down it would look like he welcomed the man's company. "So what do you want?" he said.

"I wanted to congratulate you. A deputy sheriff. The first step in what promises to be a long and exciting career as a crime buster."

"Not me," said Calhoun.

"I mean it," said the Man in the Suit. "You made the right decision. So how's it going?"

"What's it to you?"

The Man in the Suit smiled. "That's the big question, isn't it?" He leaned forward. "Stoney, I wish I could speak more candidly with you, I really do. Maybe someday I'll be able to. But let's put it this way for now. You are investigating a couple of interesting crimes. You are, I have no doubt, discovering talents and knowledge that you didn't know you had. You're remembering new things, learning more about yourself. Am I right?"

Calhoun shook his head. "I just do what the sheriff tells me to do, that's all. I drive him around, mainly. I don't have any particular talent or knowledge that I'm aware of. I'm just helping him out. It's no big deal."

The Man in the Suit smiled. "You can be up-front with me, Stoney. I'm your friend."

Calhoun had danced this dance with the Man in the Suit before.

He had no intention of being up-front with him. "I know that," he said. "I'm just telling you how it is."

The Man in the Suit peered at Calhoun over the rim of his coffee mug. He took a sip, then put it down. "There is much about yourself that you don't know, Stoney, and that I do know. Quid pro quo, remember?"

"I got no quid for you," said Calhoun. "Sorry."

"Your family," the Man in the Suit said, as if Calhoun hadn't spoken. "Your education. Where you lived. What you did. What you were good at. Who you loved. Who loved you."

"I don't care about that," said Calhoun. "I got a chance to start my life over again, and it's going pretty good."

"That's not how I hear it."

"What do you hear?" said Calhoun before he could stop himself.

The Man in the Suit shrugged. "I hear Kate dumped you, for one thing."

"She didn't—" He clamped his mouth shut, then took a deep breath. "That's none of your God damn business."

The Man in the Suit shrugged. He finished his mug of coffee, put the mug down, and stood up. "Maybe next time I come by you'll be in a better mood, Stoney."

"Don't bother coming by," said Calhoun. "This is my mood whenever I see you."

"We haven't talked about your relatives lately," said the Man in the Suit.

Calhoun knew this was how the man hoped to manipulate him, but he couldn't help himself. "What relatives?"

"Well," said the Man in the Suit, "for example, it occurred to me that you might have wondered if you had any children."

Calhoun clenched his teeth so that he wouldn't speak before he thought about what to say.

Then he said, "I don't care about that."

The Man in the Suit smiled and nodded. "Right. Okay, Stoney. Maybe another time." He went down the steps to his Audi. He opened the door, looked up and waved, and got into his car.

Calhoun stood there and watched him head up the driveway

until his headlights stopped winking through the woods and the purr of the Audi's engine died in the distance.

He knew it was going to be hard not to think about children, now that the Man in the Suit had stuck that idea into his head.

But he planned to try.

CHAPTER NINE

Calhoun woke up with gray light and a cacophony of birdsong seeping in through the bedroom window screen. It had been another lousy night's sleep. The last time he remembered sleeping decently was several nights earlier with Kate beside him, their legs all tangled together, her hair in his face, her skin slick against his.

That was before she told him she wasn't going to come to his house anymore, and before Paul Vecchio showed up dead, and before Ralph disappeared.

The dreams, as usual, faded too fast for him to nail them down, and he was left with that familiar sadness, the vague certainty that things were not right. He often had vivid dreams, and he understood that if he could remember them and analyze them, they would give him a window into his life before ten thousand volts of lightning had pulverized all of his conscious memories.

He could never recall them, though. He'd tried instructing himself to wake up in the middle of a dream so he could write it down for later analysis, and he had managed to do it a few times, but in the sharp rational light of morning wakefulness, his notes made no sense whatsoever. "Woman with no eyes waving her hat at me," he'd written once about a dream that had left him feeling panicky. Another time: "Naked in the desert surrounded by children with heads like tennis racquets."

The doctors at the VA hospital in Virginia had explained that his memories of the first thirty-odd years of his life weren't really gone. They resided in remote and mysterious corners of his unconscious mind. But his wiring had short-circuited. The electronic connections, the network of ganglions and synapses that allowed thoughts to move back and forth between the conscious and the unconscious parts of the normal mind, had been fried in Calhoun's. Sometimes there would be a spark—a dream fragment, a song lyric, an evocative smell—and a distorted impulse would plow into his consciousness, daring him to make sense of it, which, so far, he hadn't had much luck at.

So Stoney Calhoun was left with weird, quickly forgotten dreams, and jolts of déjà vu, and apparitions. They were the gifts— and the curses—of a lightning-zapped brain, and he accepted them as his own version of normality.

Then along would come the Man in the Suit hinting that maybe he had children, or he'd get a particularly vivid flash of déjà vu, or a gray nun who'd been dead for eighty years would cry out to him from Quarantine Island, and even if he couldn't figure out what it meant, or if it was just random and meaningless, it would leave him jangly and depressed—sometimes only until he came fully awake, but sometimes for the whole day.

He hoped today wasn't going to be one of those days.

He poured a mug of coffee, took it down to Bitch Creek, and sat on his usual boulder. Ralph sat beside him. Calhoun thought about Lyle, as he always did when he visited Bitch Creek. He remembered how Lyle had brought a little Brittany puppy to him, telling him that a man living alone in the woods needed company. For a young guy, Lyle was pretty wise. Calhoun always missed him.

They looked for feeding trout, but there were none to be seen this morning. No ghostly dead bodies came drifting down on the currents, either, and whatever it was that had been tugging at Calhoun's memory recently did not reveal itself.

They went back to the house. He fed Ralph and made a toasted peanut-butter sandwich for himself. They ate on the deck while the sun rose into a pure blue September sky, but Calhoun's cloud of hopeless sadness continued to envelop him.

He spent the morning splitting and stacking firewood, and gradually the intense, hard, repetitive exercise cleared his head and calmed his spirit.

A little before eleven Calhoun and Ralph piled into the truck and headed for the shop. Sundays had been dead since Labor Day, but Kate insisted that they open up for a few hours anyway. If you closed the shop when business was slow, she said, business would just get worse. He supposed she was right. Anyway, Kate was the boss.

So he opened up, turned on the classical music station, checked the voice mail for messages, made some coffee, then sat at the bench to tie some more flies for the Boston guys.

Kate had set up the fly-tying bench in the middle of the store, and she encouraged Calhoun to tie flies whenever he wasn't actually with a customer. She theorized that a man tying flies would be an attraction to any potential customers who wandered into the shop. Plus, it would give them something to talk about with Calhoun, who was uninterested in holding idle conversations with strangers.

A little after two o'clock, the bell over the door dinged. Calhoun looked up. A woman had stepped inside.

Ralph got up from where he was lying beside Calhoun and went over to her with his stubby little tail all awag, and she knelt on the floor and bent her face down so Ralph could lick it. He could hear her cooing and nice-dogging at him. Ralph couldn't get enough of that kind of attention.

At first he didn't recognize the woman. A long reddish-blond braid hung out of the back of her Boston Red Sox cap. She was wearing dirty sneakers and tight-fitting blue jeans and a dark leather vest over a man's untucked white shirt.

It was Dr. Sam Surry, the medical examiner. She looked more like a college art student than a doctor.

After a minute she straightened up, looked around, and spotted Calhoun. She smiled and waved and came over, with Ralph trailing behind her trying to sniff at her cuffs.

"Hey," she said.

"Hey, yourself. Where's your stethoscope?"

She smiled. "This is Ralph, right?"

Calhoun nodded.

"He came back. I'm so glad. I was worried about him, I really was." She bent over and gave Ralph's forehead a scratch. "He's a nice doggie. He must smell Quincy on my pants."

Quincy, Calhoun remembered, was her springer. "Ralph's a bird dog," he said. "He's got an excellent nose."

"You're tying flies. That's so cool." She came over and stood behind him. "It's hard to reconcile, a big tough guy like you making those delicate little things out of feathers and thread and fluffy stuff."

"I ain't that tough," said Calhoun.

She put her hand on his shoulder and leaned over to look at what he was doing. Her fingers burned, the way they had left heat the other night when she'd touched him. Her hair smelled soapy. "Do you give lessons?" she said. Her mouth was very close to his ear.

He shrugged. "Kate and I have talked about doing that. Holding fly-tying classes in the winter when things are slow. It would bring people into the shop, give us more exposure, maybe even create some new fishermen, new customers. That's her idea, anyway. I think it's probably worth a shot, though I'm not sure I have the patience for it. Maybe we'll try it this year."

"If you do," she said, "I'll sign up. I almost went into surgery because I like to do precise work with my hands. It must be satisfying to catch fish on flies you made yourself."

Calhoun nodded. "Ayuh. It is." He wondered why Dr. Sam Surry had come into the shop, but he couldn't come up with a polite way of asking.

"I bet you'd make a wonderful teacher," she said. Her hand was still on his shoulder. He wondered if she'd forgotten it was there, or if she was as aware of it as he was.

He shifted in his chair, and she finally took away her hand, which was a relief.

"We got a big clearance sale going on," he said after a minute.

"Fifty percent off all the clothing. Or, if you like, you can get two of something for the price of one. Whichever you prefer. We're making room for next year's outdoor activewear fashions."

She was smiling at his cumbersome change of subject. "Are next year's outdoor activewear fashions better than this year's?"

Calhoun shrugged. "I am the last person you should ask about fashion. I was just trying to do my job and sell you a damn shirt."

"Would it be awful if I didn't buy anything?"

"You didn't come here looking for a bargain?"

"No," she said. "I came looking for you." She hesitated. "I thought you'd want to know that they did the ballistics, and your pistol was not the weapon that Mr. Vecchio was shot with."

"I was pretty sure of that," said Calhoun.

"You should get it back in a few days."

He nodded. "That's good. I appreciate you dropping by to tell me."

She shrugged. "I was in the neighborhood. Thought you'd like to know that you're no longer a suspect."

"I've been wondering whether I did it or not."

She smiled.

"You want some coffee?" he said.

She looked at her wristwatch, then at him. "Okay. Sure."

"Milk and sugar?"

She shook her head. "Just black."

Calhoun got up, went back to the coffee urn, filled two mugs, and brought them back to the fly-tying bench.

Dr. Sam Surry had picked up one of the featherwing streamers he'd made the other day. She was holding it up to the light, squinting at it. "This is gorgeous," she said. "A work of art."

"It's called a Gray Ghost."

"It's too pretty for some old fish to chew on."

He handed her a mug of coffee. "I'll make one for you, if you want. Show you how it's done."

"I'd like that," she said.

She hitched up a chair beside him, and he proceeded to tie a Gray Ghost for her. He explained what each piece of material and each part of the fly was called, and he told her that Mrs. Carrie Stevens, who'd invented several Ghosts—gray, green, and black that he knew of, maybe others—tied beautiful flies without a vise, holding the hook and manipulating the thread and the materials with her fingers.

He was just stroking back the wings and whip-finishing the head when the bell over the door dinged and Kate came in. She looked around, and then her eyes lit on Calhoun with Dr. Sam Surry sitting beside him. She arched her eyebrows, smiled quickly, and came over.

"How's it going?" she said to Calhoun.

"Slow." He dabbed a drop of head cement on the Gray Ghost. "This is Dr. Surry," he said to Kate. "She's the medical examiner on Mr. Vecchio's case." To Sam Surry, he said, "This here is Kate Balaban. She's my boss. She owns the place."

Kate gave Dr. Surry a quick smile. "Stoney and I are partners, actually," she said.

"He was showing me how he ties a Gray Ghost," said Dr. Surry.

"He's an artist, all right," said Kate.

"I thought you were taking the day off," said Calhoun.

Kate nodded. "I know you did. I need some stuff in my office. I'll be out of your hair in a minute."

She went into her office in the back of the store, and after a few minutes she came back out. She went behind the front counter, did something at the cash register, then waved and left the store.

"Kate's a spectacular-looking woman," said Dr. Surry.

Calhoun nodded. "She surely is."

Dr. Surry stood up. "Well," she said, "I guess I should get going."

"Don't forget your fly," said Calhoun. He put the Gray Ghost he'd tied for her into a transparent envelope. "Go catch something with it."

"I think I'll have it framed," she said. She headed for the door.

Calhoun got up and followed her. "Sure I can't interest you in a nice half-price Patagonia shirt?"

She smiled. "I've already got a shirt. Thanks for the fly. If I hear anything new on the case, I'll let you know." She gave him a little wave and went out the door.

Calhoun watched her walk away, then shrugged and went back to his fly-tying bench. He had the feeling that between Sam Surry and Kate Balaban, he'd missed something, but he decided not to dwell on it. There was no point to trying to understand the ways of women.

Calhoun was putting away the fly-tying stuff, getting ready to close up the shop, when the sheriff came in.

"You want to buy something," said Calhoun, "or are you on the job?"

"On the job, I'm afraid. Two murder cases, Stoney. Can't really take a day off, even if it is a Sunday. Jane doesn't like it, but what are you going to do?"

"Take her out to dinner."

He nodded. "Already thought of that. We're going to try that new Mexican place. I'd ask you to come along, but . . ."

Calhoun smiled. "If you did, I know enough to turn you down. So what's up?"

"Just wanted to update you. They haven't been able to check the dental records yet, it being the weekend and all, but the body size and age and everything of that burned corpse matches what they know about Errol Watson. It's not a positive identification, but everything fits and I'm prepared to pursue it. He served four and a half of a seven-year sentence for fondling a twelve-year-old girl, exposing himself to her, showing her pornographic photographs. Got out a year and a half ago. I got the names of the victim's parents and the ADA who prosecuted the case and the PD who defended him. I figure we should try to talk to all of them."

"We?" said Calhoun.

The sheriff nodded. "I'm hoping you'll come with me, Stoney. I'd value your insights."

"You talking about tomorrow?"

The sheriff nodded. "The sooner the better. Your shop's closed on Mondays, if I recall."

Calhoun shrugged. "I got nothing better to do."

"I also want to talk to Mattie Perkins's parents," said the sheriff.

"Suspects," said Calhoun.

"Sure. The other thing is, Gilsum says his cops never went to Vecchio's house. I had the feeling he never even thought of it, though what he said was, they hadn't gotten around to it yet."

"You tell him I was there?"

"Had to," said the sheriff. "Had to tell him you were working with me."

"What'd he say about that?"

"Nothing. I think he'd've liked it if you were a good suspect. But you're not, and he knows it. Gilsum's a pragmatist. He just wants the case solved. He doesn't much care how it happens."

"So," said Calhoun, "whoever killed Vecchio took his keys and went to his house up in Sheepscot and grabbed his laptop and stuff."

"We don't know that," said the sheriff, "but it's a reasonable supposition."

"Reasonable supposition," repeated Calhoun. "You sound like a damn lawyer."

The sheriff smiled and glanced at his watch. "Jane's waiting. I'll pick you up around nine in the morning?"

"Come early," said Calhoun, "we'll have coffee."

Thick black clouds were hanging low in the sky Monday morning when Calhoun and Ralph went down to Bitch Creek with their coffee. The air was still and heavy. It smelled damp and organic, and moisture was dripping off the trees. Calhoun wondered if a line storm was going to come blasting through from the northeast, ripping the leaves off the trees and blowing the warm summery air away, leaving the crisp chill of autumn in its wake. It was the season for line storms—the autumn nor'easters that demarcated the line between summer and fall in New England.

He supposed he could check the weather forecast on the radio, but he didn't see the point. There was nothing you could do about it.

It had rained overnight, and the boulders along the stream were wet. Calhoun and Ralph sat on them anyway. The surface of the stream was littered with yellow poplar leaves. They swirled like little sailboats in the eddies and gathered in rafts along the edges of the stream, but right in the current seam where the stream was narrowed by the remains of the old bridge and the quick water rubbed against the slow water, Calhoun spotted the dimply rise of a trout. Probably eating some ants or beetles that got blown onto the water along with the leaves.

He hoped Lyle liked the idea of having his ashes mingled with clean spring water and trout and mayflies in Bitch Creek.

After a while, he heard the sheriff's Explorer coming down the driveway. Then he heard the car door slam. Then the sheriff appeared at the top of the slope.

Calhoun made a show of looking at his wrist where a watch would've been if he'd worn one.

"Okay, dammit," said the sheriff. "So I'm twenty minutes later than I said I'd be. If you carried that cell phone around with you like I told you to, you'd know why. Now I'm going up to your house, and I'm going to pour myself some coffee, and then I'm going to dry off a chair and sit on your deck, and the sooner you come up and join me, the sooner I can fill you in and we can get going."

Calhoun smiled. The sheriff sounded kind of pissed. He wasn't usually that long-winded.

"Let's go," he said to Ralph.

Ralph scurried up the hill, and Calhoun followed behind, and when he climbed up on the deck, the sheriff was sitting there sipping coffee with his reading glasses perched low on his nose, peering at a notebook that he had propped up on the arm of the chair, and Ralph was lying on the deck beside him.

The sheriff looked up over the tops of his glasses. Then he reached into his pants pocket and took out a thin electric cord with a heavy square plug on one end. He put it on the table. "Use this to recharge your phone," he said. "We got to be able to keep in touch, Stoney. You didn't lose it, did you?"

"I got it somewhere," said Calhoun.

"I tried to call you about an hour ago. Wanted to tell you I was going to be a little late and fill you in."

"Fill me in now," said Calhoun.

The sheriff looked down at his notebook for a minute. "Okay. First off, the reason I'm late, I was talking with the ME's office up in Augusta. They matched up Errol Watson's prison dental records with the X-rays of that corpse we found on Quarantine Island. So we got ourselves a positive ID, which is pretty damn big progress all by itself. I managed to track down the whereabouts of the assistant district attorney who prosecuted Watson, guy name of Acworth, though I wasn't able to talk to him, inasmuch as he's presently residing in a cemetery."

"He's dead?" said Calhoun.

The sheriff nodded. "Drowned three summers ago. Jet Ski accident."

"I guess he didn't kill Errol Watson, then," said Calhoun.

"No," said the sheriff, "and he won't be helping us figure out who did, either." He looked at his notebook for a minute. "I got a meeting with Detective Gilsum this afternoon."

Calhoun felt a twinge of panic. "A meeting," he said.

The sheriff laughed. "You aren't invited, Stoney. This is just me and Gilsum and maybe Enfield. Gilsum wants to keep this thing organized and coordinated, and I'm all for that. He's got some Portland detectives talking to Watson's neighbors and coworkers and anybody else they can track down who knew him. He's also lined up some state cops up there in Augusta to question people about Paul Vecchio. At this point, Gilsum is treating Watson and Vecchio as separate cases."

"That don't make any sense," said Calhoun. "It's pretty obvious—"

"It doesn't matter," said the sheriff. "The point is, Gilsum has got competent people doing what needs to be done, tracking down people and interrogating them, and that is good for us, Stoney, because it's necessary, but it's the kind of legwork can be terribly boring and unproductive."

"Does that mean they're going to follow up with Mattie Perkins?"

The sheriff shook his head. "I told Gilsum we already made a connection with that family, and we'd try to catch up with Mattie's mother this afternoon, get her story ourselves."

Calhoun nodded. "Okay. Good."

"I also made an appointment for us to talk to the PD who handled Watson's case," said the sheriff. "Fella name of"—he squinted at his notebook—"Maxner. Otis Maxner. He's got an office down in Westbrook. Does real estate law now. I talked to him on the phone for a minute on the way over here. He said he remembers the Watson case. We're supposed to be there at eleven. And after that— around twelve thirty—we're going to drop in on Judge Roper, who heard the case. He's retired now, said he'd be at the marina and we better not be late, as he's going fishing. His Honor August Roper. Sat on the bench for close to thirty years. Ever run into him?"

Calhoun shook his head.

"Reputation for being tough but fair. Salty old bastard. So anyway, how's all that sound to you?"

Calhoun shrugged. "Sounds like a lot of damn talking. You said for starters. What else you got in mind?"

"I want to talk to the parents of Watson's victim. Folks name of Dunbar. They live down in Biddeford."

"You make an appointment with them?"

"We'll drop in on them unannounced," said the sheriff, "see how it goes. They both work. Their daughter, Watson's victim, she's off to college. They got a teenage son who goes to school. We'll show up on their doorstep this evening around dinnertime, flash our badges at them."

"Disrupt 'em," said Calhoun.

The sheriff smiled.

"Catch 'em off guard."

"Sure."

"Don't give 'em time to get their stories straight," said Calhoun. "You're gonna treat these poor folks as suspects?"

"Everybody's possible suspects," said the sheriff. "But I believe the parents of some child that's been molested would have the world's best motive to cut off a guy's dick, wouldn't you say?"

"Wouldn't blame 'em one bit," said Calhoun. "What about the child herself?"

"I guess she'd have a motive, all right," said the sheriff, "though it's kind of hard to imagine her actually doing it."

"Where's she go to school?"

"California," said the sheriff.

"So much for that idea."

The sheriff pushed himself to his feet. "So what do you say, Stoney? How's that sound to you?"

Calhoun shrugged. "Not sure what you want me tagging along for."

"You got a good shit detector, Stoney." The sheriff pushed himself to his feet and hitched up his pants. "Ready to rock and roll?"

Calhoun stood up. "You're the sheriff. I'm a mere deputy. You want me to drive?"

"Why don't you follow me. We'll leave my vehicle at Kate's shop. Then we won't have to come all the way back here before my meeting with Gilsum."

"Sounds like a plan," said Calhoun. He looked at Ralph, who was snoozing on the deck beside them. "Why don't you go get in the truck."

Ralph lifted his head, looked at Calhoun, and yawned. Then he got to his feet and trotted down the steps. He paused to lift his leg against a bush before he went over and sat beside the truck.

"You sure you want to bring Ralph?" said the sheriff. "He'll be cooped up in the truck all day."

"Ralph don't mind that. He likes riding."

"I don't know, Stoney," said the sheriff. "He'd probably be happier staying home, running around, swimming in the creek."

"Maybe he would," said Calhoun. "But I wouldn't. Last time I left him home, I thought I lost him."

CHAPTER TEN

Attorney Otis Maxner's office suite occupied the bottom floor of a big yellow Victorian on Main Street, which ran along the Presumscot River in downtown Westbrook. When Calhoun and Sheriff Dickman walked in, the receptionist, a middle-aged woman with a round face and a well-practiced smile, asked for their names, then waved at some sofas and chairs, suggested that they have a seat and relax, and said she'd let Mr. Maxner know they were there, and could she get them some coffee?

"Our appointment's at eleven," said the sheriff. He looked pointedly at his wristwatch. "It's eleven right now."

"I'll be sure Mr. Maxner knows you're here, sir," she said. "Please make yourselves comfortable. What about some coffee while you're waiting?"

The sheriff said, "We don't want to be comfortable. We don't want coffee, and we don't want to wait. We want to talk to the lawyer. We have an appointment with him at eleven, and it is eleven, and we do not intend to be kept waiting."

The secretary was nodding and smiling. "Of course, sir. If you'll just—"

"We are not clients," continued the sheriff. "I am the sheriff and this is my deputy. We're not here for legal advice. Our hours with the lawyer will not be billable. We're here because Mr. Maxner, who is a lawyer and therefore an officer of the court, might be able to help us enforce the law, and as far as I'm concerned, eleven o'clock means eleven o'clock." He cocked his wrist and looked at his watch. "And it is now one minute past eleven."

The secretary's smile never wavered during the sheriff's assault. "No coffee, then," she said when he stopped for a breath. "I'll let Mr. Maxner know you're here."

She picked up her phone, spoke softly into it, hung up, and shifted her smile back to Calhoun and the sheriff, and right then the door beside her desk opened.

Otis Maxner was a tall, thin guy with close-cut sandy hair and pale skin and round glasses. He wore chino pants, a navy blazer, and a blue striped shirt, no necktie. He looked like a college kid to Calhoun, but he had to be somewhere in his early thirties, at least, if he'd defended Errol Watson in court six years ago.

He came at them with his hand extended. "Otie Maxner," he said. "Hope I didn't keep you waiting."

The sheriff and Calhoun both shook hands with him. "We just got here," said the sheriff.

"Come on," Maxner said, "we'll go into my office. Did Rita offer you coffee?"

"She certainly did," said the sheriff. "We declined."

"Water? Juice?"

"We're all set."

They followed Maxner into a large office that Calhoun figured had once been a parlor in the old Victorian. There was a brick fireplace in one corner. The ceiling was high and the windows were tall. Maxner's desk had its back to the wall facing the doorway. Four upholstered chairs encircled a round glass-topped coffee table under the windows. On the other side of the room sat a long conference table lined with straight-backed wooden chairs.

Maxner gestured at the upholstered chairs, and Calhoun and the sheriff sat down.

"Sure I can't get you something?" said Maxner.

"We're good," said the sheriff. He took his notebook out of his jacket pocket. "Sit down, please."

Maxner sat down, crossed his ankle over his knee, and plucked at the crease in his pants. "You wanted to talk about the Errol Watson case, you said."

The sheriff nodded. "Whatever you can remember about it."

"May I ask you why?"

"No."

Maxner smiled uncertainly, as if he thought the sheriff was joking. Then he said, "What's Watson done now?"

The sheriff said nothing.

Maxner smiled. "I just figured, he's probably out by now, so he's probably in trouble again."

"Why would you think that?"

Maxner shrugged. "The crimes he commits. He can't help himself. He's that kind of man."

"Tell me about the case, Mr. Maxner, will you?"

"Sure. Okay." Maxner cleared his throat. "I was a PD back then, fresh out of law school, looking for experience and action, hoping to make some connections. I really didn't know what I wanted to do, or even if I wanted to practice law. I was, you know, young and idealistic, and defending indigent people, making sure their rights were respected, it seemed like a good thing to do." Maxner shook his head. "That was before I started meeting my clients. Wife beaters, child molesters, armed convenience-store robbers, drunk drivers, drug dealers."

Calhoun noticed how the sheriff nodded and smiled now and then, encouraging Otis Maxner to talk without giving him any direction or feedback.

"What I'm trying to say," said Maxner, "is that a public defender's idealism is tested constantly. It's always safe to assume that your clients are guilty, although they always lie to you. Usually they're guilty of really nasty things. So you have to keep telling yourself, your job isn't to win the case, it's to make sure that the prosecution doesn't cheat."

"Errol Watson," said the sheriff.

Maxner nodded. "Right. Well, Watson was one of them. Maybe not the meanest, nastiest client I ever had, but he was right up there, though you'd never know it to look at him. Very ordinary-looking man. You wouldn't even notice him. He was a clerk in a hardware

store. Wore a shirt with his name stitched over the pocket. Errol."
Maxner smiled. "He was accused of showing pornographic photographs to a minor child, exposing himself to her, making her touch
him, and, um, fondling her. She wasn't quite twelve years old, just a
child, a sixth grader, and I dreaded the possibility that the prosecution
would put her on the stand so that I'd have to cross-examine her."

"They didn't?" said the sheriff.

Maxner shook his head. "The parents refused to allow it. Good
for our case, bad for theirs. Without her testimony, it was all pretty
much hearsay. I was unable to keep his dirty photos from being en-
tered as evidence, though, and they were pretty damning. Watson
could've gotten eighteen years—probably should have—and he
only got seven. That was over six years ago. He's probably out by
now. Seven usually means four served. I did a good job for him.
Seven years was way better than he had any right to expect. Not that
he was exactly grateful, of course. He thought I should've gotten
him off. Claimed he was innocent. It was all a big misunderstand-
ing." Maxner looked at the sheriff as if he expected a comment or a
question, or maybe a commendation.

The sheriff just looked back at him, and after a minute, Maxner
kind of laughed and looked out the window. "I'm not sure how I can
help you, Sheriff," he said. "You haven't told me why we're talking
about Errol Watson. I mean, it's not like I knew the man. I just rep-
resented him that one time, and I had a lot of other clients, too."

"You seem to remember him pretty well," said the sheriff.

Maxner shrugged. "Errol Watson was hard to forget."

"Any chance he was innocent?"

Maxner rolled his eyes.

"Aren't these the kind of cases a public defender tries to plead
out?"

"Sure," said Maxner. "I did try. The ADA wouldn't hear of it.
This was before the trial, when he thought he was going to have the
victim on the stand, nail Watson to the cross. When the parents re-
neged on that, the trial was practically over, and Judge Roper
wanted to hear it to the end."

The sheriff nodded. "Tell me about the trial."

"When we couldn't work out a plea, we waived our right to a jury trial. I figured we had a better chance at impartiality from a judge, and I turned out to be right. I kept Watson off the stand, needless to say. A jury would've interpreted that as evidence of his guilt instead of just your right as an accused person, but a judge knows better. Plus, of course, the victim's parents both testified for the prosecution, and it was quite emotional. Would've had a jury in tears." Maxner laughed quickly. "Practically had me in tears."

"What was the gist of the parents' testimony?" said the sheriff.

Maxner shrugged. "The mother described how their little girl had nightmares, refused to go anywhere alone, cried any time she saw a strange man. Mailman, UPS guy, just somebody walking down the street, she'd see him and go running up to her room. All men upset her. Couldn't even hug her father. They spent thousands of dollars on therapy, no end in sight, and they had to send her to a special school for, um, disturbed girls. The mother was a good witness. Calm, articulate, factual. I cross-examined her, got nowhere with her, figured I was doing my client more harm than good, so I cut it short. The father, he was a different story. Very emotional. At one point, he stood up in his witness chair, tears streaming down his face, and he pointed his finger at Watson, and said something like, if there was any justice in this world, he'd be castrated."

"Castrated," said the sheriff.

Maxner shrugged. "He didn't say castrated, exactly. You get the idea."

"What did he say, exactly?"

"He said he should have his, um, his penis cut off, and—"

"Did he use the word penis?" asked the sheriff.

"Actually, I believe he did." Maxner shrugged. "The judge threatened to have the poor man removed from the courtroom if he didn't get himself under control, which he did after a minute, and apologized. I didn't even try to cross-examine him."

"Who else testified?" said the sheriff.

"The girl's therapist," said Maxner. "A doctor, too. Also someone who saw Watson with the little girl on the afternoon of the, um, alleged crime."

"Who'd you put on the stand?"

Maxner shook his head. "Nobody."

"Nobody? No witnesses for the defense?"

"Watson had no alibi," he said, "and he couldn't suggest any character witnesses. I moved to dismiss on the grounds of insufficient evidence. The judge, no surprise, denied my motion."

The sheriff glanced at Calhoun, who shrugged. It was interesting, watching the sheriff work.

"What else can you tell us about the man?" said the sheriff.

Maxner shrugged. "I just defended him that one time. He went to prison, and that was the end of it."

"Well, okay, then. Thank you, Mr. Maxner. We appreciate your cooperation." The sheriff slapped his thighs and stood up.

Calhoun stood up, too, and so did Maxner.

"I'm very curious, Sheriff," said Maxner. "After all this time, Errol Watson? He's out and doing it again, am I right?"

"Of course you're curious," said the sheriff. He held out his hand. "Thanks a lot for your time."

Otis Maxner looked at the sheriff, then frowned at his extended hand, then shrugged and shook it. Then he shook hands with Calhoun and ushered them out the door to the waiting room, where the ever-smiling Rita ordered them to have a nice day.

Back at Calhoun's truck, they let Ralph out to putter around and lift his leg on some bushes. Calhoun emptied a bottle of Poland Spring water into the plastic bowl he kept in back. Ralph lapped it all up and then went looking for more bushes to pee on.

The sheriff was leaning against the side of the truck, tapping his hat against the side of his leg. "Castration," he said. "You hear what he said, Stoney?"

"I heard it."

"You thinking what I'm thinking?"

"Well," said Calhoun, "the obvious thought is that the father there, Mr.—what'd you say the parents' name was?"

"Dunbar," said the sheriff.

"Mr. Dunbar," said Calhoun, "went and did what he thought needed to be done to Errol Watson."

"Castrated him," said the sheriff. "That's the obvious thought."

"Of course," said Calhoun, "anybody could've performed that operation. Mr. Dunbar had a good idea, and anybody who heard him say it no doubt agreed with him. In fact, you wouldn't've had to hear that poor fella's testimony to come up with the idea all by yourself. It's the logical thing."

"Somebody not only had the idea," said the sheriff. "They went ahead and actually did it. And Mr. Dunbar is the most obvious one, him having not only articulated the concept in court but also having the kind of motive that can actually get stronger with time. Usually, in this business, what's obvious turns out to be what's true."

"I'm not saying Mr. Dunbar didn't do it," said Calhoun. "I just said it was kind of obvious."

"We'll talk to him tonight," said the sheriff. He glanced at his watch. "Let's go see how the judge remembers it."

The sheriff directed Calhoun to the Yacht Club in Falmouth. He parked his truck between a new Lexus SUV and a Porsche with the top down, and he and Ralph followed the sheriff across the crushed-seashell area and out onto a long floating dock.

The sheriff turned onto one of the finger docks that branched off the main dock and stopped at a center-console fishing boat named *Hard Time*. A small man wearing a grease-stained T-shirt and baggy blue jeans was kneeling inside the boat fiddling with a bunch of spinning rods.

"Judge Roper," said the sheriff.

The man looked up. He had about five days' worth of gray stubble on his cheeks and the stub of an unlit cigar clenched in his teeth. He nodded. "Sheriff Dickman," he said. "Come aboard."

The sheriff climbed in. Calhoun stayed on the dock. Ralph curled up beside him on the sunwarmed wooden planks.

The judge cocked his head at Calhoun, then held out his hand. "Gus Roper," he said.

Calhoun reached over and shook his hand. The judge had a big bony hand and a strong grip. "Stoney Calhoun," he said. He pointed at Ralph with his chin. "This here's Ralph."

"You this man's deputy?"

"Sort of."

Roper glanced at his watch, then turned to the sheriff. "You got fifteen minutes. Then I got a date with some bluefish. You mentioned the Errol Watson case. I refreshed my memory after you called."

The sheriff nodded. "We found his body. Throat sliced ear to ear, penis cut off and stuffed in his mouth. Body burned to a crisp out on Quarantine Island."

The judge nodded. "I heard about that. Unfortunately, the state of Maine frowns upon judges handing down such punishments, but it's a good one, all right. All I can do is put 'em in prison. You want to know who killed him, I suppose."

The sheriff nodded.

"You got a lot of suspects," said the judge. "Start with everyone whose daughter or girlfriend he ever molested."

"I was only aware of that one case."

"There was only the one case. You aren't so naive as to think that was his one and only offense, are you?"

"I guess not," said the sheriff. "It's just the only one we know about."

Roper nodded. "Well, me, too. I'm just suggesting."

"Right. Who'd know about other instances?"

"The victims and their families, whoever they are. Watson himself."

"Not sure how I can use that, Judge."

He shrugged. "Me, neither. You're the sheriff. Far as that particular case was concerned, you understand that I can't talk about it beyond what's in the record. It was a pretty run-of-the-mill case, as child molestation cases go." The judge shrugged.

"I understand the victim's father was pretty passionate."

"I had to warn him," said the judge. "It was moving as hell, but way out of line. That's all in the record. You're looking for an obvious murderer, you couldn't go wrong with him."

"The father," said the sheriff.

Judge Roper nodded.

The sheriff looked at Calhoun. "You think of anything, Stoney?"

"What about that prosecutor?" said Calhoun.

"I don't think he did it," said the judge, "inasmuch as he's been dead for a few years now."

"I understand that. I only meant, the job he did. Any suggestions that he was bagging the case?"

"Don't know why you'd think that," said Roper, "but I sure as hell can't comment on it. Read the record and figure it out for yourself. Acworth was a tough prosecutor, I can tell you that. Some people don't think that Jet Ski accident was any accident. He pissed a lot of people off." The judge picked up his rods and set them into the racks under the gunwales. "I did what I could. I found the man guilty and put him in prison. Made sure that when he got out, he'd have a target painted on him."

"The sex offender registry, you mean," said the sheriff.

"Yep. It makes anybody with a computer a suspect, wouldn't you say?" He looked at his watch. "Okay, your time's up, Sheriff. Was there something else?"

"Guess not. If anything occurs to you . . ."

"Sure. I'll call you. Now get your ass off my boat so I can go fishing. I been waiting a long time to be retired, and I don't want to waste it rehashing old cases or dwelling on the murders of men who deserve to be murdered."

The sheriff shook hands with Judge Roper and stepped onto the dock.

The judge looked at Calhoun and touched his forefinger to his eyebrow. "Deputy," he said.

"Good to meet you, Judge," said Calhoun, and he and Ralph turned to follow the sheriff back to his truck.

A battered brown Volkswagen Rabbit that hadn't been there on Saturday now sat in front of the green ranch house where Mattie Perkins lived. Calhoun pulled his truck in behind the Rabbit.

They got out and went to the front door. The sheriff rang the bell, and a minute later the inside door opened and a woman looked out at them through the screen door. She was holding a cigarette down alongside her leg, as if she were trying to hide it. The smoke twirled out through the screen.

"Mrs. Perkins?" said the sheriff.

"Yes," she said. "I'm Allison Perkins. And judging by your uniform, you're the sheriff. And you," she added, jabbing her cigarette at Calhoun, "must be the deputy. You boys've already interrogated my daughter. I got to say, this is a lot of fuss over a dog that tips over trash cans and howls at night."

"Can we talk with you, ma'am?" said the sheriff.

"Sure." She pushed open the screen door and stepped outside. She was wearing shorts and sandals and a sleeveless jersey. She had muscular legs and arms. Calhoun thought she had intelligent eyes, and he liked her cynical smile. "I'd invite you in," she said, "but it's a mess. I clean rooms at the Ramada, and I can't keep my own place picked up. As if cleaning rooms was my career. You want to talk about Errol Watson, right?"

The sheriff nodded. "That's right."

"Not about his dog, huh?"

The sheriff shrugged.

"I'm biased," said Allison Perkins. "I happen to know what Errol Watson is, and I've got a teenage daughter, and I'm not at all happy to have that man living in my neighborhood."

"How did you find out about Watson?" said the sheriff.

"One of the neighbors told me, and I looked him up on that website. It's hard to know how to tell your daughter that the man across the street is a convicted sex offender."

"What did you tell her?"

She shrugged. "I just told her to steer clear of him. I didn't tell her why. Maybe I should have, I don't know. They don't tell you how to handle something like this in the child-rearing manuals. So I just let Mattie think I'm being overly protective, which I have always been anyway, and she knows it. She can be mad at me, I don't care, as long as she does what I tell her."

"Did you ever speak to Mr. Watson?"

"About Mattie, you mean?" She dropped her cigarette on the dirt and ground it out under her sandal. "Not me. Mattie disobeyed me once. I found out she was over there. She swore she was just watching the man work on his motorcycle. I gave her hell, but I was so scared that I got Mattie's father to come and, um, explain our position to Errol Watson. That is one thing that Lawrence Perkins is very good at. Explaining his position. He doesn't always find just the right words for it, but he makes his meaning clear so that you have no doubt what he wants out of you and what will happen if you don't do it. Or, in this case, refrain from doing it."

The sheriff smiled. "You mean he yells."

Allison Perkins nodded. "Yells and swears and threatens to knock the shit out of you, which, among other things, accounts for the fact that he and I are divorced. Lawrence Perkins always manages to get his message across loud and clear. Especially loud."

"Did he threaten Errol Watson?"

"Sure he did. You can ask anybody in the neighborhood, because he wasn't exactly soft-spoken about it. He told him if he touched our daughter, if he said hello to her, if he even looked at her, he, Lawrence Perkins, would personally be back for him, and when he was done with him, he wouldn't ever think about little girls again."

"What'd he mean by that?" said the sheriff.

She shrugged. "You'd have to ask him. Near as I could tell, Watson took him seriously. Mattie says she hasn't even seen him since then. We figured he was hiding inside his house, afraid to show his face."

"When did this, um, conversation between Mr. Perkins and Mr. Watson take place, do you remember?"

"Sometime in July? A few weeks after we moved down here, which was right after school got out." She looked at the sheriff, then at Calhoun. "We were living in Madrid and I lost my job. I was the elementary school reading specialist, and they were having budget problems, so they eliminated my job. If you have tenure, they can't fire you without cause, but they can eliminate your job, and then it's just tough shit. I can tell you, there isn't a lot of work for a reading specialist up in that neck of the Maine woods, so I brought Mattie down here to the city, such as it is, hoping I could find something." She laughed quickly. "So here I am, cleaning rooms at the Ramada, circulating my résumé, hoping to get some interviews. I've got a master's degree and eleven years' experience and good references, and I'm changing sheets and scrubbing toilets for a living."

Calhoun noticed that Allison Perkins pronounced "Madrid" the same way Mattie had, with the emphasis on the first syllable.

"Errol Watson," said the sheriff. "He hasn't been a problem, then?"

"His dog has been," she said. "I called about him tipping over our trash cans, howling all night long." She smiled. "Next thing I know there's a sheriff and a deputy at my door."

"Just his dog, then?"

"Except for that one time with Mattie, and truthfully, that was her fault." Allison Perkins fished a cardboard pack of cigarettes from the hip pocket of her shorts. She flipped it open with her thumb, plucked out a cigarette with her lips, lit it with a plastic lighter, and turned her head so she wouldn't exhale in the direction of the sheriff. "Near as I can tell," she said, "Watson didn't do anything wrong. Mattie said he wouldn't even talk to her. Still, it scared me, knowing what kind of man he is."

"When did you see him last, do you remember?" said the sheriff.

She took a puff on her cigarette and looked up at the sky for a moment. Then she shrugged. "I don't remember. It's been a while. A few weeks, anyway. Like I said, after my ex confronted him that time, he laid pretty low. I can tell you that his dog was pestering us for quite some time. I had to make four or five phone calls before the animal people finally showed up. Why? Has something happened to Errol Watson? Where is he?"

"What about your neighbors?" said the sheriff. "Any of them have any, um, confrontations with Mr. Watson?"

Allison Perkins shrugged. "Not that I know of. I mean, it wouldn't surprise me, but I can't say. I don't see much of my neighbors. I'm off working a lot of the time. I take all the hours they'll give me."

"And Mattie?" said the sheriff. "She's staying away from him?"

"Mattie is a good kid," she said. "Now and then I ask her. I'll say, 'You been over to Mr. Watson's house?' or, 'You talk to Errol Watson lately?' And Mattie says, 'No, not since you told me not to.' And I can see in her eyes that she's not lying to me, because I can always tell when she does lie to me. She knows she can't lie to me, and she doesn't bother trying anymore. I say, 'Matilda Louise'—she hates it when I call her by her whole name like that—I ask her, 'Have you been smoking?' And she just goes, 'How did you know?' And I give her a little punishment, but I tell her it would be a lot worse if she tried to lie about it." She smiled. "Anyway, I do believe Mattie has stayed away from him, and him from her, too, ever since that one time. Which still doesn't make me happy that he's living across the street."

"What about visitors?" said the sheriff. "Does he have friends, people who drop in on him or who come home with him?"

"Not that I ever noticed," said Allison Perkins. "I don't recall ever seeing a strange car parked over there, or anybody going in and out. Doesn't mean it doesn't happen. Just that I never saw it." She looked at her watch. "I've got to be at the Ramada at three, and before that I've got to have some lunch and take a shower and put on my uniform and make some dinner for Mattie, so . . ."

"Mattie's at school?" said Calhoun.

She turned and smiled at him. "I didn't know you could talk, Mr. Deputy."

"I prefer not to," he said. "The sheriff's better at it than me."

"Mattie's at school, yes. Eighth grade. A terrible grade to teach, by the way. She's on the field hockey team, so she doesn't get home till suppertime. I don't like it, but we're making it work for now. I'd rather have a job in a school, I can tell you that."

"Can you tell us how to find your husband?" Calhoun said.

"My ex-husband," she said. "He works on marine engines at Antrim's boatyard down in Kittery."

CHAPTER ELEVEN

Calhoun dropped the sheriff off at the shop where he'd left his vehicle, and then he and Ralph headed down to Kittery. It took about an
hour on the turnpike, and then another ten or fifteen minutes to find
the Antrim Boatyard, which was located on the banks of the Pis-
cataqua River across from Portsmouth.

A ten-foot chain-link fence topped by barbed wire surrounded
the boatyard, which appeared to cover several acres. The entire en-
closed area was crowded with boats of all descriptions in dry
dock—motorboats and speedboats, tugboats and launches, sailboats and yachts, fishing boats and lobster boats. There were several
large hangar-like buildings with metal roofs, and here and there
the neck of a crane poked high into the sky. Along the river side of
the yard Calhoun could see some docks where more boats were
moored.

He found the entry gates open, and inside the entrance he spotted a white tin-roofed building, a miniature of the big boat hangars,
with a sign that said OFFICE on the wall beside the door. He parked
in front and went in.

The inner walls were dark fake-wood paneling. They were cov-
ered with photographs of boats. A thirtyish woman wearing a pink
T-shirt sat behind an L-shaped steel desk talking on the telephone.
She was poking at her reddish hair with the eraser end of a pencil.
Her desk was piled with papers and catalogs and manila folders. A

computer sat on the short leg of the L. A big floor fan was blowing the warm air around.

The woman arched her eyebrows at Calhoun, gave him a quick smile and lifted a finger at him, then shifted her eyes back to the ceiling and continued her conversation. As near as he could tell, she was talking to a teenager about getting his homework done before he went out with his friends.

Calhoun turned his back on her and looked at some of the boat photos. In one of them he recognized the first President Bush grinning from the stern of a long skinny speedboat. He was holding a spinning rod in one hand and a big bluefish in the other.

"Can I help you, sir?" said the woman.

Calhoun turned. "You got a man named Lawrence Perkins working here?"

She frowned. "Who wants to know?"

He fished the leather case that held his deputy badge from his pants pocket and flipped it open. "Sheriff's business," he said. "I'm Calhoun."

"I hope Perk ain't in trouble?" said the woman, making it a question.

"I just need to talk to him," said Calhoun.

She cocked her head and looked at him for a moment, as if she could read something in his face. Then she said, "I'll get him for you." She picked up the phone, poked a couple of buttons, then said, "Man here needs to talk to Perkins . . . I don't know, Harry, but . . . yeah, right now. Good. Thanks." She hung up. "He's on his way. Do your business outside, okay?"

"Sure," said Calhoun. "Thanks."

He went outside and leaned against his truck, and a few minutes later a big man came lumbering up from the direction of the water. He was wearing a gray T-shirt with the sleeves cut off and baggy blue jeans and a backward baseball cap. He had a thick blond beard, and stringy sun-bleached hair curled out from under his cap.

As he got closer, Calhoun saw that his arms were enormous and that each biceps was plastered with an elaborate tattoo—an angel with its wings spread on the right one with the word HEAVEN under it, and a red Satan rising from a blaze of fire on the left, which, of course, was labeled HELL.

The man frowned at Calhoun. He was wiping his hands on a greasy-looking rag. A V of sweat stained the front of his T-shirt. "You lookin' for me?"

"Mr. Perkins?"

He nodded. "Who are you?"

"Name's Calhoun." He showed Perkins his badge.

Perkins glanced at it and shrugged, as if he'd seen plenty of badges in his life. "So what'd I do now?"

"Nothing, far as I know," said Calhoun. "I just need to ask you a few questions."

"Allie sent you, didn't she?" he said. "She said if I was late again, she'd report me. I told her I'm tryin' to do my best. I know my responsibility."

Calhoun shook his head. "It's nothing like that, Mr. Perkins. I just want to ask you about Errol Watson."

Perkins frowned. "Who?"

"Errol Watson," said Calhoun. "Lives across the street from your wife and daughter?"

"Oh, him," said Perkins. "Allie's not my wife. We're divorced. It was her idea, getting divorced, but I'm still s'pose to give her child support every month."

"I don't care about any of that," said Calhoun. "Tell me about Watson."

"What do you want me to say? God damn convicted sex pervert living practically next door to my baby daughter, never mind my ex-wife? That ain't right. People like that, they should keep 'em locked up."

"You had words with him, I understand," said Calhoun.

"Words?" Perkins laughed. "I told him if I heard he went anywheres near Mattie—or Allie, for that matter—if he spoke to them or even looked at them, he'd be sorry."

"Meaning what?"

"I don't know," said Perkins. "It's just what I said. I guess I'd kill him. Wouldn't you?"

Calhoun smiled. "When was the last time you saw Errol Watson?"

"First time, last time, only time," said Perkins. "Allie calls me, this is a couple months ago, right after she and Mattie moved down to Portland, she's crying and swearing and sputtering, I never heard her so mad, I can barely make sense out of what she's saying, she's telling me this freak's tryin' to, I don't know, seduce my little girl. So I piled into my truck and I went up there and I did what Allie wanted me to do."

"She wanted you to . . . what? Threaten him?"

He rolled his eyes. "Allie's this sweet little schoolteacher, right? You know her?"

"I met her," said Calhoun.

"She's a ball buster," said Perkins. "I mean, believe me, she could've done a better job than me, scaring the shit out of that Watson. She can be pretty scary, believe me. I think she was disappointed I only yelled at the guy."

"What did she expect?"

He shrugged. "You never know with her. All I know is, no matter what I do, it ain't right, or it ain't enough."

"Are you saying that the only reason you confronted Watson was because your ex-wife asked you to?"

He shrugged. "I wouldn't've even known about him if she didn't call me."

"But you were just doing it for her?"

"For her?" Perkins laughed. "Not hardly. Doin' it for me, too, man. I don't mind telling you, I was pretty pissed. The idea of a person like that living in a . . . a neighborhood. I had to control myself not to hammer the sonofabitch."

"And you haven't seen Errol Watson since that one time?"

"That's right. Just that once."

"Have you talked to your ex-wife about him since then?"

He shook his head. "I don't talk to her that much about anything. Mostly, she just wants to know where her child support is. That's mainly what we talk about. I'm pretty sure if there was still a problem with that Watson, though, she'd've told me."

"What about Mattie? Do you talk with her?"

"Sure," said Perkins. "She's my little girl. We get together once or twice a week, have a clam roll and ice cream, maybe go for a boat ride or something. I talk with her on the phone, too."

"Has she mentioned Watson?"

He shook his head. "Nope. She hasn't said nothing and I sure haven't asked. It's not a subject I want to talk about. I don't even want to think about it." He looked at Calhoun. "How come you're asking about this Watson? Hey, he didn't do something to Mattie, did he?"

Calhoun shook his head. "Nothing like that." He took out his wallet, removed one of the sheriff's business cards, and gave it to Perkins. "If you remember anything else about Errol Watson, give us a call."

Perkins took the card, looked at it, shrugged, and stuffed it into his pants pocket. "So, we done?"

Calhoun nodded. "We're done for now. Thanks for your time."

Lawrence Perkins nodded and said, "Sure. Okay." Then he turned and trudged back in the direction he had come from, his big arms swinging at his sides like clubs.

When they got home, Calhoun found a Coke in his refrigerator, and he and Ralph went down to the brook. It was about fifteen degrees cooler in Calhoun's piney woods down by the running water of Bitch Creek than it had been in the boatyard in Kittery. Ralph waded into the pool below the old bridge abutments and dog-paddled around, snorting and lapping the water as he swam.

Calhoun fished the sheriff's cellular telephone from his pants pocket, pressed the button on the side, said, "Dickman," and pressed it against his ear. It rang five times, and then the sheriff's recorded voice said, "It's Sheriff Marshall Dickman. Leave your number and a brief message after the beep, and I'll get back to you."

After the beep, Calhoun said, "It's Calhoun. I talked to Perkins, if you want to hear about it. Anyway, you're coming by my house to pick me up, right? We can talk then, I guess. What time? Seven?"

He pressed the red button, then sat there on the rock, sipping his Coke and holding the phone in his hand and listening to the gurgle of Bitch Creek. Sometimes he imagined he could hear Lyle humming one of his Beatles tunes in the rhythmic babbling music of the brook.

After a few minutes, Ralph hauled himself out of the water, shook himself dry, and came over and sat beside Calhoun. He gave Ralph's forehead an absentminded scratch. He had to fight the urge to use the cell phone to call Kate. All he had to do was poke her numbers and hit the green button.

He wasn't looking for some heavy conversation about love and loyalty and responsibility and guilt. He just wanted to tell her about talking to Lawrence Perkins, how the man was split from his wife and daughter but it was obvious that he still loved them, how he'd ripped the sleeves off his T-shirt so you could see these big apocalyptic tattoos on his giant biceps.

He thought Kate would enjoy that. They always used to talk about such things, interesting people they met, clients and customers, or about how she'd spotted a mixed school of bluefish and stripers crashing bait near the mouth of the Presumscot River by the B&M bean factory and how she threw every fly she had at them and couldn't get a hit, or about how the guys from Boston were asking Calhoun about buying property up near Moosehead, just sharing unimportant stories, knowing what amused each other . . .

He stood up and shoved the phone into his pocket. He couldn't imagine having one of those conversations with Kate now. Things were too intense. There was too much going on. He, for one, couldn't stop wondering if it really was all over with her, if she'd decided that loving Walter meant she couldn't love Calhoun after all, if she never again would come to his house at night in her swirling dress wearing her turquoise jewelry.

And if that was the case, what the hell was he supposed to do for the rest of his life?

You couldn't tell stories about some guy's tattoos when you had things like that on your mind.

He was mixing dry dog food with half a can of Alpo in Ralph's bowl when his pants vibrated. This time it only took him a second to realize it was his cell phone.

He fished it out, hit the green button, and said, "Hey, Sheriff? That you?"

He heard the tinkle of a woman's laughter. "No, Stoney. Sorry to disappoint you. It's Sam. Sam Surry."

Before he could help himself, he said, "I ain't disappointed at all. How'd you get ahold of this number?"

"Just got out of a meeting," she said. "Sheriff Dickman was there. I mentioned that I needed to get ahold of you and he gave it to me."

"Who else did he give it to?"

"I don't know," she said. "You mad?"

"Mad?" he said. "Nope."

"You sound mad."

"The sheriff told me he was the only one who'd be calling me on this damn telephone, that's all. So I didn't expect it to be somebody else."

"Well, you shouldn't be too mad at him," she said. "I kind of wheedled your number out of him. Blame me."

"I ain't mad," said Calhoun. "So what'd you want?"

She laughed again. "You're fairly blunt, aren't you?"

"You saying I'm rude? I didn't mean to be rude. I apologize."

"Not rude, no. You're straightforward, and it's refreshing. What I wanted was, I wondered if I could hire you to take me fishing in your boat."

"Sure," said Calhoun. "What did you have in mind?"

"I was thinking of, like, half a day? Take your boat out on the bay, see if we can catch a fish? Do you do that? Half a day, I mean? Just because I never get a whole day off."

"We can do that," said Calhoun. "Four hours, give or take. That's half a trip. I don't put you on the clock. Half a tide. Best bet is the two hours on either side of a high tide. When'd you have in mind?"

"Friday?" she said. "I can get out of the clinic around three, could meet you by four? Would that work?"

Calhoun did a quick calculation. "On the water by four thirty. That'll give us a turning tide. Not ideal for catching fish, but I know a few tricks. We'll have a few hours before sunset, but if you're up for it and the weather's okay, we'll fish into dark. Sometimes it really heats up after the sun's off the water."

"We could stay out all night," she said. "Wouldn't that be fun?"

"Let's stick to the half day," said Calhoun. "Consider yourself booked. Meet me at the shop Friday afternoon. I'll have my boat trailered up and ready to go."

"Oh, that's excellent," she said. "What should I bring?"

"Long sleeves, long pants, wide-brimmed hat, sunglasses. Something warm for after the sun goes down, something water-proof in case it rains. I got everything else."

There was a hesitation. "Hey, Stoney?" she said.

"Yup?"

"I've fly-fished like maybe five times in my whole life. I know it's fun, but I'm not that good at it."

"That's all right."

"I just wanted you to know, if we don't catch a bunch of fish, I won't blame you. I won't even mind. I don't care that much about catching fish."

"It's better to catch 'em, though."

She laughed. "It's always better to catch 'em than not catch 'em. Fish, and anything else you're after."

"We'll see what we can do," he said, wondering what the hell she was trying to say.

"Okay," she said. "See you Friday."

He said good-bye to Dr. Sam Surry, pressed the red button on the phone, and slipped it back into his pocket.

He finished mixing Ralph's dinner and put it out on the deck for him. Then he poked around in the refrigerator, looking for something he could make a sandwich out of, and found a wedge of extra-sharp Vermont cheddar. He put the cheese on a cutting board, grabbed a knife and a loaf of crusty Italian bread and a can of Coke, and took his supper out on the deck with Ralph.

So Dr. Sam Surry wanted to go fishing. From the sound of it, she'd be happy with a nice quiet boat ride around the bay. Busy person like her, all that responsibility, getting out on the water on a Friday afternoon after a long week of work would be the perfect way to relax. He could show her some of the islands, tell her their stories. Maybe they'd see some seals lying on the rocks. If it didn't rain, they'd watch the sun set behind the city and the moon rise over the bay, and with any luck they'd spot a crazy bloody frenzy of birds and baitfish and predators, and Sam Surry would find a big bluefish or striper bending her rod, and maybe that would teach her the difference between catching fish and not catching fish.

Calhoun was pouring himself a travel mug of coffee when he heard the sheriff's Explorer come rumbling down his driveway. He filled a second travel mug and took them both out onto the deck.

Ralph scampered down the steps to greet the sheriff when he stepped out of his truck. The sheriff bent down, gave Ralph's ears a rub, then looked up at Calhoun. "We ought to get going, Stoney. Why'nt you come on down?"

"I got some coffee for you," said Calhoun.

"Wonderful."

Calhoun took the two mugs of coffee down the steps and handed one to the sheriff.

"Thanks, Deputy," said the sheriff. "You drive, I'll navigate. Okay by you?"

"The deputy should do the driving and all the other menial tasks," said Calhoun. He went around to the passenger side of the sheriff's vehicle, opened the door, gave a little bow, and said, "Sir?"

The sheriff rolled his eyes, muttered, "Jesus Christ," and got in.

Calhoun shut the door, went around to the other side, opened the driver's door, and snapped his fingers at Ralph.

Ralph stood there with his stubby tail wagging, looking at Calhoun.

"You coming?" said Calhoun.

Ralph sat on the ground.

"Come on. Get in."

Ralph didn't move.

"Looks like he doesn't want to come along," said the sheriff from inside the truck.

"I want him to," said Calhoun, "and I'm supposed to be the boss."

"He'll be all right."

"Last time I left him home, he ran off."

"He probably ran off for a good reason," said the sheriff. "Anyway, he did come back. You've got to trust him."

"I thought he was gone," said Calhoun. "It was the worst feeling." He went over and scooched down beside Ralph. "If you want to stay, you better be here when I get back."

Ralph licked his hand.

He gave Ralph's muzzle a scratch, then climbed into the sheriff's Explorer. He turned it around and headed out the driveway. In the rearview mirror, he saw Ralph get up and saunter over to the deck.

He didn't know what he'd do without that dog.

After they'd turned onto the two-lane road heading southeast to Biddeford, Calhoun turned to the sheriff and said, "So who else did you give my phone number to?"

"What do you mean, who else?"

"Dr. Surry called me on my damn cell phone a little while ago."

Calhoun had his eyes on the road, but he sensed that the sheriff was smiling.

"Police business, I assume?" said the sheriff.

Calhoun shrugged.

"Actually," said the sheriff, "that's my cell phone, which I asked you to carry with you to facilitate our work together. I explained to everybody at the meeting today how you were involved in this case, working closely with me. They all have the number. In case they need to transact police business with you."

"Your phone," said Calhoun. "In my pants."

"I'll ask Dr. Surry not to pester you, if you want."

"She asked me to take her fishing."

"That," said the sheriff, "doesn't sound like police business. I'll speak to her."

"A little late for that," said Calhoun. "I'll handle it."

"She is kinda cute," said the sheriff.

Calhoun grunted. "Big meeting today, huh?"

"Gilsum, Enfield, Dr. Surry, me, couple of Portland detectives. Comparing notes."

"Any progress on Paul Vecchio?"

The sheriff blew out a breath. "Not really. They've questioned people who knew him, mostly at the college where he worked. About the only thing we know for sure is that he had a computer in his house that he did his writing on, and now it's gone."

"His killer stole it," said Calhoun.

"Most likely." The sheriff paused to sip some coffee. "The picture is of a quiet man, respected teacher, no scandal in his background. Married once, divorced years ago, ex-wife remarried and living in Arizona. Vecchio lived alone, kept to himself. No current girlfriend, or boyfriend, for that matter. No love affairs that anybody would mention. No close friends, apparently. Into his writing and his teaching. Kind of a typical professor."

"Nobody's typical," said Calhoun. "Was he working on a story?"

"If he was, he was pretty secretive. Nobody seemed to know anything about it."

"In other words, that investigation is going nowhere."

"Gilsum's got some people on it," said the sheriff. "We're assuming it's connected with the Watson case. We're doing a little better with that one."

"I wouldn't have said we were doing all that well," said Calhoun.

"Well," said the sheriff, "the ME in Augusta estimates that Watson had been dead between nine and ten days when we found him. That narrows the time of death down to about forty-eight hours. That's something."

Calhoun thought for a minute. "We found him last Tuesday morning. Today's Monday. That makes it . . . two weeks ago this past weekend. So it probably happened sometime on the weekend."

"That's exactly right," said the sheriff. "Saturday would be ten days, Sunday nine, and given that, we can pin down the time of death even closer, because Watson worked his shift in the lumber-yard that Saturday. He was scheduled to work Monday morning and didn't show up."

"Sometime Saturday night, Sunday, or Sunday night, then."

The sheriff grunted. "They couldn't find anybody who'd seen him after he left work on Saturday. None of the neighbors could remember seeing him that Sunday."

"Would they've seen him?" said Calhoun.

"Not necessarily," said the sheriff. "Anyway, for lack of anything more specific, I'm figuring this happened Saturday night. Last time he was seen alive, as far as we can tell, was Saturday around six in the afternoon."

"Any complaints about Watson since he got out?" said Calhoun.

"Gilsum checked that very question. The answer is no. No formal complaints were filed, anyway, if you don't count the one Miz Perkins made about his dog. Not to say he behaved himself, but if he didn't, nobody reported it, nor did any of the people the cops talked to mention it." The sheriff paused. "I got something you'll find interesting, I think." He reached around into the backseat and hefted a briefcase onto his lap. He opened it and pulled out a manila folder. "Transcript of Watson's trial."

"Yes," said Calhoun. "I'm interested."

The sheriff riffled through some papers. "Okay," he said after a minute. "Here we go. Cast of characters. Mr. Acworth—that is, the late Mr. Acworth, now deceased from a Jet Ski accident. He's the ADA who prosecuted the case, questioning his witness, Mr. Dunbar, who is the father of the alleged victim, Bonnie Dunbar. Mr. Maxner, of course, is our friend the public defender. Judge Roper is, well, the judge who we talked with. Got all that?"

"Got it." Calhoun was holding down his speed. He was interested in what the sheriff had to say, but he was trying to concentrate on his driving, too, keeping a careful watch on the narrow road. It wound through the rolling countryside, past swamps and woodlands, pastures and cornfields, in the general direction of Biddeford on the coast just south of Portland. Darkness was settling over the landscape, and he wanted to be alert for deer leaping in front of the vehicle, or for a skunk or cottontail rabbit or raccoon frozen by his headlights in the middle of the road. He didn't want to run over any small innocent creatures, and swerving to avoid a deer—or colliding with one, for that matter—could get him and the sheriff killed. So he drove attentively.

"Okay," said the sheriff. "So Franklin Dunbar, the father, is on the stand. Acworth, the prosecutor, says—I'm reading this here—he says: 'Sir, please tell the court how your daughter has been doing since the incident.' And Dunbar says, 'She's lost weight. She barely eats anything. She won't go to school. She won't even leave the house. Whenever I'm home, she goes to her room and closes the door, because she can't bear to look at me, never mind talk to me or . . . or let me hug her. I'm her father, and just seeing me makes her sick. Physically sick, I mean. I understand. Her therapist explained it, and my wife keeps telling me. It's not me. It's any man. All men. So I'm not supposed to take it personally. I'm supposed to be patient and hope my dear Bonnie gets better. It's because of what that man did to her. That man right there. He ruined her. She'll never be the same. He— he might as well have killed her. He killed the girl she was, do you see? She's practically dead. Her spirit is dead. Do you understand, you son of a bitch? Are you listening to me? Yes, you. Look at me, damn you. That's what you did. You killed my little girl's spirit. You might as well have shot her or stabbed her. She was a sweet, trusting child, all the time singing. Loved animals. Loved people. Trusted people. She was just an innocent child. Wanted to be a doctor so she could cure sick children. Now . . . I can't imagine her having a boyfriend, getting married. Having any kind of normal life. You. I said look at me. You deserve to die. You are a horrible, disgusting animal. You are evil. You should burn in hell forever and ever. I pray for that. You should have that . . . that evil penis of yours cut off with a dull knife. Somebody should hack it off slowly, and—' Here," the sheriff said, "a bit tardy, I might say, our friend Otis Maxner, the public defender, objects, and Judge Roper grants the objection, and Acworth, the ADA, no doubt quite pleased with his witness's testimony, says, 'No further questions.' And the judge says, 'Your witness, Mr. Maxner,' and Maxner says, 'I have no questions for this witness, Your Honor.' "

"Heavy stuff," said Calhoun. "You did a really nice job reading it, too."

"So this Dunbar," said the sheriff, "he's who we're on our way to visit. Be interesting to see what he has to say now, whatever it is, six or seven years later."

"Burn in hell," said Calhoun. "When we talked to Maxner, he mentioned the cutting off his evil penis part, but he didn't mention the burning in hell part."

"That caught my attention," said the sheriff. "Burn in hell and have his organ hacked off, the man said. Pretty much the fate that actually befell Mr. Errol Watson."

"Doesn't sound like a coincidence, what happened to him," said Calhoun. "Wonder how many people heard or read about what Dunbar said."

"Who knows?" said the sheriff. "Besides the people there in the courtroom, it must've been reported on TV and in the papers. Maybe Mr. Dunbar gave out interviews."

"When you think about it," said Calhoun, "it's kind of obvious. Cutting off his pecker and then setting him afire."

"A damn good idea," said the sheriff.

"But not all that original. Anybody could've thought of it."

"True enough," said the sheriff. "Except this Dunbar's the one who actually said it."

CHAPTER TWELVE

It was dusk, and orange streetlights lit the tree-lined suburban street in Biddeford. The houses, Colonials and dormered Capes, were set back from the sidewalks on what Calhoun guessed were one-acre lots. Newish automobiles, mostly big square SUVs, were parked in front of the garages. The lawns and gardens appeared to be well tended. The maples and birches were just beginning to turn yellow.

Calhoun was driving slowly. The sheriff was trying to read house numbers off the mailboxes and doorframes.

The clock on the dashboard of the Explorer read seven thirteen when the sheriff said, "Here we go. Pull over here."

Calhoun stopped in front of a big white Colonial house framed by a pair of big maple trees. When they started walking down the driveway, a floodlight on the peak of the garage roof, apparently motion activated, flashed on and lit up the area. A basketball hoop on a steel pole stood at the side of the paved area. The garage had four doors and was nearly as big as the house.

The sheriff went to the garage and peered through the windows. Then he took out his flashlight and shined it inside. "Come here, Stoney," he said. "Look at this."

Calhoun went over and looked in. There were four bays. One was occupied by a canoe upside down on sawhorses. Cars were parked in the other three. There was a blue Subaru Legacy, a black

Honda Accord, and a dark red Saab sedan. All three vehicles looked quite new.

"The Saab," said Calhoun. "Dark red."

"Burgundy," said the sheriff. "With a sunroof. To quote Sherlock Holmes, 'Aha.'"

"I don't think Sherlock Holmes ever actually said 'Aha,'" said Calhoun. "He might've said 'Egad' or 'Zounds' or 'The game's afoot.'"

"That doesn't sound right, either," said the sheriff. "Let's talk to the Dunbars."

They went up to the front door. The sheriff rang the bell.

The light over the door flicked on, and then the inside door opened. A boy stood there on the other side of the screen. He looked sixteen or seventeen, Calhoun thought. He was tall and gangly, a good-looking kid with dark curly hair. "My parents don't talk to salesmen or Mormon missionaries," he said.

"We're not salesmen or missionaries," said the sheriff. He held up his badge. "I'm the sheriff and this is my deputy."

The boy narrowed his eyes at the sheriff's badge, said, "Hang on a minute," and disappeared.

A minute later a man appeared. He had a cloth napkin in his hand. He wore a white shirt with the cuffs turned up at his wrists and a necktie pulled loose at the throat. "Can I help you?" he said.

"I'm Sheriff Dickman," said the sheriff. "This is Deputy Calhoun. We'd like to talk to you."

"Me?" said the man.

"You are Franklin Dunbar?"

"Yes, I am. But—"

"Your wife is Meredith, and your daughter is Bonnie? And the young man who came to the door is your son?"

"That's Benjie," he said. "Yes. What's this about?"

"May we come in?" said the sheriff.

"We're just finishing up our dinner," said Dunbar. "It's really not a good time. Can't it wait?"

"No," said the sheriff.

Dunbar frowned for a moment, then wiped his mouth with his

napkin and unlatched the screen door. "Well, all right. Come in, then."

The sheriff and Calhoun stepped into a small flagstone entryway, and Dunbar led them into the living room. There was an Oriental rug on a wide-plank pine floor, new-looking square furniture, a glass-and-steel coffee table, a big flat-screen TV mounted on one wall, a huge abstract oil painting on the other wall, and a brick fireplace. The lights were recessed in the vaulted ceiling except for a track light that illuminated the painting.

Calhoun noticed the absence of family photos or, for that matter, any personal memorabilia in the room. It appeared to have been professionally decorated in preparation for a magazine photo shoot.

Dunbar gestured to an L-shaped sofa. "Have a seat," he said.

Calhoun and the sheriff sat.

Dunbar remained standing. He was a bigger man than he'd appeared to be at first. He had dark, curly hair like Benjie, his son, except Franklin Dunbar's was flecked with gray. "So what do you want?" he said.

"I could use a glass of water," said the sheriff. "How about you, Deputy?"

"I wouldn't mind some water," said Calhoun.

A woman came into the room. She peered at the sheriff and Calhoun, then said, "What's going on, Franklin? I was about to serve dessert."

"This is Sheriff Dickman and Deputy Calhoun," said Dunbar. "They haven't yet said what they want."

A sudden smile appeared on the woman's face. Calhoun figured she was one of those people who could smile on demand regardless of what she might be feeling. She stepped forward and held out her hand. "I'm Meredith Dunbar. Did Franklin offer you some coffee?"

"He offered water," said the sheriff. "We accepted."

Dunbar left the room. The sheriff and Calhoun both shook Meredith Dunbar's hand. Then she sat across from them. She wore a white blouse and dark tailored slacks. She was slender to the point of being skinny. Her blond-streaked hair was cut short and straight. She wore clever makeup around her eyes that made them look larger and wider-spaced than they were. Calhoun guessed she was around fifty. He pegged her husband as a few years younger.

Franklin Dunbar came back with a pitcher of water and four glasses on a tray, which he put on the coffee table. Then he sat beside his wife. "Okay," he said. "Here's some water. Help yourself. I'm sorry if I was impolite. I had a long day on the road, and I was just relaxing with my family over dinner, and . . ."

"And we interrupted," said the sheriff. Calhoun noticed he didn't apologize. "We want to talk to you about Errol Watson."

Dunbar frowned. "Who?"

His wife, almost simultaneously, said, "Oh, my God. What has that monster done now?"

Dunbar turned and frowned at her. Then he said, "Oh. Him." He looked back at the sheriff. "What about him?"

The sheriff said, "You didn't remember his name?"

"Of course I remember," said Dunbar. "I don't like to think about him, that's all."

"Have you seen Errol Watson recently?"

Dunbar opened his mouth, then shut it. He reached for the water pitcher, poured some into a glass, picked up the glass, and took a sip. "Watson's in prison, isn't he?"

"He's been out for over a year," said the sheriff.

Calhoun was watching the woman. She was frowning at her husband. "Ma'am," he said, "you knew he was out, right?"

She nodded. "We heard. He served a total of four and a half years. Which is ridiculous, after what he did. I supposed he's . . . molesting children again?"

"You knew he was out," said the sheriff to Dunbar.

"I guess so."

"Why did you lie?"

Dunbar shrugged. "I was denying, not lying. This is an unpleasant subject."

"You said you haven't seen him?"

"That's right. Why would I see him?"

"Which of you drives the Saab?"

"I do," said Dunbar.

"Your car was seen at Watson's house a few weeks ago," said the sheriff.

Dunbar opened his mouth to speak, but his wife put her hand on his leg and said, "Franklin, you didn't!"

He looked at her. "What? Well, what if I did?"

"You were there," said the sheriff.

"Look," said Dunbar. "All right. I can't tell you how I hate that man. He haunts my thoughts constantly. He has wrecked our lives. My poor daughter is ruined. My marriage is . . ." He glanced at his wife, who looked away. "It's not the same. Never will be. Nothing will ever be the same. Can you understand how this one evil person could poison the innocent lives of an entire family?"

"So what did you do?" said the sheriff.

"Do?"

"When you went to Watson's house?"

"I wanted to see him. I wanted to see if he had changed. I wanted to know if he had . . . repented. In court he never said anything, never looked at us, never conveyed any emotion whatsoever. I wanted to give him the chance to say he was sorry, to say he regretted what he had done."

"Why?"

"Why?" Dunbar blew out a breath. "I don't know. I thought it would make me feel better."

"What happened?" said the sheriff.

"Nothing. He wouldn't talk to me. He wouldn't let me in."

"So what did you do?"

Dunbar shrugged. "I left."

"Was that the only time you were there?"

He nodded. "Yes. Just that once."

"You want to think about that?" said the sheriff.

Dunbar blinked, glanced at his wife, then said, "Okay. I went back. It was a few nights later. But I just drove past his house. I didn't know what to do. I was angry and frustrated."

"So what did you do?"

"Do? I didn't do anything. I drove by, that's all. And then I came home."

"What about the other times?"

"There was only—what do you mean?"

Meredith Dunbar took her husband's hand in both of hers. "You should just tell them the truth," she said.

"Which truth?" he said. "The truth about how he destroyed us? The truth about how he barely got his wrist slapped in court? The truth about how they set him free so he could wreck other families?"

"Just tell them what you did," she said softly.

Dunbar looked at the sheriff. "I didn't do anything. That's my shame. What kind of man am I, I can't take care of my family, correct this horrible thing that's been done to my daughter, to us. Why can't I do what I want to do?"

"What do you want to do?" said the sheriff.

"What do I want to do? I want to go back in time to before Errol Watson lured my little girl into his house to show her his puppies, and I want to kill the man right then, before he could do what he did." Dunbar took in a deep breath. Calhoun noticed that his eyes were glittering. "But I can't do that, can I? It's too late, isn't it? So now? Now I just want him dead. I want him to suffer. I want to know he's burning in hell."

Calhoun was watching Dunbar's wife. She was hard to read. She kept her eyes on her husband's face as he talked, and her lips were moving slightly, as if she were trying to speak for him.

"You went to his house to kill him," the sheriff said to Dunbar, making it a statement, not a question.

"No, no." Dunbar shook his head. "I don't know why I went there. Not to kill him. I don't think I could do that."

"What exactly do you want with us?" said Meredith Dunbar. "What's happened to that man?"

"Why do you think something happened to him?" said the sheriff.

She shrugged. "Why else would you be here?"

The sheriff turned to Dunbar. "Where were you two weeks ago last Saturday night?"

Dunbar frowned. "I don't know. What was the date?"

"August thirty-first."

"We were home that whole weekend," said Meredith Dunbar. "That was right after Bonnie left. She's attending college in California. It's a small Catholic girls' school. Very strict. Very regimented. It's what she needs. She's doing a little better. Her therapist is optimistic. We hope she's going to be all right."

"Yes," said the sheriff. "Good. So what about that Saturday night? Where were you?"

"We were here."

"Just the two of you?"

"Yes," she said. "Benjie was away for the weekend. That would be the weekend before he started school. Labor Day weekend. He was up at the lake. His friend Charles—Charles's parents, that is—they have a place on Long Lake. They do a lot of waterskiing. He came back Monday afternoon."

"Did you have guests or visitors that evening?"

"That Saturday, you mean?"

The sheriff just looked at her.

"No," she said. "It was just the two of us."

"What did you do?"

"I don't know," she said. "It was just another Saturday night. Watched television, I suppose. We don't do much anymore. We don't go out. We don't have friends. Franklin goes off to work. He's on the road a lot. I volunteer at the library. As many hours as I can get. We try to keep busy. We don't have any fun."

The sheriff said, "Since . . ."

She nodded. "Yes. Since that happened." She cocked her head at him. "Errol Watson has been murdered, hasn't he?"

"Why would you say that?" said the sheriff.

"Why else would you be here, asking us these questions? We—Franklin, I mean—he's your best suspect. He threatened Watson in court, and he's been seen at his house." She smiled. "You don't know my husband. He couldn't do that. He—he has trouble doing much of anything. He thinks and agonizes and ponders, and he looks at things from all possible angles, and he ends up doing nothing."

"What about you?" said the sheriff.

"I could do it," she said. "I didn't, but I could. I am very clear about the difference between right and wrong. Killing Errol Watson would not be wrong. If somebody killed him, they did the right thing. If my husband did it, I will take back every bad thing I've said about him over the past seven years." She turned to Dunbar. "Did you do it, Franklin?"

He shook his head. "No."

She smiled. "Well, if he's dead, maybe our family can begin to heal. Maybe it will give us closure, finally." She narrowed her eyes at the sheriff. "Is he dead?"

He nodded. "Yes, he is."

Meredith Dunbar nodded. "Good. I'm sorry to tell you, we didn't do it. So do you have any other questions for us, Sheriff?"

The sheriff glanced at Calhoun, who shook his head. "No, I think that's it for now." He pushed himself to his feet, then reached into his pocket and pulled out a business card. He handed it to Franklin Dunbar. "If you think of anything you forgot to tell us, please give me a call."

Dunbar ran the ball of his thumb over the front of the sheriff's card, then tucked it into his shirt pocket. "Sure," he said. "Of course."

They went to the front door. Watson pulled it open.

"Do you like fishing?" said Calhoun.

"Fishing?" said Dunbar. "Yes, I guess so. I used to like fishing."

"Do you have a boat?"

Dunbar nodded. "Sure. Everybody around here has a boat. Having a boat, spending time on the water, that's why people choose to live near the coast of Maine, isn't it?"

Calhoun nodded. "What kind of boat?"

"Ours?" said Dunbar. "Boston Whaler. It's just an eighteen-foot runabout with a forty-horse motor. Nothing fancy. I got it before . . . what happened. I thought, you know, it would be fun to take the family out in the boat, spend some time on the water, have picnics on the islands, explore the rivers, dig some clams, do some trolling." He shook his head. "Since . . . well, we pretty much stopped doing family outings. Benjie uses the boat mostly, now."

"Where do you keep it?"

"At the marina. The Saco Marina, right there in the river." He frowned. "Why are you asking about my boat?"

Calhoun smiled. "I'm interested in boats, that's all."

"Well," said Dunbar, "I'd sell that damn thing if it wasn't for Benjie. You know what it costs to rent a slip in a marina? He keeps saying he might want to try lobstering, and I think it would be good for him, a good thing for a boy to do, if he could ever got off his butt."

Calhoun nodded and pushed open the screen door. From somewhere outside came a rhythmic thumping sound that he identified as a ball bouncing on pavement.

The sheriff turned to Meredith Dunbar and said, "I wonder if I could use your bathroom?"

"Of course," she said, and led him back into the house.

Calhoun went outside. Benjie Dunbar was shooting a basketball at the hoop on the side of the driveway. He was working hard at it. He'd shoot a long jump shot, then go charging in to grab the ball before it hit the pavement, and he'd shoot again. Then he'd grab the ball, dribble back a distance, make a couple of fakes and pivots, and shoot again.

He hardly ever missed.

After a minute, Calhoun said, "You on the team?"

The boy stopped suddenly and looked over. "Jesus," he said. "You scared the shit out of me, man."

"Sorry. I was watching you. You're very good."

"Yeah," said Benjie. "I'm hoping to be a starter this year. I don't know. I've got to work on my left hand." He suddenly snapped the ball at Calhoun.

Calhoun reached up, snagged it with one hand, and bounced it tentatively. It felt familiar, and he knew that he had dribbled a basketball before. Without thinking about it, he raised the ball over his head and flicked it toward the hoop in a smooth, comfortable motion that felt utterly natural, and he knew that his muscles had repeated that motion hundreds of times.

His shot ticked off the front of the rim and fell short.

Benjie grabbed the rebound and laid it in. "You gotta follow through," he said. He held up his arm and flopped his hand forward at the wrist.

Calhoun clapped his hands. Benjie passed him the ball. He shot again, this time following through with his hand and wrist, and it slipped through the net without touching the hoop.

"There you go," said Benjie. "Lookin' good." He retrieved the ball and passed it back to Calhoun.

He fired again. Swish.

Benjie grabbed the ball, dribbled to where Calhoun was standing, and handed it to him. "Come on," he said. "Give me your best move." He bent his knees and held his hands loose at his sides.

Calhoun figured that if he thought about it, he'd probably trip over his own feet, so he blanked his mind, and the next thing he knew, he had twitched his hip, dropped his shoulder, and rocked back, and then he took one big crossover step around Benjie, dribbled for the basket, launched himself into the air, twisted his body, and dropped the ball through the hoop from the other side.

Benjie caught the ball as it came through the net and zipped it at Calhoun. "Try that again."

Calhoun held up his hand. "I'm an old man. You want me to have a heart attack?"

"I wasn't ready for you," said Benjie. "I can stop you."

"Sure," said Calhoun. "I know you can." He bounced the ball toward the boy.

Benjie picked it up, made a ball-fake at Calhoun, then pivoted and tossed in a fallaway jumper. He retrieved the ball and threw it hard at Calhoun.

Calhoun knocked the pass down, then picked up the ball. "You mad at me or something?"

"You beat me once and then you quit? You can't do that."

"Sure I can."

"Come on, man," said Benjie. "See if you can stop me."

"Sure," said Calhoun. "Okay."

They moved out about twenty feet from the basket. Calhoun gave Benjie a bounce pass, then got down into a defensive position.

Benjie held the ball in both hands, his elbows out, knees bent, weaving his head side to side, and Calhoun knew he was going to fake left, hesitate, give him a quick jam step, then drive to the right.

When Benjie did it, Calhoun pretended to go for the fake, and Benjie drove in for a fancy over-the-shoulder layup.

Calhoun trailed behind him and caught the ball as it fell through the net. "Nice move. I left my jock back there somewhere."

"Wanna go again?"

Calhoun blew out a breath. "Nope. I was lucky once. Let's leave it at that." He handed the ball to Benjie.

Benjie shrugged. "A move like that isn't luck. You played in college, right? I mean, you're pretty good for somebody your age. Where'd you play?"

Calhoun shrugged. He had no idea when or where he'd played basketball. It was one of the myriad things that had happened before a bolt of lightning obliterated his memory. Still, it was pretty obvious that he had played, and the memory of it lived in his muscles, if not his brain.

Benjie put the basketball down on the blacktop and sat on it.

Calhoun squatted beside him. He was breathing hard. "Wow," he said. "I'm out of shape."

"So somebody killed that bastard who raped my sister, huh?" said Benjie.

"I'm not supposed to talk about it."

Benjie laughed harshly. "Yeah, me, neither. It's the big family shame, our terrible secret. You wouldn't know it, but before that happened, my dad was a hot-shit guy. Took us fishing and camping, played ball with me, told jokes. He hasn't shot hoops with me since then. Not once."

Calhoun glanced at Benjie and saw that tears were glittering in the boy's eyes. He stood up and looked back toward the house so Benjie wouldn't see that he'd noticed.

The sheriff was standing there on the edge of the driveway with his arms folded across his chest, watching them.

"Look," said Calhoun to Benjie, "I've got to go. You want to talk sometime, give me a call." He found one of the shop's business cards in his wallet. "Call me here. It's where I work when I'm not playing deputy sheriff. If I'm not there, leave a message. I'll get it. Maybe we could go fishing sometime."

Benjie swiped his wrist across his eyes, then took the card and looked at it. "Calhoun, huh?"

"Stoney. That's what they call me." He held out his hand.

Benjie shook it. "Thanks, man. Maybe I'll do that." He put the card in his pocket, then picked up the basketball and held it out to Calhoun. "Try another move on me."

Calhoun held up both hands. "That was my only move. It works only once. I better quit while I'm ahead. You take it easy."

Benjie grinned. "You, too."

Calhoun turned and went over to where the sheriff was standing. "Ready to go?"

The sheriff was shaking his head. "You keep surprising me, Stoney Calhoun."

"Me, too," said Calhoun.

When they were in the Explorer headed back to Calhoun's house, the sheriff said, "So what do you think, Deputy?"

"What Watson did wrecked that family," he said. "Bonnie wasn't the only victim. All of them are screwed up. It's hard to feel bad about what happened to that son of a bitch. He got what he deserved."

"Somebody murdered him," said the sheriff. "Don't lose track of that."

"I know." Calhoun nodded. "Paul Vecchio's the one I care about, though. I wouldn't be here with you doing this if it was just about what happened to Errol Watson."

"I figure," said the sheriff, "if we find who killed Watson, we'll also have the man who killed Vecchio."

"I guess so," said Calhoun. "You think Dunbar's a good suspect?"

"He had means, motive, and opportunity," said the sheriff. "He's a very good suspect. That was excellent, Stoney, by the way, asking about the boat. That establishes that Dunbar had the means to get Watson out to Quarantine Island."

"I guess his wife could've helped him."

"Or his son," said the sheriff.

Calhoun nodded. "That kid's got a lot bottled up in him. He doesn't like his father very much. Wanted to take my head off back there. Couldn't stand it that I beat him one-on-one."

The sheriff was smiling. "That was a helluva move."

"Don't ask me where it came from." Calhoun shook his head. "It's hard to imagine any of those people doing something like what happened to Watson."

"It always is." The sheriff chuckled. "It's hard to imagine you as a basketball star. You want to stop for some coffee?"

"No," said Calhoun. "I want to get home."

"You worried about Ralph?"

"I guess so."

They drove in silence for a few minutes. Then Calhoun said, "So now what happens?"

"Now," said the sheriff, "I'm going to write up a report for Lieutenant Gilsum. I'm going to remind him that what Dunbar said in court actually happened. Watson had his dick cut off, and then he was set on fire, just like Dunbar said. I'm going to report that Dunbar's burgundy-colored Saab was seen at Watson's house, and that he admitted going there, and that he lied about it at first. I'm going to say that he also lied about knowing that Watson was out of prison, and that, in fact, he tried to do a lot of lying, but he wasn't very good at it. I'm going to say that he has no alibi for the Saturday night when Watson was probably killed. I'm going to say that we'll never find anybody with a better motive than Franklin Dunbar."

"Then what?"

"Then?" The sheriff blew out a breath. "That's up to Gilsum. I'd be surprised if he didn't haul Dunbar in and give him a good grilling. Maybe the wife, too. Question them separately. We were pretty gentle with them."

Calhoun was shaking his head. "All that," he said, "but I still don't see Dunbar doing it."

"Not the type? That what you're thinking?"

Calhoun nodded. "Yeah, maybe. He seems too . . . passive. He's a broken man. Defeated. Just full of regret and sadness. He's beyond anger or revenge. I don't see him doing much of anything. You know what I'm saying?"

"People lie," said the sheriff. "Everybody lies. Everybody's got something to lie about. Most people aren't any good at it, but some are. They lie and dissemble, and the only way you can tell is by getting the right facts. In this business, you've got to assume they're lying."

"I know that," said Calhoun.

"There is no type," said the sheriff. "Anybody can do anything."

CHAPTER THIRTEEN

When Calhoun steered the sheriff's Explorer into the yard, Ralph came bounding out of the darkness. Calhoun got out and squatted down so Ralph could jump on him and lick his face. He realized that all the time he'd been gone, the possibility that Ralph wouldn't be there when he got back had been tugging at the edges of his mind.

The sheriff got out and came around to the driver's side.

"You want some coffee or something?" said Calhoun.

The sheriff shook his head. "Better not. Jane's expecting me."

"That's nice," said Calhoun, "having a woman at home waiting for you, caring where you've been."

"You've got a dog," said the sheriff. "Notice that he didn't look at his watch, tap his foot, and tell you he's been worried."

After the sheriff drove off, Calhoun went up to the house. He found a Milk-Bone in the cabinet and a Coke in the refrigerator and took them out to the deck. He gave Ralph the Milk-Bone and took a long swig of Coke. He wanted to wash away the bad taste in his mouth. Grilling a devastated family about the murder of the man who'd destroyed them was unpleasant business.

He could do it, and he understood the necessity of it, but he didn't like it.

He had to agree with the sheriff. Objectively, Franklin Dunbar made a very likely suspect. He supposed he could imagine Dunbar's ice-eyed wife or hotheaded son doing it, too. He could imagine all three of them doing it together.

What he couldn't imagine was punishing them for it. Four and a half years in prison was no punishment for what Errol Watson had done to them. Having his dick cut off and stuffed down his throat and then going up in flames, that was more like it. It was hard to feel too bad about that.

If Franklin Dunbar killed the man who wrecked his family, he deserved a big round of applause.

It would be a different story, though, if Dunbar murdered Watson and then turned around and shot Paul Vecchio.

As the sheriff said, anybody could do anything. You couldn't know what went on inside another person's head. An outwardly weak, shattered man like Franklin Dunbar might have a cold, steely center to him. Calhoun knew the sheriff was right in theory, but in this case, he did not believe that Franklin Dunbar—or his wife or their son—was capable of murdering a man like Paul Vecchio.

So Calhoun was left with a logical conundrum. Errol Watson and Paul Vecchio had been murdered. By the timing of it, and by the fact that Vecchio had discovered Watson's body shortly before getting killed himself—and by the fact that both murders were connected to Calhoun, too, for that matter—it logically followed that both men had been murdered by the same person.

Franklin Dunbar was the best suspect for the Watson murder, but there didn't appear to be any reason why he'd kill Paul Vecchio.

Maybe the two murders were unrelated, and all of the connections were coincidental. Or maybe Franklin Dunbar didn't kill either of them. Or maybe he killed both Watson and Vecchio, in which case, they needed to find his connection with Vecchio.

They were going at it wrong. They were looking for Watson's killer because it was easier. Watson was an evil man, the kind of man who accumulated enemies and had no friends. You could understand why someone would want to kill him. Anybody who knew the man made a good suspect. So there were plenty of possible killers with plausible motives, and you could keep yourself busy tracking them all down and interrogating them, and you'd feel like you were doing a good job.

But what did it matter? Watson was dead, and he deserved to be dead, and there was no justice in punishing his killer.

Calhoun just didn't want to do it anymore. He didn't care if they caught Errol Watson's killer. Actually, he kind of hoped they wouldn't. He couldn't see punishing Franklin Dunbar, if that's who did it. He should be given a medal.

He sat there in his Adirondack chair with his head tilted back looking up at the stars and listening to the owls. He knew what he wanted to do. He wanted to quit the whole distasteful business. His instincts had been right the first time. He should never have gotten involved.

He decided to do it. He would quit. He'd tell the sheriff first thing in the morning. He'd return the badge and the damn cell phone, shake his hand, wish him luck, tell him most sincerely he hoped they'd still be friends. Then he'd go back to guiding fishermen and tying flies and chopping wood and working in the shop. Life was too damn short and uncertain to keep doing things that didn't feel right and that you didn't believe in.

The instant he made the decision, he felt better.

He stood up, and so did Ralph, who'd been lying on the deck beside him, and they went into the house. Calhoun took the deputy badge and the sheriff's cell phone out of his pocket and put them on the table. Then he loaded the automatic coffeemaker, made sure Ralph's water dish was full, brushed his teeth, and went to bed.

Quitting the case made him feel pure and clean, and he fell asleep almost instantly.

Calhoun woke up thinking about Paul Vecchio. Through his bedroom window, he could see the black sky dotted with bright stars and the pine boughs waving in the breeze. His internal clock read five forty in the morning.

He felt twisted-up and conflicted all over again, the way he'd been feeling before he decided to quit working with the sheriff.

There had been a dream, of course, but he had no specific memory of it. Just that Vecchio had been in it. That was part of the tension he was feeling. His dreams always did that.

Calhoun had spent enough time with Paul Vecchio to know that he liked him. You share a boat with a man, chase some fish, it doesn't take long to get a pretty good idea of what kind of man he is. Vecchio was solid. He was smart and self-contained. He didn't take himself too seriously. He liked the ocean and fishing.

It hadn't been enough time to say they were friends, but it was enough time to believe that he and Paul Vecchio would've ended up being friends. If he hadn't been murdered.

Calhoun had decided to quit working with the sheriff. It wasn't quit that simple, though. He couldn't quit on Paul Vecchio.

With Vecchio's murder, unlike Errol Watson's, you started without any motive. Vecchio appeared to have no enemies. He wasn't a drug dealer or pornographer or rapist. Calhoun felt sure that he was just what he appeared to be, an inoffensive college professor. Nothing that Gilsum's detectives had learned so far contradicted that. There was no place to start with Vecchio. Without a motive, you had no suspects, and no way to start looking for them.

Apparently whoever killed Paul Vecchio had followed him to Calhoun's house in the woods. It was a good, solitary place to commit a murder, and that made it personal for Calhoun.

Not even to mention the fact that when they came to kill Vecchio, Ralph ran away and took his time coming back. Ralph wouldn't do that unless they'd taken a shot at him or tried to kick him. That made it very personal.

The question was: Why did Paul Vecchio go to Calhoun's house two days after their fishing trip?

Calhoun lay there in the dark and replayed that morning in the boat with Vecchio, beginning with the first time he laid eyes on the man two hours before sunrise under the orange lights of the parking area at the East End boat landing. They shook hands. Vecchio had a couple of rod cases in his hand and his black L.L.Bean gear bag slung over his shoulder. Calhoun told him he didn't need his fly rods, then pointed at the bag and gave his little speech about forbidding electronic gadgets on his boat. Vecchio went back to his Subaru to leave his rods and his cell phone. Then they went down to the boat. Vecchio patted Ralph, stored his gear bag in the waterproof locker under the seat, and . . .

Calhoun fast-forwarded through the morning to the sheriff telling Vecchio he couldn't go back to Quarantine Island with them, and Vecchio reluctantly getting out of the boat, then standing there watching them go, disappointed, maybe a little pissed off, not waving.

Calhoun studied that picture in his memory. He clearly saw that Paul Vecchio did not have his L.L.Bean gear bag in his hand or slung over his shoulder or sitting on the ground beside him.

He remembered that right before they landed on Quarantine Island, Vecchio had taken the bag out of the waterproof compartment under the middle seat. He held it on his lap, sitting on the front seat facing forward, and he rummaged around in it. After a couple of minutes, he lathered himself with sunscreen. Then he zipped up the bag, turned around, and put it back under the middle seat.

Sunscreen. There was that bottle of sunscreen on the deck beside Paul Vecchio's dead body, as if he'd been applying sunscreen when he got shot.

Except you didn't put on sunscreen at the end of the day, which was when Vecchio had gone to Calhoun's house. So he'd left it there for a different reason. It was a message for Calhoun from a man who realized he was about to be killed.

The gear bag. That's what had been nagging at the edges of Calhoun's memory for the past few days. Paul Vecchio had left his gear bag in the boat that day.

Maybe that's why he came to Calhoun's house. He wanted to retrieve his L.L.Bean bag, which was still in the boat, trailered there in the yard.

That's when he got murdered.

So why hadn't he called Calhoun at the shop or at home, told him he'd forgotten his bag, and arranged for Calhoun to get it back to him? Why had he come all the way to Calhoun's house in

Dublin? What was in the bag that was so important that he couldn't wait to get it back?

He rewound the scene and replayed it, and he heard Vecchio tell him what he kept in his gear bag. Windbreaker, camera, pliers, fish knife, boxes of flies, dry socks, sunscreen, insect repellent.

He took out the camera before he stored the bag in the compartment under the seat. He used the sunscreen in the boat.

If the killer was after something in the bag, then Vecchio hadn't told Calhoun everything, because nobody committed murder for a pair of socks or a box of flies.

Well, if the bag wasn't in the boat now, it meant the killer had taken it.

If it was still there in the waterproof compartment under the middle seat, Calhoun would open it up and see if it contained something of particular and unusual value to Paul Vecchio, and maybe to his killer.

Or maybe the bag had nothing to do with his getting killed. Coming to Calhoun's isolated house to retrieve it just created a convenient opportunity for the killer.

No. Vecchio had dropped that bottle of sunscreen on the deck to remind Calhoun about his gear bag.

Calhoun turned on the light beside his bed, got up, and pulled on his pants.

Ralph, who was curled on the floor at the foot of the bed, lifted his head and blinked at him.

"Go back to sleep," said Calhoun. "I'll be right back."

He turned on the floodlights, went down to where his boat was parked, and lifted the lid of the middle seat. Paul Vecchio's L.L. Bean gear bag was there.

He took it out and carried it back up to the house. He put it on the kitchen table, opened it up, and put everything he found inside on the table.

Socks, fly boxes, sunscreen, insect repellent, rolled-up windbreaker, pliers, fish knife.

He picked up each item, looked at it, turned it over, put it back on the table.

When he unrolled the windbreaker, he found a wrinkled scrap of notebook paper tucked inside.

He smoothed the paper on the table.

Keelhaul Albie 9/6 9:00 was written on it.

The letters were slightly blurred, as if they'd been exposed to dampness, but clearly legible, printed with a black felt-tip pen.

He turned the paper over. On the reverse side was an abstract design scratched with a pencil. It was a big inverted letter *U,* like an upside-down bowl or an umbrella, with a dozen or more crudely shaped roundish blobs of various sizes scattered around the paper as if they'd spilled from the bowl. Four of the little blobs had *X*'s crossed through them.

Calhoun looked at it. It didn't mean anything to him. Just a big upside-down *U* and a bunch of shapeless circles.

He figured it probably meant something to Paul Vecchio.

He flipped the paper over again. *Keelhaul Albie,* it said, with what appeared to be a date and time—9/6 9:00. That would be September 6, nine o'clock. He counted back. The sixth was the Saturday before he took Paul Vecchio fishing. Exactly a week after the ME said Errol Watson had been killed.

Vecchio, Calhoun remembered, had called the shop Sunday afternoon, the seventh, to arrange their trip., and he'd talked to Kate. Calhoun recalled her telling him about her conversation with this new client. He'd told her he was really eager to go, hoped to go out that same day, if possible, or Monday would be good. Said he didn't care whether he went with Kate or Calhoun. Kate had explained that it was too late to go out Sunday and they were closed on Monday, so Tuesday was the first date that anybody was available for guiding, and that it was Calhoun's turn.

Maybe this scrap of paper wasn't connected in any way to what happened to Paul Vecchio, but it was the closest thing to a clue anybody had come up with so far.

Was fetching this piece of paper the reason Paul Vecchio had come to Calhoun's house? Was it what got him killed?

Keelhaul Albie?

Was Calhoun's fishing trip with Paul Vecchio on Tuesday the

ninth the result of somebody named Albie getting keelhauled on Saturday the sixth at nine o'clock?'

Keelhauling was a traditional form of punishment at sea. It was way more severe than tying a misbehaving sailor to the mast and lashing him. To keelhaul a man, you tied ropes to his arms and legs and lowered him over the bow, and the crew held the ropes taut so that the victim was spreadeagled, and they walked back to the stern, dragging the poor outstretched bastard under the vessel, scraping him along the keel.

Victims of keelhauling who didn't drown first generally died from having their flesh flayed off by barnacles.

Maybe "keelhaul" was figurative. Maybe it just meant: Punish Albie severely and cruelly. Or maybe it meant kill. Keelhauling was usually fatal.

So who was Albie? Had he been keelhauled—or punished in some way, or killed—on Saturday, September 6, at nine o'clock?

And what, if anything, did that have to do with going fishing on Tuesday?

Errol Watson had been punished cruelly and severely, but being incinerated was nothing like being keelhauled.

Well, Paul Vecchio was a college professor. He probably liked metaphors and figurative language.

Another thought: "Albie" was what fishermen sometimes called false albacore, the small schooling tuna that occasionally appeared in the coastal waters off Maine and, more abundantly, around Cape Cod and Martha's Vineyard. Albies—and their cousins the bonito—were especially prized by fly fishermen.

But keelhauling a fish? That made no sense.

He waited until eight thirty to call the sheriff. He didn't want to interrupt the man's breakfast and hoped he would catch him after he was done in the bathroom.

Jane answered and said her damn workaholic husband, who'd been out till after midnight the previous night, had already left for the office, and you could probably catch him on his cell.

So Calhoun picked up his cell phone, pressed the button on the side, and said, "Dickman." After a couple of rings, the sheriff said, "Stoney? What's up?"

"I got something to show you."

"What kind of something?"

"It's this piece of paper I found in Paul Vecchio's L. L. Bean gear bag, which he left in my boat. It's got writing on one side and some kind of abstract design on the other side, and I'm thinking he came to my house to fetch it, and I think he dropped that bottle of sunscreen to remind me about his gear bag, and it might be connected to him getting killed."

"Piece of paper, huh?"

"A scrap of notebook paper, yes."

"A clue, eh, Sherlock?"

"You don't need to be sarcastic with me," said Calhoun.

"Sorry, Stoney. That is what you're thinking, though, right? This piece of paper's some kind of clue?"

"Ayuh. That is what I was thinking."

"You're right. It might be." The sheriff hesitated. "Okay, look. I'm just pulling into the parking lot at the state police headquarters. Got a big meeting with Lieutenant Gilsum and his crew. Enfield, the DA, he's going to be there, too. They want my report on our meeting with Franklin Dunbar. We're all supposed to be comparing notes, getting reorganized and coordinated. I don't know how long it'll take. Gilsum does love his damn meetings, and he will no doubt want to do some showing off for Enfield. What can you tell me about this piece of paper?"

Calhoun told him what it said and tried to describe the design with the upside-down U and the crude shapes, some with X's drawn through them.

"Hm," said the sheriff after a minute. "Interesting. I bet you've given it some thought, and I want to hear it. Myself, I can't think about it now. You gonna be at the shop today?"

"Ten till four," said Calhoun. "It's Tuesday."

"I'll meet you there. Gotta go."

Calhoun hit the Off button, hesitated, then shoved the phone into his pocket. He picked up the deputy badge, bounced it in the palm of his hand for a minute, then stuck that in his pocket, too. He wasn't sure anymore if he was going to quit. It all depended on whether he'd be able to focus on the Paul Vecchio case.

He was definitely done with the Errol Watson investigation.

He folded Vecchio's scrap of notebook paper and stuck it in his shirt pocket. Then he poured himself a travel mug full of coffee and took it, along with Paul Vecchio's gear bag, down to his truck. He stuck the gear bag in the back, hitched up his boat, opened the driver's door so Ralph could jump in, and headed for the shop in Portland.

He wanted to keep the boat handy to the water. He had that fishing trip with Dr. Sam Surry coming up on Friday, and maybe they'd pick up another trip before that. Maybe someone would even call wanting to go out today. He could park the boat in the lot beside the shop and be ready.

He got there a little before ten. Kate had already opened up. She was at her desk in the back office talking on the phone when Calhoun walked in. She arched her eyebrows and wiggled her fingers and gave him a quick smile, then looked down at something she was reading on her desk.

Calhoun felt a familiar tingle. It was nice to see Kate smile, however briefly. She hadn't been doing much smiling lately.

Ralph went over and lay down beside her. She reached down and gave his shoulder a scratch.

Calhoun poured himself a mug of coffee and took it up front to the counter. He opened the trip book and wrote in Dr. Surry's name for four o'clock on Friday. There were no other trips scheduled before or after that.

He was tying some more landlocked salmon featherwing streamers when Kate came out of her office. She stopped by the fly-tying bench, watched Calhoun for a minute, then said, "We ran low on your Deceivers and sand eels this year, you know. People really liked them. Maybe you can make more of them for next season?"

He looked up at her. "You saying I shouldn't be tying these streamers for the Boston boys?"

"I was saying no such thing," she said.

He shrugged. "My mistake."

"You seem kind of cranky this morning, Stoney. You okay?"

He wanted to say: I am not okay. I don't like pretending that nothing's wrong between us. I don't like it that I can't even hope you'll come to my house some night. I don't like thinking that we are over with.

What he said was: "I'm fine. This business of working with the sheriff is kind of stressful, that's all."

"Making any progress?"

"I don't know."

She touched his shoulder for a moment, then went behind the counter.

His shoulder tingled where she'd touched him.

A few minutes later, from behind the counter, Kate said, "You booked yourself a trip, I see."

"Friday afternoon," he said. "Half a day."

"Dr. Sam Surry. That cute redhead, huh?"

He looked up at her. He didn't know how he was supposed to answer. If he said yes, would that mean that he agreed that Dr. Surry was cute?

Kate had her elbows on the counter with her chin in her hands, looking at him, neither smiling nor frowning. "We take turns, Stoney," she said. "You know that's our rule. You had the last trip. This one should be mine."

"Dr. Surry specifically asked me to take her out," said Calhoun. "What was I supposed to say?"

"We've been over this before," she said. "You don't get to take out who you want and refuse to take out who you don't want. That's not professional. That's not how we agreed to do it."

"It was her who asked to go out with me," he said. "Not the other way around."

"Hard to blame her, charming rogue like you." Kate was not smiling. "She'll have way more fun with you, I'm sure."

"You want me to tell her you'll be the one taking her out instead of me?" he said. "I can do that."

She smiled quickly. "Oh, we wouldn't want to disappoint the client. I bet she's a big fan of yours."

"It's not like we've got all these trips lined up," said Calhoun.

Kate narrowed her eyes at him. "That's for God damn sure." She slammed the trip book shut, turned, stalked back to her office at the rear of the shop, and kicked the door closed behind her.

Calhoun was at the front counter talking on the phone with the Simms sales rep, listening to what he had to say about next year's line of breathable waders, when Kate came out of her office, where she'd been holed up all morning. She stood there pretending to straighten out the display of rain gear until Calhoun hung up. Then she said, "You want a sandwich or something?"

"Sure. Tuna would be great. Onions and lettuce. Whole wheat bread."

She smiled. "I guess I know what you like on your tunafish sandwiches."

You know as much about me as I do, he wanted to say. You know every square inch of my skin. You know how my crazy brain works. I have no secrets from you.

Instead, he said, "Why don't you bring Ralph with you? He's been cooped up all morning."

She gave him a little smile that did not reach up to her eyes. "I'm sorry, Stoney. About how I've been acting. It's me, not you. I'm the cranky one."

"Don't worry about it," he said. "How's Walter doing?"

She gave her head a quick shake. "He gets a little worse each day."

"Tell him hello for me."

"Sure," she said. "I'll do that."

Calhoun and Kate were sitting on the front steps of the shop finishing up their sandwiches and Cokes and enjoying the midday September sunshine when the sheriff's Explorer pulled into the lot.

Ralph, who had been lying there attentively, alert for errant sandwich crumbs, got to his feet and trotted over to the Explorer.

The sheriff climbed out, leaned over, gave Ralph a pat, then went over to where Calhoun and Kate were sitting. He touched the brim of his hat, nodded to Kate, said, "Ma'am," and turned to Calhoun. "You going to be free around five today, Deputy?"

"We close up at four," said Calhoun. "Anytime after that."

"I'll shoot for sooner," said the sheriff, "but it'll likely be sometime after five."

"I'll be here," said Calhoun, "unless you want me to help you interrogate families whose daughter has been raped and molested, in which case you'll find me back home stacking firewood, and don't bother comin' after me."

The sheriff glanced at Kate, who seemed to be watching them with an amused little smile playing around her mouth. Then he turned back to Calhoun and nodded. "I do understand, Stoney."

"I'm pretty interested in what happened to Paul Vecchio," said Calhoun, "but I've lost interest in what happened to Errol Watson. I decided I ain't going to work on that case anymore. I just want you to know that."

"Watson was an evil man, all right," said the sheriff. "That doesn't make murdering him okay."

Calhoun shrugged.

"Anyway," said the sheriff, "you're off the hook. Lieutenant Gilsum figures he's got what he needs to close that case. He wanted me to tell you he appreciates your good work."

"Franklin Dunbar?"

The sheriff looked at his watch. "As we speak, with the blessing of District Attorney Enfield himself, Gilsum is hauling Mr. Dunbar and his wife and son in for questioning, reading them their rights, and getting warrants to search their house, with particular emphasis on the family computer. Also their boat and car."

Calhoun shook his head. "You know as well as I do that Dunbar couldn't do something like that."

"I know no such thing." The sheriff smiled. "Anyway, that right there is the best reason I can think of for you not to quit on me."

CHAPTER FOURTEEN

Around four, Kate said she was leaving for the day, going to go visit Walter. Calhoun was sitting at the fly-tying bench, still turning out landlocked salmon streamers for the Boston guys. He reminded her to say hello to Walter for him.

She looked at him for a minute, then nodded and gave him a tiny little smile. She scootched down and patted Ralph, straightened up, waved her hand, and left.

Calhoun got up, put on the classical music station, and went back to tying flies. Some time later he felt a vibration against his leg. He fished out his cell phone, hit the green button, put it to his ear, and said, "Sheriff? That you? Everything okay?"

"I'm just leaving this damn meeting," said the sheriff. "Sorry it's so late. I'll be there in about fifteen minutes. Don't go anywhere."

"What time is it, anyway?" said Calhoun.

"After six."

"What—"

"Don't ask."

When the sheriff came in, he said, "I could use a drink." Somewhere along the way he'd changed out of his uniform. Now he wore a red-and-black-checked flannel shirt, baggy blue jeans, and a black windbreaker, no hat covering his bald head.

"I got Coke," said Calhoun. "Coffee's still hot."

"That's not what I had in mind, but I'll take a Coke."

Calhoun went to the refrigerator in back, fetched two cans of Coke, and brought them to the front of the shop. The sheriff had pulled a chair up to the fly-tying bench. He was looking at the flies Calhoun had tied. They were lined up neatly, stuck into the foam strip along the side of the bench while their laquered heads dried.

"These are nice flies, Stoney. You do good work. What's this one here called?"

"That's a Warden's Worry. Classic old Maine streamer fly. That one there's a Gray Ghost, and we got a few Black Ghosts and Green Ghosts, too. Right there, and there." Calhoun pointed at the various flies.

The sheriff was peering at them, apparently fascinated.

"So you gonna tell me what's been going on," said Calhoun, "tied up in meetings till six o'clock?"

The sheriff looked up. "They're holding Franklin Dunbar."

"Case closed, huh? You don't seem exactly triumphant."

"It doesn't feel good to me," said the sheriff. "We got no witnesses or physical evidence, just for starters. Gilsum figures the motive is enough at this point, that plus Dunbar having no alibi. He's confident they'll come up with something."

"How about you?"

The sheriff shrugged. "I guess I wouldn't be surprised if Dunbar did it. If I were him, I probably would. Still, I'm uncomfortable with it. Uncomfortable with Gilsum, really. He's too damn hot to make his arrest, close his case. You should've seen him grill poor Dunbar."

"He didn't confess, did he?"

"No such luck," said the sheriff.

"What about the Vecchio murder?" said Calhoun.

"I guess Dunbar could've done that, though it's harder to make sense of. He's got no alibi for that night. Claims he was on the road, says he has no idea who Paul Vecchio is. Gilsum's going to check Dunbar's phone and e-mail records, try to catch him in another lie." The sheriff shook his head, then took a long swig of Coke. "You got that piece of paper you were telling me about?"

Calhoun took it out of his pocket and unfolded it on the table.

"You said Vecchio had it in his gear bag?"

Calhoun nodded. "When we were on the water, he took the bag out of the compartment under the seat and pretended to be digging around for some sunscreen. I was looking for fish, trying to watch where I was going, not paying much attention to Mr. Vecchio, but I can see it in my head, him with his bag on his lap, his back to me, bent over looking at something."

"Looking at this piece of paper, you think?"

"What I see in my memory, it's not clear. Like I said, his back is to me, but he's looking at something, and it could be this piece of paper. After a minute, he puts it back, finds his sunscreen, makes a big show of lathering himself up with it."

"Hm," said the sheriff. "Interesting." He squinted at the printed words, *Keelhaul Albie 9/6 9:00*. Then he turned the paper over and looked at the design with the inverted *U* and all the misshapen circles, some of them with *X*'s crossed through them. He looked up at Calhoun and jabbed his forefinger at the paper. "This make any kind of sense to you, Stoney?"

Calhoun shook his head. "Just a bunch of shapes."

The sheriff turned the paper over again and pointed at the words and numbers that were printed there. "So what do you make of this?"

"I've been thinking about it. Haven't come up with much of anything worth sharing. I don't think they keelhaul sailors anymore, do they?"

The sheriff smiled. "September sixth was a Saturday, right? Exactly a week after the ME said Watson died?"

Calhoun nodded. "Right."

"I have one thought," the sheriff said. "It occurred to me this morning after we talked on the phone, when you read this to me. There's a place called the Keelhaul Cafe down an alley off of Wharf Street in the Old Port part of town. Know it?"

"Never heard of it," said Calhoun. "I guess if I did, I might've made that connection myself."

"I'm sure you would have," said the sheriff. "You don't forget anything. The Keelhaul's what you might call a downscale kind of place. I made a drug bust there last winter, I think it was. Mostly fishermen, lobstermen, sailors, the odd freelance hooker hang out there."

"Maybe some guy named Albie hangs out there, too," said Calhoun.

The sheriff drained his Coke, crushed the can in his hand, tossed it into the wastebasket, and stood up. "Exactly what I was thinking," he said. "Why don't we go see?"

At that, Ralph, who'd been lying under Calhoun's feet, yawned and got up and trotted over to the door.

"Does that dog understand everything?" said the sheriff.

"Only if it's in English," said Calhoun.

It was nearly dark when the sheriff pulled his Explorer into the shadowy alley off Wharf Street. The entry to the Keelhaul Cafe was on the left. Some trash cans were lined up along the blank wall on the right. Aside from the double-sized oak door with the faded wooden sign and the dim light hanging over it, both walls were tall and flat and blank.

Calhoun and the sheriff climbed out of the truck. Ralph remained curled up on the backseat.

When they went inside, Calhoun was hit by the sour smell of decades of spilled booze and out-of-service toilets and stubbed-out cigarettes. Some female country singer was crooning about a snake, by which Calhoun surmised she meant a man.

The bar ran across the back wall of the low-ceilinged rectangular room. On the left side were half a dozen square wooden tables. A big-screen wall-mounted television set, muted, was showing a baseball game.

The right side of the room was dominated by a pool table. A young guy with a ponytail was shooting a game with a blond girl in tight, low-slung blue jeans and a cropped tank top. Four or five middle-aged men at the bar were craning their necks around, watching the pool game. Watching the girl, Calhoun supposed. The way she bent over the table, stuck her butt up in the air, wiggled it around as she lined up a shot, showed all that skin between the top of her jeans and the bottom of her shirt, she knew she was putting on a show for them, and the way the guy in the ponytail was grinning and glancing toward the men at the bar, he was enjoying the attention she was attracting from them.

The sheriff slid onto a bar stool. Calhoun climbed onto the one beside him. The bartender was down at the other end talking to the four other guys.

Calhoun looked around. Fishing nets draped on the walls, lobster buoys hanging from the rafters, weathered wood-plank walls and floor. There were six fake portholes in a line behind the bar. The heavy round frames looked authentic enough, but behind the glass, it was just blue paint on the splintery wall.

After a few minutes, the bartender was still down there talking to the other guys, and Calhoun decided they were being ignored. He slid off his stool, went down to the other end of the bar, wedged himself between two guys on stools, and stood directly in front of the bartender. "Hey," he said.

The bartender glanced at him, then turned and said something to one of the men he'd been talking to.

"You," said Calhoun. "Mr. Bartender. You planning on waiting on us? Me and my friend need a drink."

The bartender glanced toward the sheriff, then looked at Calhoun. He had bulky arms, a deeply creased face, curly gray hair. "You're keepin' bad company there, if that man's your friend."

"You know who he is?"

The bartender smiled.

Calhoun leaned across the bar and crooked his finger at the bartender. "Come here," he said. "I want to tell you something."

The bartender shrugged and bent toward Calhoun.

Calhoun wrapped his hand around the back of the man's neck, squeezed it hard, and hauled him off his feet.

"Hey, shit," gurgled the bartender. "What the hell you doing?"

Calhoun pushed his face right up to the bartender's. "That bad company down there," he said, "that's your county sheriff, the man who keeps you and your family safe and secure, and if you don't get your ass down there and ask him politely what you can bring him to drink, you're going to find one of them pool cues shoved all the way up your ass. Okay?"

The guy nodded. "I know who he is," he said. "I was just bustin' his balls a little. I'll be right with you, okay?"

Calhoun let go of his neck. "Thank you."

He gave the bartender's cheek a pat, then went back and sat beside the sheriff, who had a bemused smile on his face. "Was that necessary, Stoney?"

"I don't know. I have a high tolerance for a lot of behavior, but purposeful rudeness just gets to me."

A minute later the bartender came down and swiped his rag over the bar in front of Calhoun and the sheriff. "Sheriff," he said. "How you doin'?"

"Not too bad, Leon," said the sheriff. "How 'bout you? You behaving?"

Leon shrugged. "Tryin'. What can I get you?"

"Draft beer for me."

"Coffee," said Calhoun. "Black."

Leon went off to fetch their drinks.

The sheriff leaned to Calhoun. "I hassled some of Leon's customers about selling drugs here in this establishment last winter," he said. "He took it personally."

Leon came back with a mug of coffee and a glass of beer. He set them in front of Calhoun and the sheriff. "So what's up?" he said to the sheriff. "I don't figure you came here for the ambience."

"Ambience," said the sheriff.

Leon smiled.

"You know somebody named Albie?"

"Old fisherman? Lives on his boat down near the mouth of the Stroudwater?"

The sheriff shrugged. "Sounds right. What's his last name?"

"Wazlewski? That ain't quite right, but something like that. Polack name, begins with a *W*, ends with-'ski.' That who you mean?"

"Was he in here at nine o'clock on the sixth?"

Leon frowned. "The sixth . . ."

"Week ago Saturday night. Were you here?"

"I'm always here," said Leon. He looked up at the ceiling for a minute, then nodded. "Yeah, Albie was here that night."

"You remember that specifically?"

"Matter of fact, I do," said Leon. "What about it?"

"Tell me what you remember," said the sheriff.

"Saturday," said Leon. "Always busy. Albie liked that corner table"—he pointed toward one of the tables—"where he could watch the TV, eat some soup, chew on some bread, sip on a beer. When we were busy I'd make him sit at the bar. Didn't want to waste a whole table on one person, you know? The reason I remember about that particular night was, Albie was with somebody. I mean, some of the regulars might go sit with him, shoot the shit for a minute, but this was some guy I never seen before. Not the kind of gentleman normally comes into this dump, and not the kind of guy you'd expect to be conferring with Albie."

"What'd he look like," said the sheriff, "this stranger?"

"Tall, salt-and-pepper beard. Somewhere in his late forties, early fifties. Wearing a sport coat, creased pants, shined shoes, you know?"

"Ever see this man before that time?"

Leon shook his head. "Nope."

"You sure?"

"Yep. I'd've remembered him."

"You've got a good memory for this," said the sheriff. "Any reason you'd remember this particular man so well?"

"I remember everybody. We always got the same customers. Regulars. That's the kind of place the Keelhaul is. Somebody new, you remember him." Leon shrugged. "So this well-dressed guy you'd expect to see in some fancy restaurant with a classy blonde, he's huddling with old Albie? You remember something like that. It didn't fit, you know what I mean?"

"Sure," said the sheriff. "What were they huddling about, do you know?"

He shook his head. "Couldn't tell you. I remember, though, they had a piece of paper on the table between them. Albie was poking at it, writing on it. I didn't get a look at it."

"Writing with a pen or a pencil?" said Calhoun.

Leon darted his eyes at Calhoun. "How would I know? I'm standing here, they're sitting over there, you know?"

"You catch the guy's name?" said Calhoun.

Leon shook his head.

"Did you hear anything they were saying?" said the sheriff.

Leon shook his head. "Joanie was waiting tables that night. Maybe she did." He looked at Calhoun. "Maybe she caught a name, saw if he was using a pen or pencil."

"Joanie," said the sheriff. "She coming in tonight?"

"She's only on Fridays and Saturdays."

"I'll need her full name, address, phone number."

"It's Joan McMurphy. You want to hang on, I'll get that information for you."

"In a minute," said the sheriff. "You said Albie comes in all the time. You expect him tonight?"

"What I said was," said Leon, "he used to come in all the time. I ain't seen him in a while." He paused. "Maybe not since that night, I'm not sure."

"That Saturday night. The sixth."

"Right," said Leon.

"The night you saw him huddling with the guy with the beard."

Leon frowned. "He might've come in the next night. It's been a while, though."

"Try to remember the last time you saw him," said the sheriff.

He shrugged. "I can't remember. A week? Not recently. Hey!" Leon yelled at the men at the other end of the bar. "When'd you see Albie last?"

The guys mumbled among themselves for a minute. Then one of them said, "It was like a week ago. I wanna say Sunday?"

One of the others nodded. "Yeah. I ain't seen him for at least a week. I remember that Sunday. Albie was here."

Leon looked at the sheriff and shrugged. "So Sunday."

"What can you tell me about Albie?" said the sheriff.

Leon shrugged. "Fisherman. Used to run blue-water charters. Stopped doing that, I don't know, six or eight years ago. Not sure why. Couldn't make a go of it, I guess. Plus, he's always complaining about his arthritis, bad knees. Let his boat get run-down, couldn't find anybody to work with him. Competitive business, sport fishing. Expensive. I suppose Albie just couldn't keep up. Nice guy, though. He's got a lot of stories, even if after a while you start hearing the same ones all over again."

"You said he lives on his boat?"

Leon nodded. "He talks about it all the time. Had a bad money situation few years ago. Lived with his mother down in Stroudwater. She was sick for quite a while. Big medical bills. When she finally died, Albie sold the house, used all the money to pay off her bills, managed to hang on to his boat. That's all he ended up with. That boat. That was his choice. Keep the boat, sell his mother's house. He says it was a no-brainer. Keeps her moored in the Fore River up near where the Stroudwater comes in. Takes her down to South Carolina for the winter. He'll probably be leaving pretty soon. Likes to wait for the end of hurricane season." Leon frowned. "What's its name? Can't think of the name of the damn boat." He waved at the men at the end of the bar. "Any o' you guys remember what old Albie calls his boat?"

One of the men said, "What is this, a quiz?"

Another guy raised his hand and said, "I know, I know."

"Jesus Christ," muttered Leon. "So what is it?"

"*Friendly Fire*," the guy said. "Painted across the transom. She's a dumpy old tub, white with black and red trim."

"*Friendly Fire*," said Calhoun. "Odd name for a boat."

"Well, sure," said Leon. "Albie's an odd guy. He was in Vietnam. Doesn't talk about it much, but you can tell it haunts him. I s'pose that's where he got the name for his boat."

One of the other guys said, "Nah, that ain't it. Albie told me he named her after his mother. I guess she was always giving him a hard time."

Calhoun turned to the sheriff. "I got an idea where she's moored. Maybe we ought to go talk to Albie."

"I guess we better." The sheriff looked at Leon. "So how will I know it's Albie when I see him?"

Leon gazed up at the ceiling for a minute. "Well, he's a small man. Not very tall, and kinda scrawny. Tough little bird, though. You wouldn't want to mess with him. Gray hair, what's left of it. Wears glasses. Tattoos all over his arms from his time in Vietnam. He's in his late fifties, I'd say. That help?"

"Sure. Thanks." The sheriff took out his wallet and laid a five-dollar bill on the bartop. "That cover it?" he said to Leon. "A Coke and a coffee?"

Leon pushed the bill back at him. "Drinks're on the house. On account of me being discourteous to you. Least I can do."

"Keep it," said the sheriff. "We can't take freebies. You know that."

Leon left the bill on the bar.

"Anything else you can tell us about Albie?" said the sheriff.

"Maybe if you told me why you're askin' about him . . ."

The sheriff just smiled.

"Well," said Leon, "there is one thing."

"What's that?"

"Albie's had a little money to throw around lately. Usually he's broke, just a couple of crumpled-up dollar bills from selling some lobsters or a bushel of littlenecks or a few bluefish, and I charge him whatever he's got, which means he ends up paying for his beer and gets a free bowl of soup and a dinner roll. Lately, though, he's ordering fried chicken, a pork chop, like that, pays with nice crisp tens and twenties. I asked him, I said, Albie, you must've had a rich uncle die or something, leave you some money. Albie, he just gives me this look, like, I've got a secret, man."

"When did this start?" said the sheriff. "Albie with the money?"

"Oh, just the last little while. Not long. Few weeks, maybe. I don't know exactly."

"Before that Saturday night we mentioned? The sixth?"

"Oh, yeah, week or two before that. I guess if Albie came into some money, he's probably found a classier joint than the Keelhaul to hang out in, which may be why I haven't seen him lately. Look. Lemme get that information about Joanie for you."

Leon disappeared through a doorway behind the bar. He was back a minute later holding an index card, which he handed to the sheriff. "Joanie's a good kid. Hope you don't hassle her too bad."

"I don't hassle people." The sheriff stuck the card in his shirt pocket. "Not me." He slid off his bar stool, reached his hand across the bar, and said, "Thanks, Leon."

Leon shook his hand. "No hard feelings, okay?"

The sheriff jerked his chin at Calhoun. "Talk to my deputy."

Leon held out his hand to Calhoun. "Sorry about being un-friendly."

Calhoun shook his hand. "Always be nice to your local sheriff."

They left the Keelhaul and climbed into the sheriff's Explorer. Ralph lifted his head from the backseat, saw who it was, and tucked his nose back under his little stubby tail.

"So you want to go talk with Albie?" said Calhoun.

"I sure do," said the sheriff. "What are we waiting for? You say you know where he's got his boat moored?"

Calhoun nodded. "I know the area. There's no marina or dock there. There's some boats anchored in the deep water out in the middle of the cove, and if we're gonna go knocking on Albie's door, ask him about his meeting with Mr. Vecchio, we need to get my boat."

They drove back to the shop and hitched Calhoun's boat up to his truck. The sheriff retrieved some foul-weather gear and a big flashlight from his truck while Ralph peed. Then they drove to the East End boat landing.

Calhoun asked Ralph whether he'd rather stay warm and dry in the truck. Ralph gave him his *Are you serious?* look and hopped into the boat.

They launched the boat and putted out of the harbor and followed the shoreline southerly. Aside from the city lights, blurry in the fog off to the west, it was a black night, and the freshening easterly breeze was heavy with moisture.

The sheriff braced himself in the front of the boat, and Calhoun stood in the stern running the motor. The city of Portland lay off to their starboard side, and off to port lay Cape Elizabeth. After a while they turned due west and went under the Veterans Memorial Bridge and then the Route 295 bridge where Long Creek came into the Fore River.

Calhoun cut back on the throttle. "It should be up here ahead of us," he said to the sheriff. "Get your flashlight out."

There were a few scattered boats moored in the river, ghostly through the fog in the beam of the sheriff's light. Calhoun wound among them while the sheriff shined his light on their transoms.

"Here we go," said the sheriff after a few minutes.

His light illuminated the words *Friendly Fire* on the transom of a sport-fishing boat with a tuna tower and folded-back outriggers and red-and-black trim.

Calhoun shifted into neutral. Over the quiet burbling of the motor, he heard the clank of rigging and the slosh of waves slapping against the side of Albie's boat and the wet swish of trucks passing over the bridge behind them. The sheriff scanned the area with his big flashlight. It showed four or five other boats moored in the area, none very close to Albie's, none showing lights.

"Shine on *Friendly Fire* again," said Calhoun.

The sheriff did.

"Hm," said Calhoun.

"Tell me what you're thinking," said the sheriff.

"Don't look like Albie's aboard," said Calhoun.

"She appears deserted, all right."

"That ain't what I meant," said Calhoun. "What I meant was, I don't see any dinghy or rubber boat tied up to her."

"So how could he get here," said the sheriff. "That what you mean?"

"Ayup. Doubt he swam. Must've locked her down and rowed himself ashore, left his dinghy there."

"Hey," the sheriff called. "Hey, Albie? You aboard?"

There was no rustle or bump of movement, no light flicking on, no response of any kind from inside the boat.

"Well," said the sheriff, "he's not there, and that's that. We can't go aboard if we're not invited. A boat's like a man's house. Damn sorry to've wasted your whole damn evening, Stoney, never mind half a tank of boat gas. I'll make it up to you."

"I can go aboard," said Calhoun.

"The hell you can. You're my deputy, and I'm telling you, we're not going aboard."

Calhoun took his badge out of his pocket and put it on the seat. "I quit, then. Now I ain't your deputy, and I can do whatever the hell I want to do, and I want to board this damn boat."

The sheriff turned and shined his light on Calhoun for a moment. Then he said, "Ah, the hell with it. Pick up the damn badge. Let's go see what's on Albie's boat."

Calhoun shoved the badge back into his pocket, then put the motor in gear and putted over alongside *Friendly Fire*. The sheriff grabbed on to the ladder. Calhoun turned off his motor.

"Tie us off," said Calhoun. "There's a line in the locker under the bow."

The sheriff found the line, hitched it around their bow cleat, and tied the other end to the ladder on Albie's boat. Then he climbed aboard.

Ralph roused himself from his spot on the bottom of the boat. He went to the bow, looked up at Albie's boat, and started making a little squeaky sound in his throat.

"What's with you?" said Calhoun.

Ralph turned around, came all the way to the back of the boat, and sat at Calhoun's feet. He continued whining.

Calhoun patted his head. "You can stay here. I ain't gonna make you climb that ladder. We'll be back." He stepped over Ralph, walked down the middle of the boat to the front, checked the sheriff's knots, then followed him up the ladder onto *Friendly Fire*.

Ralph sat in the back of Calhoun's boat, whining softly.

The sheriff was shining his light around the inside of Albie's boat. There were three or four mossy lobster pots piled in a corner, along with some loosely coiled line. Scraps of seaweed and dried bait and seagull splatters littered the floor. "Nobody home," said the sheriff. "Looks like he hasn't been aboard for a while."

Calhoun went over to the cabin, which was shut tight. He tried the handle, and it turned in his hand. "He forgot to lock up when he left," he said.

He pulled open the door that led below to the galley and the berths and the head—and the smell that came blasting out drove him three stumbling steps backward.

"Jesus," said the sheriff. "I hope that's not what I think it is."

"Afraid it is," said Calhoun. He pressed his jacket over his nose and mouth. "Dead human body," he mumbled. "You never forget that smell, even when you can't remember where you smelled it. You better shine your light in here."

CHAPTER FIFTEEN

He was slumped on the floor, half sitting, his back wedged into the forward corner where the two lower berths met. His chest and arms were naked and caked and crusty with dried black blood. His chin was slumped down on his chest. His wrists and ankles were bound with duct tape.

He was a small, sinewy man with thin gray hair. Both arms were plastered with tattoos.

"Looks like we found Albie," said Calhoun.

In the white glow of the sheriff's light, Albie's skin was purplish and bloated. It appeared to shimmer and twitch. It took Calhoun a minute to realize that bugs and maggots were crawling all over it. It was repellent, but he forced himself to look at it, to see that it had been a living human being, not some ugly decomposing thing. A man named Albie.

"Jesus," whispered the sheriff.

"I'd say he's been dead for some time," said Calhoun.

"All that blood." The sheriff grabbed Calhoun's arm. "We've got to call it in."

Calhoun turned to move out of the cabin. Then something caught his eye. He stopped. "Shine your light there," he told the sheriff. "On the shelf by that berth there."

The sheriff moved his light and stopped it on a book. It was one of those large-format paperbacks. The pages were curled from the dampness. On the cover was a black-and-white photograph of a submarine in the fog with some rocky coastline in the background. The title was *U-Boats on Casco Bay: German Submarine Warfare on the Maine Coast.* Under the title it said: "Now a PBS miniseries."

The author was Paul R. Vecchio.

"There's your connection," said Calhoun. "That's how Albie knew about Mr. Vecchio."

The sheriff nodded. "Read his book and gave him a call, maybe." He blew out a breath. "Come on, Stoney. We gotta get out of here before I puke."

"Suits me."

They backed away from the doorway. The sheriff shined his light around the inside of Albie's boat one more time, and then they climbed down the ladder onto Calhoun's boat.

Calhoun went back and sat on the stern seat. Ralph, who was lying on the floor, looked up at him. Calhoun scratched his muzzle. "Another damn dead body," he told him. "You smelled it, didn't you?"

The sheriff sat up front and took out his cell phone and made a call. Calhoun couldn't hear what he was saying.

After a minute, the sheriff folded his phone and jammed it back into his pants pocket. "They're on their way. We're supposed to wait here. Sorry, Stoney. This might take a while."

"Okay by me," said Calhoun. "I got no appointments. Wish we'd brought some coffee is all."

The fog had thickened into mist. Calhoun and the sheriff pulled on their rain jackets.

Pretty soon the mist turned into rain. They huddled in Calhoun's aluminum boat, tied up to *Friendly Fire*, the three of them, waiting for the troops to arrive. The sheriff sat up front with his back to Calhoun. They didn't talk. There wasn't much to say.

After a little while, Ralph crawled up on the seat beside Calhoun. He sat there for a minute, then twirled around a couple of times and flopped down with his chin resting on Calhoun's thigh.

It probably was no more than an hour, but it seemed longer, until the Coast Guard boat came burbling down the river with all of its lights blazing through the misty rain and its searchlight sweeping the river.

"You called the Coast Guard?" asked Calhoun.

"Ayup," said the sheriff. "Murder on a boat on the high seas, which includes the tidal part of rivers, is their jurisdiction. Those islands in the bay where you found Errol Watson, they're part of Portland. It was Gilsum who I talked to. He called the Coast Guard. There'll be local and state cops along with the feds. Talk about chaos."

Someone called over a bullhorn: "Sheriff Dickman? Are you there? Is that you?"

The sheriff squinted into the searchlight and raised his arm.

"Go aboard *Friendly Fire* and wait for us. Leave your deputy where he is."

The sheriff waved, then turned in his seat. "Okay by you, Stoney?"

"I don't care," said Calhoun. "Do your job. I'll wait for you."

The sheriff climbed the ladder onto Albie's boat. A minute later the Coast Guard boat slid alongside. Calhoun saw the sheriff reach over and give somebody a hand. The man was wearing a rain slicker with USCG printed on the back. Calhoun knew some Coast Guard people, but he didn't recognize this one. Then Lieutenant Gilsum boarded, and he and the Coast Guard guy shined their lights around Albie's boat and down the hatch into the cabin where the body was. They conferred with the sheriff for a while.

Then, while Calhoun sat there in the rain with Ralph shivering beside him, several other people climbed over the gunwales of the Coast Guard boat onto Albie's. Among them was Dr. Sam Surry, wearing an oversized yellow slicker with the hood covering her red hair. She was lugging her old black leather bag.

There ensued a confusion of lights and voices and winking camera flashes on *Friendly Fire*.

After a little while, the sheriff leaned over the side of Albie's boat and said, "Hey, Stoney."

"I'm right here," said Calhoun, "being obedient."

"You can go home. I got a ride."

Calhoun shrugged. "I ain't a suspect? They don't want to interrogate me?"

The sheriff laughed. "No. Not now, anyway. Go home, get dry, feed Ralph. I'll catch up with you tomorrow."

"Okay. I ain't going to argue with you."

The sheriff waved and ducked away from the side of the boat.

Calhoun walked up to the front of his boat, untied the line from the ladder, and cast off from *Friendly Fire.* Just as he turned to move back to the stern where he could start the motor, a soft voice above him said, "Hey, Stoney."

He looked up. Dr. Sam Surry was smiling down at him.

Calhoun grabbed ahold of Albie's ladder so the tide wouldn't drift him away and said, "Hi, Doc."

"So we meet again," she said.

"Yup. Another dead body."

"I'm looking forward to Friday."

Calhoun had to think for a minute. Right. Their half-day fishing trip. Four o'clock Friday afternoon. "Me, too," he said. "Let's hope to hell it ain't raining."

"I heard that fish bite better in the rain."

"That's a damn myth," said Calhoun. "Fish under the water don't know what it's doing in the air. Only good that rain does is keep the other fisherman away."

"Rain or whatever," she said, "it'll be fun, and I can't wait. Anyway, go get warm. See you then." She gave a quick wave and turned away.

Calhoun let go of Albie's boat, went to the stern seat, started up his motor, turned his boat around, and headed back through the rain to the East End boat landing.

By the time he got to the landing, backed down the trailer, hitched up his boat, and got the truck headed to his house in Dublin, he figured it was sometime after eleven. A long day, and neither he nor Ralph had had any supper.

Whenever he drove past a meadow or pasture or some other open area, the rain came sweeping across the road at an angle. At times it came so hard that it drummed on the truck's roof like hand-fuls of buckshot. The winding two-lane roads from Portland west to Dublin were slick and shiny in the headlights and littered with broken pine branches and windblown wet leaves.

It was a classic New England autumn nor'easter. Behind the storm would come a high-pressure front, with crisp, dry days and cold nights. Mud puddles would be frozen in the morning. Frost would coat the pumpkins in the fields and blacken the annual flower plants. The leaves would fall from the maples and poplars and oaks. The striped bass and bluefish would hasten their southward migra-tion, and so would the Canada geese and black ducks, and pretty soon it would be winter.

Ralph was curled up on the passenger seat. Calhoun reached over and stroked his back. His fur was wet. Calhoun turned up the truck's heater and switched on the fan.

By the time he turned off the road onto his driveway, he figured it was after midnight.

As he started down the long, sloping, unpaved driveway that ended at his house in the woods, he noticed fresh tire tracks in the muddy ruts. He stopped, pulled on the emergency brake, and got out, leaving the door hanging open. In the truck's headlights, he scootched down to look at the tracks. They'd been made by a small truck, not an automobile, which ruled out the Man in the Suit, who drove an Audi sedan. Dirty rainwater had begun to seep into the grooves the treads had cut in the mud, but the edges were still sharp. Calhoun figured they'd been made less than an hour earlier.

He stood up and scanned what he could see of his driveway in the headlights. There was just one set of tracks. Whoever had driven in had not driven back out.

He went back to the truck, where Ralph was now sitting up and looking around. "You better come with me," said Calhoun. "I'll want you to heel."

Ralph stood up on the seat, stretched and yawned, then slith-ered out.

Calhoun reached behind the seat and retrieved his Winchester

Model 94. He levered a cartridge into the chamber. Then he shut off the truck lights, turned off the ignition, pocketed the keys, and eased the door silently shut.

He stood still for several minutes, waiting for his eyes to adjust to the darkness. Without moon or stars, it was all shades of blackness, but gradually he was able to sense, if not actually see, how his driveway twisted down through the woods.

"Okay, let's go," he hissed at Ralph. "We got ourselves another damn visitor, and I just hope to hell he ain't dead. And for Christ sake, you better heel. I don't want something happening to you again."

Ralph plodded along a few feet behind Calhoun's left heel, and they moved down the driveway. Calhoun hugged the right side, outside the muddy ruts where the weeds were bent down and the footing wasn't too bad.

He knew they were approaching the opening in the woods where his house stood by the way the driveway began to flatten out, and a minute later he detected a new lighter shade of black that signified the opening in the woods that was his yard and parking area.

Then he saw something else, so quick and sudden that he wasn't sure he'd actually seen it. It was a momentary spark of orange light in the place where he usually parked his truck.

He whispered, "Whoa," to Ralph.

They both stood there. Calhoun looked hard at the place he'd seen the light. Then he saw it again, and this time the spark lingered a bit longer.

"Stay," he said to Ralph.

He didn't bother checking. He knew Ralph would stay right there, sitting on the ground, for five minutes or for an hour or for however long it was until Calhoun released him.

He had his finger on the trigger of the short-barreled deer rifle. He carried it in both hands, ready to fire from the hip if necessary.

He crept closer to where he'd seen the wink of orange light. Then he identified the gray outline of a pickup truck parked there. Another spark of orange. It was coming through the back window from inside the truck.

He was barely ten feet from the pickup when he stopped, let out a long breath, and smiled.

He went up to the driver's side and tapped the muzzle of the Winchester against the window.

A moment later the window unrolled and the business end of a handgun poked at his face.

"Don't shoot me, honey," he said.

"Jesus H. Christ, Stoney Calhoun," said Kate. She pulled her gun back. "You can't go sneaking up on a woman like that. Where's your truck? And why are you brandishing a deer rifle at me? Where have you been, anyway? I was worried half to death."

"All that's a long story," said Calhoun. "Anyhow, you ought not to go lurking around a man's house in the pitch dark after midnight, either."

"I wasn't lurking," she said. "I was waiting."

He found himself smiling in the darkness. "So what the hell are you doing in there. Lighting matches?"

She showed him the half-smoked cigarette she was holding.

"You don't smoke," he said.

"Shows what you know."

"Hell, I know you inside and out," he said. "Never saw you smoke. Never smelled smoke on you."

"Things change, Stoney," she said. "You gonna invite me in?"

"I don't know why you didn't just go in," he said. "You know it ain't locked. You know you don't need an invitation."

"I feel like I do," she said softly. "Since I . . ." She looked away.

"Come on," he said. "Ralph and I are cold, wet, and hungry. Let's go in." He turned back to where Ralph was still sitting. "Okay, bud. Come on. Let's get something to eat."

Ralph was sitting on the wet ground. His ears perked up at the word "eat."

Kate stubbed out her cigarette in her truck's ashtray, then pushed open the door and slid out. Ralph got up and trotted over to her. She leaned down to pat his head, then straightened up.

Calhoun noticed that she was wearing blue jeans and work boots and a hip-length rain jacket—not one of the dressy outfits

she used to wear when she came for sleepovers. He checked his reaction to that information and realized that he was not disappointed. He had assumed she'd never again come to his house at
night, and now she had, and that was plenty good enough for the
time being.

Calhoun held out his hand, and she took it, and they walked
hand in hand through the mud, up the steps, and into the house.

Kate went straight to the cabinet over the refrigerator where she
kept her bottle of bourbon. She poured an inch into a glass and sat at
the kitchen table. She shook a cigarette out of a pack and lit it.
"What can I use for an ashtray?" she said to Calhoun.

He half filled a coffee mug with water and put it at her elbow.
"What's with the smoking?" he said.

"You don't approve?"

"Well, first off, it's none of my business what you do, and second, that smoke smells so damn good that I'm thinking maybe I
used to smoke myself."

"Maybe you did," she said. "Before lightning zapped you.
That's a pretty extreme method of smoking cessation, but it appears
to have worked."

"What's your story? How come you took up smoking?" He
wasn't that interested in Kate's smoking, but he figured it was connected to her frame of mind and why she'd come to his house, and
that interested him very much.

She took a long drag on her cigarette and blew a plume of
smoke up at the ceiling, where it swirled around in the light. Then
she took a sip of bourbon. "I quit nine years ago," she said. "Right
after Walter got his diagnosis. Him with that disease, it seemed
fairly stupid for me to do something so unhealthy. So it's not that I
just took it up. I returned to it. I guess it's my way of saying, ah, the
hell with everything."

Calhoun was at the counter putting Ralph's supper together. He
said, "I'm sorry you're feeling that way. You want to talk about it?
That why you came here tonight?"

Kate shrugged. "I don't know why I came here. I just needed to
go someplace, and this was the only place I could think of."

He put Ralph's dish on the floor. Ralph was sitting there. "Okay," said Calhoun.

Ralph stood up and began inhaling his supper.

Calhoun went to the refrigerator and found some sliced ham and Swiss cheese and a loaf of bread and a jar of mustard. He put them on the table. "You want a sandwich?" he said to Kate.

She shook her head.

He sat down, made himself a sandwich, took a bite. "Haven't eaten since lunch," he said.

"Walter thinks we should get divorced," said Kate.

Calhoun looked at her. He didn't say anything.

She dropped her cigarette butt into the mug of water. "He says if we stay married, pretty soon we'll go bankrupt, on account of his health expenses. He says if he's single, there are ways that he can manage it. Don't ask me to explain, because I don't understand. He's been talking to an accountant."

Calhoun took another bite of his sandwich.

"I told him no," said Kate.

He nodded. "I understand."

"I doubt it," she said.

He shrugged. "You're probably right. I ain't you. How could I understand?"

"I think he's just trying to set me free, giving me permission to be happy."

"You think he's lying about the accountant?"

"I don't know," said Kate. She took another sip of bourbon. "I just can't sort it out. If it wasn't for you . . ."

"What would you do if it wasn't for me?"

"Well, I don't know. The point is, there is you, and I can't imagine there not being you. But, see, when I saw the way that damned redheaded woman was looking at you, and then you tell me you're going to take her fishing . . ."

"Dr. Surry," said Calhoun. "She's a client."

Kate grinned. "Of course she is."

"You jealous or something?"

"It's way more complicated than that, Stoney."

"Because if you are, you don't need to be."

"She's quite attractive. And sexy and smart and—"

"It's you I love," said Calhoun.

She looked at him over the rim of her bourbon glass. Then she blinked, took a sip, and put down the glass. "I know," she said. "Doesn't change how I felt when I saw how she obviously has this gigantic crush on you. I came here because I wanted to sleep with you tonight."

"What would that prove?" said Calhoun.

"You turning me down?"

"It was just a question."

Kate turned her head away. She was fumbling for another cigarette. When she got it lit, she looked at him. Her eyes were wet. "What'm I gonna do, Stoney?"

"I'm the last person you should consult on that question."

"No," she said. "You're the first person. The way I look at it, we're in this together. This is about us, not just me."

"Well," he said, "I can tell you this. I'm not enjoying the idea of us never being together. I don't like it when we try to be all businesslike and polite with each other. But I got plenty of patience. I can wait for you to figure out whatever it is you got to figure out and do what you've got to do."

"I'm asking you to help me figure it out," she said.

"What's best and what I want might not be the same thing."

She nodded quickly. "Hell, I know that. So tell me. What do you want?"

"That's easy," he said. "I want you here with me all the time. I want to sleep with you and wake up with you. I want to take showers with you and eat breakfast with you and go fishing and snowshoeing and skinny-dipping with you." He waved his hand in the air. "You know all that already."

She smiled. "It's clarifying to hear you say it."

Ralph had finished his supper and was standing at the door. Calhoun got up from the table and let him out. When he turned back to the table, Kate had stood up.

"I think I better go now," she said.

"Go where?"

"Home."

"Honey," he said, "it's way past midnight, and it's a miserable night out there. Stay here."

She shook her head. "I don't think I'm ready to . . ."

"I understand," he said. "I'll sleep on the couch. You take the bed with Ralph."

She looked sideways at him. "Can we do that?"

"I can," he said.

When Calhoun's eyes popped open, his bare feet were hanging over the armrest of his sofa and the blanket had slipped off his shoulders. He was cold all over, and one of his arms had gone tingly.

The darkness inside his house was absolute. He figured he hadn't been sleeping for more than an hour.

He tugged at the blanket, rolled onto his side, squirmed, adjusted his pillow, trying to get comfortable.

Then he remembered Kate. Smoking cigarettes, drinking bourbon. For what? Courage?

Okay, she'd said finally. *You're probably right. I'll sleep here. Just because it's late and the driving is bad.*

She gave him a quick hug—no kiss—and slipped into his bedroom. Ralph followed her, and then she shut the door.

Now he was on the sofa and she was sleeping in his bed. He thought about going in there, sliding under the covers beside her, snuggling up against her. He thought about how she'd groan and press herself against him, half asleep, reacting without thinking. He thought about burying his nose in her hair, tasting her skin, running his fingertips along the insides of her legs. He thought about kissing her neck and how she'd murmur, "Oh," in the back of her throat, and how she'd tangle her fingers in his hair and arch her back to meet him . . .

He wouldn't do it, of course. But he liked thinking about it.

He recalled that he never had gotten around to telling her that he'd been out with the sheriff tracking down another dead body.

He still wasn't clear on why she'd come to his house.

The next time he woke up, orange sunshine was angling in through the windows. He was lying on his side with his knees bent up so he'd fit between the arms of the sofa, and Ralph was curled in the nest against the back of his legs.

He sat up and yawned. Ralph lifted his head, looked around, stretched, and slithered off the sofa.

Calhoun pulled on his pants and went to the kitchen. He poured a mugful of coffee and took it out to the deck. Ralph followed along and then went padding down the steps.

When Calhoun looked over the railing, he saw that Kate's truck was gone. In its place sat his own truck with his boat trailered behind it.

He imagined her slipping out of the house in the dark, driving up the driveway in her truck, finding Calhoun's truck blocking the way, backing all the way down to the parking area, climbing the steps into the house, fishing in his pants pocket for his keys, walking out to the end of the driveway to his truck, driving it in, backing it around so the trailered boat would be where it belonged, returning his keys, and then getting into her own truck and leaving.

Calhoun figured she had to have been pretty eager to get away from him to go to all that trouble. Otherwise she would've just waited for him to wake up and help.

He sat at the table and sipped his coffee until Ralph came back.

When they went inside for breakfast, Calhoun saw Kate's note on the kitchen table. It said: *I had to leave. I'm sorry. I'll take care of the shop today. Don't come in. You need a break. You got Thursday, okay? I'll take Friday. xxoo K.*

Not I love you. Just a couple of X's and O's. Didn't even sign her name. Just K.

Still, there were those X's and O's.

He figured she didn't want him to go to the shop because she didn't want to run into him.

He didn't know how to feel. He was happy Kate had come to his house. Disappointed that they hadn't slept in the same bed. Confused that she'd left early without saying good-bye. Just that note.

Don't come in. You need a break. Meaning, Stay out of my sight. Meaning, It makes me feel uncomfortable to be around you.

He'd do it her way, of course. It was the only way he knew how to handle things with Kate.

He supposed it would work itself out one way or the other. She knew how he felt. Now all she had to do was figure out how she felt. That was progress.

He was splitting firewood out back when he heard Sheriff Dickman's Explorer come bouncing down the driveway and skid to a muddy stop in front of the house. He glanced at the sun and figured it was close to eleven o'clock.

By the time he climbed the steps onto the deck, the sheriff was sitting there having a conversation with Ralph.

He went inside, poured two mugfuls of coffee, took them out, and sat down. "What do you know about women, anyway?" he said.

"Me?" The sheriff smiled. "Less and less with every passing day."

Calhoun nodded. "I guess that answers my question."

The sheriff took a sip of coffee, then breathed out a sigh. "You get some sleep, Stoney?"

"A little."

"Not me," said the sheriff. "I been up all night with Albert Wolinski, which is our dead body's actual name. Albie. I want you to know everything I know, because as far as I'm concerned, you and I are in this together."

"I ain't sure about that," said Calhoun, "but go ahead."

"That Dr. Surry's pretty sharp," said the sheriff. "She's got some

balls, so to speak, too. The only woman in the bunch, and she's boss-
ing Gilsum and the Coast Guard guys around, and they're all going,
'Yes, ma'am,' and, 'No, ma'am.' So anyway, she observed that poor
old Albie died from having his throat cut, which, of course, didn't
take any advanced degree in detecting to figure out, but which ac-
counted for a good portion of that blood all over the front of him.
There was a fillet knife lying there, which might be the murder
weapon. We are not optimistic that there are any fingerprints on it,
but Gilsum sent it up to the lab in Augusta."

"Wait a minute," said Calhoun. "Did you say good portion? You
saying that some of the blood we saw was not from his throat?
Don't tell me . . ."

The sheriff was shaking his head. "His penis was intact. But
there were about a dozen puncture wounds on his chest and belly."

"Puncture wounds," said Calhoun.

"Dr. Surry thought the shape of the punctures matched the tip
of the fillet knife. She hypothesizes that they were inflicted slowly.
They went quite deep, some of them. Imagine it, Stoney. Pricking
the man's skin with the tip of that knife, slowly pushing it in. Very
painful. She thinks they were intended to torture the man."

"If he was tortured . . ."

The sheriff nodded. "You torture somebody to get information
out of him."

"And after you get it, you cut his throat."

"You might also cut his throat," said the sheriff, "when you figure out he doesn't know anything."

"Or when you realize he's so damned tough he'll never tell you,"
said Calhoun.

The sheriff nodded.

"Why torture Albert Wolinski?"

"You think he knows something you want to know," said the
sheriff.

"Was Errol Watson tortured?"

The sheriff frowned for a moment, then shook his head. "No.
There was nothing about torture in the ME's report."

"But they tortured Albie."

"Yep."

"What kind of information could he have had that would be worth torturing him for?"

"That's a good question," said the sheriff. "Point is, somebody tortured and murdered this Albert Wolinski, for whatever reason, sometime after he met with your friend Paul Vecchio, who himself got murdered right here on your deck shortly after—"

"After he found the body of Errol Watson out on Quarantine Island," said Calhoun.

"Right."

"Throat cut," said Calhoun. "Wrists and ankles bound with duct tape."

The sheriff nodded. "Yup. Like Errol Watson. So maybe the lab in Augusta can see if the duct tape matches, and maybe they can compare the knife wounds." He sipped his coffee and gazed out at some crows that were cawing in the top of a big oak tree. "Here's something to think about, Stoney. Albie Wolinski met with Paul Vecchio at the Keelhaul Cafe a week ago Saturday night. The following Tuesday is when you took Vecchio fishing. Two days later, Thursday, you found his body here on your deck. Okay so far?"

Calhoun nodded. "Okay."

"Last night," said the sheriff, "Dr. Surry estimated that Albie had been dead a week, give or take twenty-four hours on either side. Last night being Tuesday. You see what I'm getting at?"

"Old Albie got tortured and killed after he met with Paul Vecchio and before Vecchio himself got killed," said Calhoun.

The sheriff nodded.

"Wait a minute," said Calhoun. "You think Vecchio killed Albie?"

"The timing is right, is all I'm thinking. They had their meeting, it wasn't satisfactory, so Vecchio went to Albie's boat, and—"

"Then who killed Vecchio?"

The sheriff spread his hands. "I don't know."

"What about Errol Watson?"

"I don't know that, either. Vecchio could've done him and Albie. I guess Franklin Dunbar could've done 'em all, though I haven't come up with a scenario to account for it."

"That's what Gilsum thinks, right?" said Calhoun.

The sheriff nodded. He took a sip of coffee, then pushed himself to his feet, went to the railing, and leaned on it with his elbows. He gazed down the hill to where Bitch Creek gurgled around the old bridge abutments.

Calhoun went over and leaned on the railing beside him. It was a cloudless morning. The air felt sharp and brittle when he breathed it into his lungs. For the first time in almost a year, he smelled autumn in the air.

"That was our line storm last night," said the sheriff after a minute.

"Ayuh," said Calhoun quietly. "Yesterday was summer. Today it's fall."

They sipped their coffee and looked off to the distance. "Kate took up cigarette smoking," said Calhoun. "What do you think of that?"

"I think Kate's a woman who really ought to have some kind of vice."

Calhoun smiled. "She is kind of perfect, now that you mention it."

"I still miss it."

"Huh?"

"Smoking," said the sheriff. "Cigarettes."

A few minutes later, the sheriff said, "Where I've been this morning is tracking down that waitress."

"Joanie," said Calhoun.

"Joanie McMurphy. She was still in her bathrobe when I got there. I asked her about Albie Wolinski and Paul Vecchio that night."

Calhoun nodded. "You're like a terrier, you know that?"

The sheriff shrugged. "Got to follow up. You never know. So anyway, about all she could tell me that we didn't already know was that Albie was drawing on a piece of paper with a pencil, and it seemed like he was using the drawing to try to illustrate something for Vecchio."

"She didn't overhear what they were talking about?"

The sheriff shook his head. "You still have that piece of paper you got out of Vecchio's gear bag?"

"The one that led us to the Keelhaul and Albie, you mean?"

"That's the one," said the sheriff.

"You think that's the paper Albie was writing on?"

"One side was in pencil, right?"

Calhoun nodded. "I think it's still in the shirt I was wearing yesterday."

"Let's take another look at it," said the sheriff.

CHAPTER SIXTEEN

Calhoun found the scrap of notepaper in the pocket of his shirt, which he'd tossed on the floor behind the sofa when he went to sleep. Normally he hung his shirt in the bedroom closet, but Kate had gone in there and closed the door on him.

He went back onto the deck, hitched a chair over beside the sheriff, sat down, and unfolded the sheet of paper to the side that read *Keelhaul Albie 9/6 9:00*.

The sheriff glanced at it, then turned it over so that they were looking at the side with the inverted *U* and the random shapes with *X*'s through some of them. Except the way the sheriff had it turned, the *U* was now on the bottom, not the top. This way it looked like an open bowl, not an upside-down one.

It still didn't look like anything more than what a monkey with a pencil might draw.

"This," said the sheriff, tapping the meaningless scrawls and scribbles on the piece of notepaper, "is what Albie Wolinski was drawing for Paul Vecchio that night at the Keelhaul. It's more or less what Joanie McMurphy described to me. The way I see it, Vecchio went there with his directions written down on one side of this piece of paper. Albie was who he was meeting, the Keelhaul Cafe was the place, and there was the date and the time. When he got there, for whatever reason, Albie wanted to draw something for him. So Vecchio took out the scrap of paper he'd written his directions on, and

Albie used the other side to sketch on. This here"—the sheriff jabbed at the paper with his forefinger—"is what he sketched."

Calhoun was looking at the paper from beside the sheriff's elbow. He reached over and pulled it in front of him. "Look at it this way," he said, and he rotated the paper ninety degrees so that the U became a C. "That look familiar?"

The sheriff frowned at the paper, then shrugged. "Sorry, Stoney. Maybe you're better at spatial relations than me. You see something I don't see?"

"It's Casco Bay," said Calhoun.

The sheriff bent closer to the paper. Then he turned his head and looked at Calhoun. "You're absolutely right. I'll be damned. It's crude, it's not drawn to scale, and most of the details are missing. But it's exactly how somebody would sketch the bay." He traced the outline of the C with his forefinger. "This is the coastline. Falmouth here, here's Portland, and Cape Elizabeth here. And these"—he put his finger on one of the shapeless drawings, then on the next one— "they're some of the islands. Right? You know the bay better than I do. That the way you see it?"

Calhoun nodded. "This here's Mackworth." He moved his finger across Albie Wolinski's pencil-sketched map of the bay. "Great Diamond. Long. Great Chebeague, right? Here's Hope, and Cliff, and Jewell, and—"

"I'll be damned," said the sheriff. "That has to be Quarantine. It's got a big fat X through it."

"You thinking what I'm thinking?" said Calhoun.

The sheriff nodded slowly. "Albie drew an X through Quarantine Island for Paul Vecchio. X marks the spot. To show him where Errol Watson's body was. See, Albie had Vecchio's book, knew he was a writer, knew he lived in Sheepscot and was interested in stories about Maine. Old Albie figured Vecchio would pay him money for a juicy story. Got ahold of him, arranged to meet him at the Keelhaul. Remember how Leon said Albie suddenly seemed to have some money to spend? So he drew this map for Vecchio with these X's on it. Then Vecchio hired you to go fishing, but really what he wanted was a boat ride so he could poke around on Quarantine and see if Albie was telling the truth. He maneuvered things out there, saying he had to take a leak, stretch his legs, to get you to drop him off on the island without telling you he was looking for a man's incinerated body."

"Vecchio already knew what happened to Watson," said Calhoun, "because Albie told him. I took him there so he could confirm it."

"And," said the sheriff, "it got him killed."

"So look," said Calhoun, moving his finger over the pencil-drawn map. "There are these three other islands with X's drawn through them. You suppose . . . ?"

The sheriff straightened up, leaned back from the table, and turned to Calhoun. "You think you can follow this map, Stoney?"

Calhoun nodded. "Might be a little trial and error. There's a helluva lot of little islands in the bay. But, sure. I can find these with X's on 'em, if that's what you mean."

The sheriff puffed out his cheeks and blew out a long breath, then pushed his chair back and stood up. "Let's go take a look. You mind if we take your boat?"

As Calhoun expected, last night's storm had dragged a high-pressure system in behind it. Now, as they skimmed across Casco Bay, the sky was high and blue and utterly cloudless, the sun shone so bright you had to squint, and a sharp breeze kicked up whitecaps all across the bay and blew salt spray on their faces.

The first island on Albie's map was little more than half an acre of jumbled boulders with some scrubby brush and a few wind-bent oak trees poking up in the middle. Calhoun guessed that if the weather gods ever conspired to blow a hurricane-sized easterly wind at the bay during a full-moon high tide, the little island would end up entirely underwater.

He had to circle it twice before he spotted a patch of sand among the boulders where he could land his boat without scraping the hull. The sheriff got out and wedged the anchor between some rocks. Ralph hopped out after him and went exploring.

Calhoun followed. "If there's a body here," he said, "Ralph'll find it."

A minute later Ralph started barking.

They found him sitting on the ground with his ears laid back, whining deep in his throat and staring at the blackened body, which was propped up in a sitting position with its back against a boulder facing east. It was charred and crusty. Its face was burned off. Its ears and nose and fingers were nubs. Just like Errol Watson.

"Oh, boy," said the sheriff. He shook his head, then muttered, "Oh, boy," again. He blew out a long breath. "Well, I gotta call it in." He fished his cell phone from his pocket. "Does this island have a name, do you know?"

Calhoun shook his head. "I suppose it does, but I don't know it." He pointed. "We're due east of Bangs, there, maybe half a mile." He pointed again. "Over there's Bailey and Orr's."

The sheriff nodded. "Good enough."

As Calhoun watched, the sheriff wandered away and selected a boulder on the rim of the little island to sit on. He poked at his phone, then put it to his ear, all the while keeping his back to the dead body and gazing out toward the western horizon. Calhoun heard the murmur of the sheriff's voice, though from where he was waiting, he couldn't hear what he was saying.

After a few minutes, the sheriff stood up, shoved the phone back into his pants pocket, and came back to where Calhoun and Ralph were waiting. "You still with me, Stoney?"

Calhoun nodded. "I'm your deputy, remember? Whatever you say."

"We got two more islands with X's on them. I hope you can locate them."

"We'll find 'em," said Calhoun.

There was a burned-beyond-recognition body on each of the other two islands from Albie Wolinski's map. Both bodies had been propped up against a boulder facing east. Both had only nubs for fingers and ears. Calhoun was pretty sure their penises had been jammed into their mouths, but they didn't check to verify it.

Counting Errol Watson, that made four burned bodies, one on each of the four little Casco Bay islands that Albie Wolinski had marked with an X.

The sheriff talked for a long time on his cell phone after they found the last body. When he came back to where Calhoun and Ralph were waiting, he said, "This is going to be a long day, Stoney. You okay with that?"

Calhoun shrugged. "Kate gave me the day off."

"I told Gilsum we'd wait for him where our first body is. He'll bring a veritable posse, no doubt, and a fleet of boats. We'll need to show them where the other two bodies are."

"Whatever you want."

A little over an hour later, a flotilla of assorted motorboats materialized from behind one of the big islands and headed for them. There were seven of them altogether, and each of them managed to find a patch of beach to nose onto. Then the little island was swarming with people.

One of them was Dr. Sam Surry, wearing sneakers and khaki pants and a pale blue windbreaker. Her red hair was in a ponytail that stuck out the back of her Red Sox cap. She was lugging her old black medical bag. When she hopped off the boat, she stopped and looked around, then went straight to the rock where Calhoun and Ralph were waiting. She squatted down, rubbed Ralph's back, and looked up at Calhoun. "We've really got to stop meeting like this," she said.

Calhoun shrugged. "Better than not meeting at all."

She smiled. "I'll never be able to look at Casco Bay the same way again."

"That mean you don't want to go fishing Friday?"

"Hell, no. I'm looking forward to it. Let's just not stop off at any islands, okay?" She gave him a quick wave. "Gotta get to work." She headed over to where the others had gathered by the body.

After a while, the sheriff came over and asked Calhoun to lead the way to the second body, so he and Ralph piled into their boat, and all but two of the other boats followed along. Calhoun showed them where to land, and then he and Ralph got out and led them to where the body was propped against the boulder, facing east.

After much discussion, the various official people figured out who was going to stay there and who was going to move to the third island. Then Calhoun led two of the boats to where the last burned-up body was waiting.

Calhoun and Ralph sat there in his boat at the third island waiting for further instructions. After a while, he figured out they'd forgotten all about him. He'd done his job. They didn't need him anymore.

The sheriff and Dr. Surry had stayed back at the first island. Calhoun assumed that they'd have to check out the other two bodies before they were done.

This was going to take a while. Calhoun wasn't much good at waiting around for other people.

He remembered his cell phone. Once in a while he was glad he had it. He took it out of his pants pocket, pressed the button on the side, said, "Dickman," and held it to his one good ear.

He heard it ring. Then the sheriff's voice said, "Stoney? That you?"

"Yes, sir."

"What's up? We're kinda busy here."

"You gonna need me for anything else?"

The sheriff hesitated. "Well, actually," he said, "I guess not."

"I'll hang around if you want, but . . ."

"Nope. No reason to do that, Stoney. We got plenty of boats and more damn expertise than we can use out here. You and Ralph go on home. You did great work today, both of you. I'll catch up with you later."

"I'm pretty interested in this whole thing, you know."

"Of course you are," said the sheriff. "I'll keep you informed, I promise. Soon as I know something, you'll know it. Go home, Deputy. That's an order."

"Aye, aye, sir." Calhoun tapped Ralph on the forehead. "Okay, bud. Let's get the hell out of here."

By the time they got back to the landing and hitched up the boat, Calhoun figured it was almost two in the afternoon. He thought about stopping in at the shop, saying hello to Kate, seeing how she was doing. She had a lot on her mind. The note she'd left hinted pretty strongly that she didn't want to see him, though. So he drove straight home to Dublin.

He spent the rest of the afternoon splitting firewood and stacking it in the shed beside the house. It was good, hard, rhythmic work. He liked the way splitting a hunk of straight-grained seasoned oak required finesse and precision, and he took pride in dropping his maul in the right place and seeing two equal halves go flying off the chopping block. Wood-splitting demanded a kind of concentration that allowed one level of his mind to wander wherever it wanted, and as he watched the piles of woodstove-sized hunks of split wood grow, he allowed that semiconscious level to ponder three more burned bodies facing east from little uninhabited Casco Bay islands.

Albie Wolinski had drawn his crude map to show Paul Vecchio where the bodies were, which meant, of course, that Albie already knew their location.

Maybe it was Albie who took those four men out there, cut their throats, lopped off their penises, shoved them into their mouths, and set them afire.

That left the question of who killed Albie.

Maybe it was Paul Vecchio.

That left the question of who killed him.

Calhoun figured that some one person was doing all the killing. First the four men on the Casco Bay islands. Then Albie. Then Vecchio.

Unless it was Franklin Dunbar, which he doubted, the who and why of it was eluding him.

He didn't quit splitting wood until darkness began spilling out of the woods. Then he hung his maul on its pegs, whistled up Ralph, who'd spent the afternoon nosing around the yard, and went inside. He had a long shower, savoring the way the hot water needled into his achy shoulders, and he lingered there for a long time, thoughts of dead men mingling strangely with thoughts of Kate.

He hoped she was doing all right.

The next morning, Thursday, Calhoun and Ralph got to the shop around nine thirty. Calhoun unhitched his boat and left it in the corner of the lot, where it would be ready for his trip with Sam Surry the next day. Then they went inside. Ralph went over to his corner, turned around three times, lay down on Calhoun's old sweatshirt, tucked his nose under his tail, and went to sleep. Calhoun flipped the sign that hung in the window to OPEN, loaded up the coffee urn, and checked the phone for messages.

There were none.

Nor was there any kind of note from Kate with a report from the previous day, or a request or an instruction, or just saying hi with a happy face and a few X's and O's.

He looked over the receipts from the previous day, when Kate had been there. She'd sold four half-price shirts, a couple of Nick Lyons paperback books, and a Mel Krieger fly-casting video. She'd shipped a customer's broken Loomis eight-weight back to the company for replacement, and she'd taken one phone order from a lucky customer who had a Belize flats-fishing trip lined up for next April—four dozen bonefish flies, two dozen tarpon flies, and two dozen crab flies for permit.

That was it. Another losing end-of-the-season day at the fly shop.

He went to the office in back, turned on the shop computer, and checked their Web site for messages and orders. There were none of either.

He poured himself a mug of coffee, turned on the radio and tuned it to the classical music station, brought over the cordless phone, and sat at the fly-tying bench. He rummaged through the cabinets and drawers and lined up the materials for the fussy crab flies: tan 3/0 thread, size 1/0 stainless-steel hooks, coastal deerhair, hackle feathers,

Krystalflash, rubberlegs, lead dumbbell eyes. Production tying—producing a large number of identical flies—required the same kind of attention as splitting firewood. One part of your mind focused on the task at hand and another registered the music from the radio, leaving a less conscious part to roam wherever it wanted to.

Calhoun thought about burned bodies on uninhabited islands. He thought about a dead fisherman and a dead college professor.

He reached no conclusions.

His work was interrupted once by two guys looking for guidance to a place where they might find some blitzing stripers. In the afternoon, a few customers wandered in, checked out the merchandise, watched Calhoun tie flies, and wandered out. The phone rang three or four times. One was the Sage regional sales rep, and the others were customers placing orders.

None was Kate or the sheriff.

By four o'clock, Calhoun had tied two dozen identical crab flies and a variety of Gotchas and Crazy Charlies for bonefish. They were all lined up on the bench with their head cement drying. He liked to see them there and to remember that he had created them. He thought they were beautiful. They were symmetrical and durable, and he was proud of them. The crab flies really looked like little crabs. The bonefish flies suggested, rather than imitated, shrimp.

He'd done a good day's work.

He got up, stretched, stowed his fly-tying materials, dumped out the coffee urn and cleaned it, turned off the computer, flipped the sign to the CLOSED side, snapped his fingers at Ralph, and went out.

Ralph trotted around the corner of the building where, Calhoun knew, there were some excellent bushes to lift your leg against.

Calhoun went over to where he'd parked his trailered boat. He smelled more rain in the air, so he decided to pull the canvas cover over the boat. He wanted it to be dry and clean for his trip the next day with Dr. Sam Surry.

He was stretching the canvas over the bow and working at one of the snaps when he sensed, rather than heard, movement behind him. It might have been the bottom of a sneaker twisting on the dirt, it might have been a tiny intake of a breath, it might have been nothing more than the displacement of air when a body moves through it.

It was no conscious, considered thought. It was a quick reaction, something learned long ago and buried deep in the inaccessible recesses of Stoney Calhoun's subconscious memory that made him duck, pivot, and attack.

His left elbow smashed into ribs at the same time as his hip turned and his right hand locked onto a bony wrist. He gave it a twist and flipped his attacker onto his back.

He landed with an empty thud. His breath exploded from his lungs, and then he groaned.

Calhoun instantly dropped a knee on the man's stomach. He raised his fist, ready to smash it into his throat. The impulse to do it was powerful. He visualized the blow he would strike. He knew how it would feel against his knuckles, the soft crunching collapse of arteries and nerves, larynx and pharynx, muscle and bone. It would crush all the tissue connecting head to body, as quick and neat and certain as dropping a splitting maul on a chunk of straight-grained oak. It would be instantly lethal, and Stoney Calhoun realized in that moment between raising his fist and bringing it smashing down that he had done it before and had lost no sleep over it, and that he was fully prepared to do it again right now.

But something held his fist there where it was poised to strike. He still had a hard grip on the man's wrist. Now he saw that the hand at the end of the wrist was gripping a tire iron.

Instead of destroying the man's throat, Calhoun twisted his wrist.

The man muttered, "Ow. Jesus," and let go of the tire iron.

Then Calhoun looked at his face.

It was a boy, not a man. A tall, heavy-boned, sinewy boy, but still a boy. Benjie Dunbar, last seen a few evenings earlier shooting a basketball in his driveway in Biddeford, son of Franklin, the number-one suspect in the murder of Errol Watson, who'd served time for molesting Bonnie, his sister.

Calhoun had come within a whisker of killing him.

Ralph came trotting over. He stood beside Calhoun, rumbling a growl deep in his chest, his lips curling back from his teeth, his ears laid against the side of his head, glaring at Benjie Dunbar.

Calhoun touched Ralph's forehead and said, "It's okay, bud. You sit."

Ralph sat.

Calhoun stood up and held his hand down to Benjie who slapped it away with the back of his own hand, then pushed himself to his feet. He held his right wrist against his belly with his left hand. "If you broke my wrist . . ."

"It ain't broke," said Calhoun. "I could've, but I didn't. Wouldn't want to wreck your basketball career."

"I suppose you could've broken my ribs but decided not to do that, either."

"That's about right," said Calhoun. "And I suppose you were aiming to crack my head open with that damn tire iron."

Benjie was glaring at Calhoun out of eyes that wanted to burn holes in him. "That's right. I wanted to kill you."

Calhoun nodded. "You want a Coke?"

Benjie looked at him for a minute, then shrugged. "I wouldn't mind."

Calhoun turned and went back to the shop. He unlocked it, fetched two cans of Coke from the refrigerator in back, and took them outside.

Benjie was sitting on the steps rubbing his wrist. Ralph stood in front of him. His ears were still laid back, but he'd stopped growling.

Calhoun sat beside Benjie and handed him a Coke. "Go lie down," he said to Ralph. "Everything's under control."

Ralph gazed at Calhoun for a minute, then kind of shrugged. He climbed onto the porch and lay down.

Benjie popped the tab on the can and took a swig of Coke. He turned to Calhoun. "How'd you do that?"

"Do what?"

"You know. What you did to me. I thought you were gonna kill me."

"You'd've deserved it," said Calhoun. "Ain't that what you wanted to do to me?"

Benjie nodded. "Maybe I did. I don't know. I've been crazy lately. My life is like . . ." He took another sip, then shook his head. "Everybody thinks my dad murdered that guy."

"Everybody? How about you?"

"I don't know. No. He couldn't. You don't know him. But even my mother . . ."

"So why're you coming at me with a tire iron? You could've got seriously hurt."

Benjie shrugged. "It's your fault. You and the sheriff. Coming to our house like that, in the middle of dinner, and then the other cops coming and taking my dad away, questioning him all day, questioning me and my mom, too. Things were bad enough, my sister all messed up, my parents not talking to each other, people looking funny at me, as if your sister getting raped is something you're supposed to be ashamed of. Now everybody thinks my dad murdered somebody. I blame you for that."

"I don't think your father killed anybody," said Calhoun.

"No?" Benjie was clenching and unclenching his fists. "Then why the hell did you come to our house like that?"

"Look," said Calhoun, "the truth is, I don't give a shit who killed Errol Watson. He got what he had coming."

"I thought you were investigating the murder?"

Calhoun shrugged. "Other people have been killed. I care about them. But not Watson. I got no interest in solving that one."

"Wait," said Benjie. "You can't do that. You can't crap out now. Don't you get it? If you don't find the guy who really did it, my dad'll go to prison."

"It doesn't work that way," said Calhoun. "He won't go to prison unless he did it."

Benjie blew out a quick, ironic breath. "What planet are you from, man? Innocent people go to prison all the time. That cop Gilsum there, he's got it all figured out. My dad had to hire a lawyer, and he's saying he might have to sell our boat so he can pay him, and now my mom is talking about how hard it's going to be to pay for my college, and—"

"Cut it out." Calhoun put his hand on Benjie's arm. "You're getting way ahead of yourself. A lot of things are happening. Every-thing's going to be okay."

"What things?"

"I can't tell you. Trust me."

Benjie laughed quickly. "Why should I trust you?"

"Because I could've killed you," Calhoun said. "I had every right to. I would've been defending myself. It would've been easy. I almost did it."

"So what?"

"So I didn't. So you're alive because I decided to let you continue to live. You owe me for that. So when I say trust me, you might as well trust me. Okay?"

Benjie frowned for a moment. Then he smiled. "That makes no sense to me. But okay, maybe I'll trust you. You go find the man who killed Watson so my dad can be free. Then I'll trust you forever."

Calhoun held out his hand. "It's a deal."

Benjie hesitated, then took Calhoun's hand. They shook.

"I'm sorry I tried to smash your head in," said Benjie.

Calhoun shrugged. "Don't worry about it. It wasn't going to happen. You're not very good at sneaking up on people, and you hesitated before you raised up that tire iron. If you were any good, I'd be lying there with my head in a puddle of blood. Then how'd you feel?"

"I guess I'm glad you stopped me," said Benjie.

"You're welcome," said Calhoun.

CHAPTER SEVENTEEN

At daybreak the next morning Calhoun and Ralph were sitting on the boulders beside the pool downstream from the burned-out bridge. They were taking turns sipping from Calhoun's coffee mug and watching the Bitch Creek currents come curling around the old granite abutments. Yellow poplar leaves and scarlet swamp-maple leaves twirled like rudderless sailboats in the eddies. A soft mist was sifting down, and the woods sounds—some faraway crows cawing, a distant woodpecker hammering on a hollow tree, chickadees and nuthatches cheeping and chirping, the brook gurgling, the pine boughs and dead leaves rustling in the soft breeze—were all muffled and echoey.

Calhoun felt insulated and solitary and complete. His mind, for the moment, was empty of complicated or stressful thoughts.

It was hard to say how Ralph was feeling. He was sitting on a flat boulder with his ears perked up and his nose twitching, watching the woods. Autumn had arrived in Maine, which meant bird-hunting season, and Calhoun suspected that Ralph knew it, that some strand in his DNA sent out signals this time of year to remind him that the woodcock migrations had begun, and that it was his job—his destiny as a bird dog—to snuffle around alder patches and birch hillsides and abandoned apple orchards in the fall and to lock into a stiff point when his nostrils filled with the heady scent of a woodcock or a grouse, so that his partner, the hunter with the shotgun, could flush and shoot it.

For the hundredth time, Calhoun thought that, for Ralph's sake, he really should take up bird hunting.

His coffee mug was empty, and he was thinking it was time to climb the slope to the house to get a refill and make Ralph his breakfast when the chunk of a car door slamming came echoing through the misty air.

Calhoun recognized that particular slamming sound.

"Let's go, bud," he said to Ralph. "The sheriff's here."

They climbed the hill and found Sheriff Dickman in his khaki uniform leaning against the side of his sheriff's department Explorer talking on his cell phone. The sheriff lifted a hand by way of greeting, then turned his head away and said something into the phone. He listened for a minute, nodded, and shoved the phone into his shirt pocket. "I tried to call you a little while ago," he said to Calhoun. "Be sure you were up."

Calhoun shrugged. "I been up for a while. Want some coffee?"

"Of course." The sheriff shook his head. "I do wish you'd keep your cell phone with you."

"I know," said Calhoun.

They climbed the steps onto the deck and went into the kitchen. Calhoun refilled his own mug and filled another one for the sheriff. He put the two mugs on the table, dumped some Alpo and a cup of dry dog food into Ralph's bowl, put it on the floor for him, then sat across from the sheriff. "You here on business?"

The sheriff nodded. His Smokey the Bear hat sat on the table in front of him.

"Kind of early, ain't it?" said Calhoun. "What is it, about seven fifteen?"

The sheriff glanced at his watch. "Seven seventeen, to be precise." He smiled. "How the hell do you do that?"

"Always knowing the time?" Calhoun shrugged. "Not sure what good it does me."

"I got some information," said the sheriff. "And I got a job for you. I recall you mentioning that Kate'll be watching the shop today."

Calhoun nodded. "I got a guide trip at four. That's it."

The sheriff took a sip from his coffee mug, then pulled a small notebook from his pants pocket. He opened it, squinted at it, and looked up at Calhoun. "Those three burned-up bodies we found the other day? No surprise, I guess. They all had their throats cut and their organs lopped off and stuffed into their mouths. Their hands and ankles were bound with duct tape. All had been dead for between one and three weeks, near as Dr. Surry could guess, and their faces and fingers were burned beyond indentification. But we had a pretty good idea of how we could identify them."

"That list of sex offenders," said Calhoun.

"Right. Gilsum had his crew track down every male on the Portland registry, all one hundred and twenty-six of them. There were several who'd moved or got different jobs or something, but it didn't take them long to identify the three who'd gone missing. They'd all done time, of course, so their dental records were on file." The sheriff looked down at his notebook. "Leslie Miller, age fifty-one, rape and assault on a visiting nurse. Served nine of a sixteen-year sentence, got out three years ago. Howard LaBranche, thirty-one, trafficking in child pornography. Three of five, out year before last. Anthony Boselli, fifty-nine, sexual contact with minor boys, four and a half of ten. He just got out last February. You don't need the details."

"I don't want the damn details," said Calhoun. "It's a good thing they're dead."

"Am I going to have to give you another lecture about justice and the law, Deputy Calhoun?"

"Nope. I figure whoever killed those bad people killed Albie Wolinski and Mr. Vecchio, too. That offends me. So what do you want me to do?"

"Tell me who murdered them."

Calhoun looked at the sheriff, waiting for his smile, which came a moment later.

"Okay," said the sheriff, "if you can't do that, at least you can go talk to Otis Maxner. He defended two of them. LaBranche and Boselli."

"Maxner," said Calhoun. "That real estate lawyer we talked to, office in Westbrook, used to be a public defender?"

"Him," said the sheriff.

"What about the third guy?"

"Leslie Miller. That case got heard up in Augusta. Rape. Badder crime, bigger case, longer sentence. Miller had a real lawyer. Anyway, his trial was twelve years ago, when Maxner was probably a freshman in college."

"So you just want me to go talk to Maxner?" said Calhoun. "That's it?"

"For the moment," said the sheriff. "Me, I'm having lunch with Judge Roper. He heard the LaBranche and Boselli cases. Gilsum's got his crew interviewing the families of these guys, their neighbors and coworkers and so forth. Since you and I talked with Maxner and the judge before, we're doing the follow-up with them."

"Gilsum still think Franklin Dunbar's his culprit?"

The sheriff shrugged. "I'm not sure what Gilsum's thinking. He seemed a little disappointed that his case keeps getting more complicated."

"I ran into Benjie Dunbar yesterday."

"Benjie?" The sheriff frowned.

"The boy. The basketball player."

"What do you mean, you ran into him?"

"He stopped by the shop. Wanted to talk."

The sheriff smiled. "Nice it was you he picked to talk to."

Calhoun nodded. "Sure. Flattering." He decided not to tell the sheriff that Benjie had come at him with a tire iron, or that he'd raised his fist to kill the boy. He didn't see how that would serve any purpose. "I gave him my card when we were there the other night. He wanted to explain to me how his old man couldn't've killed anybody and how this whole thing was ripping his family apart. Bad enough his sister got molested, but now, Gilsum harassing his father . . ."

"Well," said the sheriff, "if Dunbar really didn't do it, it behooves us to figure out who did."

"That's about what I told Benjie," said Calhoun. "That we were behooved to find the real killer."

The sheriff smiled. "Maybe Otis Maxner will come up with something for us."

"Or Judge Roper."

"Or both of 'em," said the sheriff. "Roper's treating me to lunch at his yacht club. How about that?"

"You get to drink Bloody Marys and eat avocado-and-crabmeat sandwiches with the judge," said Calhoun, "and I get a cup of yesterday's coffee in some real estate lawyer's office?"

"You're merely the deputy," said the sheriff, "while me, I'm the sheriff. How it works." He glanced at his watch, then drained his coffee mug, twisted on his hat, and stood up. "Gotta get going. I got a week's worth of paperwork to clean up before lunch at the yacht club."

"Don't let the judge snow you with his club sandwiches," said Calhoun.

"Ha," said the sheriff. "Soon as you catch up with Maxner, give me a call."

"What should I ask him?" said Calhoun. "How do you want me to handle it?"

The sheriff looked at him. "Stoney," he said, "you're at least as good as me at this, whether you know it or not. Follow your instincts. We'll compare notes afterwards, see what Gilsum's people turn up, and take it from there."

Calhoun waited until a few minutes after nine to call Otis Maxner's law office in Westbrook. The secretary who answered told him that Mr. Maxner would be in Augusta all morning researching a property title. She wasn't sure when he'd be back in the office, but he had a two o'clock appointment with a client, so it would definitely be by then.

Calhoun told her to write him in for that two o'clock slot.

She said she couldn't do that. Attorney Maxner already had a two o'clock.

He reminded her that he was a deputy sheriff working on a case, and that Mr. Maxner, as an officer of the court, owed him his full cooperation.

She sighed and said, "Two o'clock, then, Mr. Calhoun. I do hope it won't take too long."

"Me, too," said Calhoun.

"Can I tell Mr. Maxner what you want to talk to him about?"

"No," said Calhoun. "I'll tell him myself."

He spent the rest of the morning tying flies, making new leaders, cleaning fly lines, organizing rods and reels and other gear, and filling the cooler with frozen bottles of water and soft drinks and snacks for his afternoon fishing trip with Dr. Sam Surry, and then loading everything into his truck.

Dr. Surry was meeting him at the shop around four. He figured if it took an hour to talk to Otis Maxner—and he didn't see why he'd need that much time—even in Friday-afternoon traffic he'd still have plenty of time to drive back from Westbrook to the shop and be there when she showed up. For some reason he couldn't quite put his finger on, he didn't want her to get there first and end up waiting in the shop when Kate was there. The way Kate had been acting, he guessed it might upset her. Lately, it was hard to predict what might upset Kate.

Two middle-aged men in suits were waiting in Otis Maxner's office when Calhoun walked in. They were thumbing through magazines, ignoring each other.

Maxner's secretary poked her head up from behind her computer monitor. "Mr. Calhoun," she said. "Mr. Maxner's not back yet. Do you want some coffee?"

"What time is it?"

"Not yet two. What about the coffee?"

He shrugged. "Sure. Black."

She jerked her thumb at a stainless-steel electric coffee machine on a table in the corner of the room. "Help yourself."

Calhoun poured himself some coffee, then sat on one of the uncomfortable wooden chairs that were lined up against the wall opposite the other two men. He found an old *Yankee* magazine in the stack on the coffee table and began to thumb through it.

A few minutes later Otis Maxner came breezing into the room. He looked at the two men in business suits and said, "Charles. Frederick. I'll be right with you." Then he seemed to notice Calhoun. He frowned. "I'm sorry, sir . . ."

"I'm Stonewall Calhoun," he said. "Sheriff Dickman's deputy. We were here last Monday. I have a two o'clock appointment with you, and you're five minutes late."

Maxner glanced at his secretary, who gave him a little nod. "Well, all right, Mr. Calhoun. Come on in." To the other two men he said, "This'll just be a minute."

Calhoun followed Maxner into his office.

Maxner sat behind his desk and waved the back of his hand at one of the client chairs. "Have a seat. I hope we can make this quick. Those two men out there are important clients. They've got a big development deal in the works." He puffed out his cheeks and blew out a breath. "So tell me how I can help you."

Calhoun sat. "I want to run some names by you." He paused, then said, "Leslie Miller. Howard LaBranche. Anthony Boselli."

Maxner looked out the window for a minute. Then he brought his gaze back to Calhoun. "Leslie Miller doesn't ring any bells, but Boselli and LaBranche were clients of mine back when I was a PD. This have any bearing on the questions you and the sheriff were asking about Errol Watson the other day?"

"What can you tell me about Boselli and LaBranche?"

"They'd both committed sex crimes," Maxner said. "They couldn't afford a lawyer, so they were assigned to me. Judge Roper heard both cases. There was nothing particularly unusual about them or the cases. Sex offenders are what they are. I did my best to defend them, which was my job, but they were guilty as hell, and they got convicted. I suppose they're out now, committing more vile crimes? Is that what this is about?"

"I wonder if you've heard anything more about Errol Watson," said Calhoun. "Since the sheriff and I were here on Monday, I mean."

Maxner nodded. "I heard he was murdered. I—oh. You telling me Boselli and LaBranche got murdered, too?"

"That's right," said Calhoun. "And that Leslie Miller, too. All of 'em sex offenders, and counting Watson, all except Miller were defended by you in Judge Roper's court."

"And you want me to help you figure out who's killing these men, is that it?"

Calhoun spread his hands. "Any ideas?"

"All my paperwork from when I was a PD is stored away," said Maxner. "I guess I could find those files for you, but it would take me a while."

Calhoun nodded. "Do that. How long is a while?"

"A couple of days? It's not on my computer. The files are in boxes in the attic of my home." He smiled. "I never imagined I'd ever have any need for all that stuff, but I save everything."

Calhoun nodded. "Good."

"I'll dig it out this weekend. I'll give you a call. Okay? Was there anything else?" Maxner pushed himself halfway out of his seat, a hint that it was time for Calhoun to leave.

Calhoun remained seated. "Tell me what you remember about those two cases of yours. Any commonalities with the Errol Watson case, for example?"

Maxner frowned. "Those cases happened several years ago, Mr. Calhoun. I had a lot of cases when I was a PD."

Calhoun nodded.

"Well," said Maxner slowly, "I do remember that the Watson case came before LaBranche and Boselli. The Watson case was memorable because of the victim's family, that heartbreaking testimony of the father. We talked about that the other day."

"Yes. Franklin Dunbar."

Maxner lifted an index finger. "There was one thing," he said.

"Now that I'm thinking about it. An interesting thing, actually. I noticed it at the time, but I didn't make too much of it. But now that I think of it . . ."

"What is it?" said Calhoun.

"Normally," said Maxner, "the people who come to watch a trial fall into three categories. One, friends and relatives. Of the victim and of the accused. Two, a few regulars, folks who think trials are high drama and show up every day. Retired folks, mostly. People with time on their hands. Three, reporters. Local papers covering the court." Otis Maxner lifted his hand, then let it fall back on his desk. "So I noticed him. Dunbar. The father of Watson's victim who made that—what would you call it? a threat?—during his testimony at Watson's trial."

"You noticed him?"

"He was there, Mr. Calhoun. At Boselli's and LaBranche's trials. He was there every day. He sat in the back of the courtroom. Just sat there watching. I remember glancing his way occasionally and seeing his eyes on my clients. Every time I looked at him, he was just staring at my clients."

"You didn't think this was strange?"

"Sure," said Maxner. "At the time, that's exactly what I thought. It was strange, bordering on downright bizarre. But anybody can sit in a courtroom, and I just figured, the poor bastard, he developed some fascination with sex crimes and sex criminals. That's not hard to understand. Anyway—" Maxner stopped suddenly. He blinked a couple of times, then said, "My God."

"What?" said Calhoun.

"Somebody's going around killing convicted sex offenders? Is that what seems to be happening?"

"Seems to be," said Calhoun.

"Franklin Dunbar," said Maxner.

"He was at those trials, huh?"

"Every day. Didn't miss a minute of testimony."

"You think Dunbar's doing this?"

"Oh, I couldn't say that," said Maxner. "I couldn't go that far. What do I know? But it's an interesting coincidence, at least, isn't it?"

"It surely is that," said Calhoun. "Can you think of any other commonalities?"

Maxner shook his head. "This other case you mentioned . . . Miller? Was that the name?"

"Leslie Miller. Yes."

"Isn't that kind of messing up your theory?"

"I don't have a theory."

"I mean, the other three, all my clients, all convicted by Judge Roper, Franklin Dunbar witnessing all three cases?"

"That ain't a theory," said Calhoun. "That's just some commonalities."

"Well," said Maxner, "if it was just those three, you'd have yourself a neat theory that poor Mr. Dunbar killed all of them, wouldn't you?"

"It would be a start," said Calhoun.

Maxner shook his head. "Well, anyway. I can't think of any other commonalities. My clients, Judge Roper's courtroom, and Franklin Dunbar. That's leaving Miller out of the equation."

"Okay," said Calhoun. "Appreciate it. You'll dig out those files for me?"

Maxner stood up. "Sure. I'll call you Monday." He came around from behind his desk. "So . . ." He held out his hand.

Calhoun stood up and shook Otis Maxner's hand. "You've been a big help. Thanks."

They went over to the door, and Maxner started to open it.

"Oh, wait," said Calhoun. "One more thing."

Maxner smiled. "I've got two very important clients out there, Mr. Calhoun. You usurped their two o'clock appointment, you know."

"Usurped." Calhoun smiled. "Right. Sorry. The names Paul Vecchio and Albert Wolinski mean anything to you?"

Maxner looked up at the ceiling for a moment, then shrugged. "No, I don't think so. Might they have been clients of mine? Are they sex offenders? Relatives of victims?"

Calhoun shrugged. "Oh, well. Just a wild shot in the dark." He waved his hand. "Don't worry about it."

Maxner was frowning. "I'm trying to think."

"Forget it," said Calhoun. "Thanks for your help."

Maxner nodded, then opened his office door and held it for Calhoun, who went out into he reception area.

Maxner stepped out and said, "Charles? Frederick? Sorry to keep you waiting. Come on in."

The two men in business suits stood up and walked past Maxner into his office. Maxner patted each man on the shoulder, nodded at Calhoun, then went in and shut the door behind him.

Calhoun stood there for a minute.

The secretary said, "Mr. Calhoun? Is there anything I can do for you?"

He turned to look at her. "Something I forgot to ask Mr. Maxner about. Local man name of Albert Wolinski. He sold his house down in Stroudwater a couple years ago. He wasn't Mr. Maxner's client, was he?"

She looked at him. "I can't talk about our clients, you know. Attorney-client privilege."

"We're just talking about selling a damn house," said Calhoun.

She shook her head.

"I was wondering if he was a client. That's all. This ain't about state secrets."

She shrugged. "Sorry."

Calhoun grinned. "Okay. Thanks anyway."

Back outside, the misty fog seemed to be thickening. Calhoun thought about his fishing trip with Dr. Sam Surry. He hoped she'd remember to bring some foul-weather gear.

Well, she might decide to cancel. It wasn't going to be much of an afternoon for a boat ride.

The fishing might be pretty good, though. He decided if she called, he'd encourage her to give it a try. Put a fly rod in her hand, hook her up with a blue or a striper, even a small one, and he guessed she'd have a pretty good time.

He let Ralph out of the truck. The dog went sniffing among the damp shrubbery alongside the sidewalk.

Calhoun took his cell phone from his pocket, pressed the button on the side, and said, "Dickman." It rang a few times, and then the sheriff's voice mail invited him to leave a message.

"It's your faithful deputy," said Calhoun. "Just talked with Otis Maxner. Couple things to think about. One, he mentioned that Franklin Dunbar was in the courtroom for the trials of both Anthony Boselli and Howard LaBranche. They were both in Judge Roper's court, so you might want to ask the judge if he remembers it the same way. The second thing I'm wondering is if Maxner handled Albie Wolinski's closing when he sold his house. Albie's name didn't ring any bells with Maxner. His secretary wouldn't say one way or the other. Just a thought. Okay. That's all. I'm going fishing."

He put the phone back into his pocket and whistled up Ralph. "Want to go for a boat ride?"

Ralph jumped into the truck and sat on the passenger seat with his ears perked up. He was ready to go.

Calhoun drove back to the shop in Portland through the fog. The closer he got to the coast, the thicker it became. Even though it wasn't yet four in the afternoon—still nearly three hours before sunset—the traffic was moving under the speed limit, and all the vehicles had their headlights on.

He wondered if Dr. Sam Surry would be spooked by the fog. On Casco Bay, visibility would be under a hundred feet.

He guessed it was about ten of four when he pulled into the parking lot beside the shop. Kate's pickup was parked next to his trailered boat. A little black Honda SUV was pulled up near the door.

Calhoun parked beside Kate's truck, and he and Ralph got out. Ralph messed around in the bushes for a few minutes. Calhoun waited for him to finish, then snapped his fingers. Ralph came over and looked up at him. "Heel," said Calhoun.

When he opened the shop door, he heard that Kate had put on the Portland oldies station. Calhoun sometimes liked listening to that old time rock 'n' roll. He found that he could sing along with songs that he'd swear he'd never heard in his life. Of course, there was that whole life that he couldn't remember. He supposed songs just got stuck in your head somewhere.

Now he stood inside the doorway mouthing "Yackity-yack, don't talk back," the tune running in his head and his mind popping up the silly lyrics as the music came along from the radio.

Kate was sitting at the fly-tying bench, and Dr. Sam Surry had pulled up a chair close beside her. They hadn't seen him come in, apparently, because they didn't even look up. Kate had a half-tied fly in the vise—it looked to Calhoun like a featherwing streamer of some kind, maybe even a Gray Ghost, the fly he'd been tying when Dr. Surry was here the other day—and she was concentrating on it, winding the thread with her right hand and holding the materials back with her left, but talking to Dr. Surry all the time.

Dr. Surry had her head tilted toward Kate, and she was leaning forward a little, watching Kate's fingers move on the half-tied fly.

Dr. Surry said something, and Kate lifted her head and looked at her and smiled, and then Dr. Surry laughed.

That's when they seemed to notice Calhoun for the first time. Kate looked up and her mouth made a surprised O, and then Calhoun had the feeling that it wasn't fly-tying they'd been talking about.

He said, "Okay," to Ralph, who was sitting on the floor behind him, and Ralph went over to Kate with his whole hind end wagging so she could pat him.

The song on the radio ended, and the familiar raspy voice of the obnoxious guy who owned the Ford agency in South Portland started yelling about great deals on new and used Ford trucks.

Calhoun went over to the radio on the shelf and turned it off. Then he looked at Kate and Sam Surry. "I can't stand that guy," he said.

They were both smiling at him, as if they were privy to some secret that they weren't going to share with him.

He figured they'd been talking about him, and he was surprised that it didn't make him uncomfortable. Actually, he kind of liked the idea.

He looked at Dr. Sam Surry and said, "Ready to go fishing?"

Kate said, "In this fog?"

He shrugged. "I ain't likely to get lost, if that's what you're worried about."

Kate turned to Dr. Surry. "He's right. He always knows where he is. It's spooky." She looked up at him. "I'll still worry, you know. I don't like fog like this. You could ram a rock. You could get run down by a tanker or some drunk teenager in a cigarette boat. What if your motor quits?"

He smiled at Kate, then shifted his gaze to Dr. Surry and arched his eyebrows. "Up to you, ma'am."

She nodded. "Let's do it."

Kate said, "I hope you got that cell phone with you." To Dr. Surry she said, "He refuses to use GPS, and he claims his boat radio's broke. He hates having electronics aboard when he goes fishing."

Calhoun patted his pocket. "I got the damn phone."

"Please don't leave it in your truck," Kate said.

"Right," he said. "So if I get lost, I can call and say, 'Help, I'm lost.' And whoever I talk to will say, 'Where are you?' And I'll say, 'How the hell should I know? If I knew, I wouldn't be lost, would I?'"

Kate smiled. "Please bring the phone."

"Phones are against the rules of my boat."

"This one time," she said, "break your damn rule. Just to make me feel better."

Dr. Surry turned to Kate. "I've got a phone," she said in a fake whisper. "I'll smuggle it aboard."

Now the two of them were conspiring. He wondered what Kate had been saying about him.

CHAPTER EIGHTEEN

There were no other vehicles parked in the lot at the East End boat landing. The fog lay in a gray wet blanket over Casco Bay. From the landing you could make out a few dark shapes out there, islands that normally were fully visible in all their colorful details.

Calhoun stopped at the top of the ramp, and he and Dr. Surry transferred all the gear from the back of the truck to the boat, while Ralph padded along the edge of the water, sniffing the seaweed and driftwood and peeing frequently.

After they got the boat loaded up, Calhoun climbed back into the truck. He backed the trailered boat into the water, pulled the emergency brake, and got out. He went around to the back, undid the safety hook, and disconnected the trailer lights. Then he un-cranked the chain, unhooked the boat, grabbed the bow line, and gave the boat a shove. He held onto the line as the boat floated off the trailer.

He handed the line to Dr. Surry. "Hang on to this while I park the truck."

She took the line. She was wearing a new-looking Simms rain outfit. It was pale blue, and it fit her nicely. She looked good in it. The blue, he noticed, made her eyes seem bigger. He wondered if Kate had sold it to her.

He thought maybe he'd have the opportunity to ask her if they'd been talking about him. Maybe she could give him some insight into Kate's frame of mind. He believed that women under-stood each other the way a man never could.

Or maybe Kate had just been showing her how to tie flies.

"Be right back," he said to Sam Surry, and she smiled and showed him that she had a good grip on the line.

He got into the truck, and Ralph hopped in with him. He drove up the ramp and parked in the lot. When he got out and looked back, his boat and Sam Surry were just blurry black-and-white shapes in the fog.

He thought about leaving his cell phone in the truck, but Kate wanted him to bring it, and he decided that no harm would come from it. Maybe he'd even give her a call when they were out there, tell her about all the stripers they were catching, ease her mind.

A rule didn't make much sense if there weren't circumstances when you should break it.

Ralph trotted along beside him as he headed back to his boat. They had just started down the sloping ramp when Ralph stopped and growled deep in his chest.

"It's just Dr. Surry," Calhoun said. "What's your—"

Then he stopped. Somebody, another human shape, was with her.

Ralph was standing there stiff-legged, his growl a low menac-ing rumble.

"Sit," Calhoun said to him. "Wait here."

Ralph sat. He continued to growl.

Calhoun went down the ramp. Dr. Surry was holding the bow line in both of her hands. The way her neck and shoulders were kind of hunched over, he thought she might be crying.

The other figure was a man. He was wearing a camouflage rain jacket with the hood pulled over his head.

When Calhoun got closer, he saw that it was Otis Maxner, the real estate lawyer, and he was pointing a semiautomatic handgun at Dr. Surry. It had the distinctive shape of a classic old Colt Woods-man .22 like the one Calhoun kept in his kitchen drawer.

About then, everything made sense.

Calhoun walked up to them. "Mr. Maxner," he said. "What's up?"

"I'm going with you," said Maxner.

"Didn't know you were an angler."

"I'm not."

"Just a killer, huh?"

"You're too smart for your own good, Mr. Calhoun. I just hope you aren't thinking about doing something stupid, because I'd hate to have to shoot this pretty lady."

"You're the man with the gun," said Calhoun. "What do you want?"

"Get into the boat. In the back."

"That's called the stern," said Calhoun.

"Do it."

Calhoun got in.

Maxner spoke to Dr. Surry. "You, drop that rope and get into the middle seat."

She climbed in and sat there facing the stern with her arms folded. She looked hard at Calhoun, and he saw in her eyes that he'd been wrong. She had not been crying. She wasn't frightened. She was pissed.

Maxner got in and sat on the bow seat, facing the stern. He kept his Woodsman pointing at Dr. Surry's back as he pulled a roll of duct tape from inside his slicker and tossed it to Calhoun. "Wrap her wrists."

"You're pretty dumb, even for a lawyer," Calhoun said. He slid his hand into his pants pocket and depressed the little button on the side of his cell phone. "Sheriff Dickman has already got you figured out." He spoke the word "Dickman" extra loud. "Be careful where you point that pistol, will you?"

"Wrap that tape on her," said Maxner.

"You want me to take you on a boat ride?" said Calhoun. "Revisit the scenes of all your crimes?"

"Oh," said Sam Surry. "I get it. Him."

"Yes, ma'am," said Calhoun.

"You talk way too much," said Maxner. "Just do what I'm telling you."

Calhoun knelt in front of Sam Surry. "It's going to be okay," he said.

She gave him a tight smile. "I know."

As he wrapped the tape around her wrists, Calhoun looked up at Maxner and said, "So, what's all this killing about? You feeling guilty or frustrated or morally conflicted or something, being forced to defend those evil sex offenders in court? Is that it? Figured you'd single-handedly rid the world of them? Otis Maxner," he said, pronouncing the name loudly and clearly for the benefit of the cell phone in his pocket, "by day a mild-mannered real estate attorney, by night some kind of avenging Spider-Man?" He was saying all this for the sheriff's benefit, hoping he'd picked up. Even if he hadn't, his voice mail would be catching it.

"You shouldn't make fun of me," said Maxner.

"Yep," said Calhoun. "It's serious business, all right. Worth torturing poor old Albie Wolinski and then plugging Mr. Vecchio. What happened? Albie betray you? Sell your secret to the writer? That what happened?"

"I paid him a lot of money," said Maxner.

"Helping you load those men on his boat, huh? Driving you out to the islands so you could set 'em afire?" He finished binding Sam Surry's wrists and tore the tape off the roll. "How's that?" he said to Maxner. "All set?"

"Tell the dog to get into the boat," said Maxner.

"Leave the dog out of it," said Calhoun.

Maxner shook his head. "Can't have him wandering around." He poked at the back of Dr. Surry's neck with his handgun. He was sitting close behind her. "Do what I say or I'll shoot her."

"Ralph," said Calhoun. "Git in the boat."

Ralph had been sitting there waiting for his instructions. Now he stood up, sauntered over to the boat, and hopped in. He sat in front of Calhoun and stared at Otis Maxner.

"He makes one false move," said Maxner, "I'll shoot him."

"Ralph never made a false move in his life," said Calhoun. "He makes nothing but true moves. He don't like you, you know. Did you take a shot at him that night you killed Mr. Vecchio?"

"Push us off," said Maxner. "Start up the motor. Let's get going."

"Where to?"

"Head for Quarantine Island."

"Quarantine Island?" Calhoun said, practically shouting for the sheriff's benefit. "Not sure I'll be able to find Quarantine in this fog."

Maxner smiled. "Oh, you'll find it. I know about you. You've got quite a reputation. Stoney Calhoun, best guide on Casco Bay, I keep hearing. Knows it like the palm of his hand. So let's go. And don't try something tricky. Mess around with me, I start shooting. First the dog. Then the lady."

"Gotcha," said Calhoun. "Quarantine it is. No need to shoot anybody."

He pushed them off with an oar, got the motor started, put it in gear, and began to chug out through the harbor. The motor thrummed softly in low gear, and even with only one functional ear, Calhoun could hear some gulls squawking and the water lapping against the sides of the aluminum boat.

"Tell him to stop looking at me like that," Maxner said.

Calhoun looked at him. "What the hell are you talking about?"

"Your dog. He's staring at me. I swear I'll shoot him."

"He won't do anything unless I tell him to," said Calhoun, "but I can't control where he decides to look."

Maxner shook his head and kind of hunched his shoulders inside of his bulky camouflage rain jacket, as if he was cold.

Calhoun supposed the sheriff's voice mail had clicked off a while ago, but just in case, he wanted to keep Maxner talking. If things didn't work out, he wanted the sheriff to know as much as possible. "So tell me," he said to Maxner, "what was it made you decide to come after me? You kind of gave yourself away, you know."

"Albie Wolinski," said Maxner. "When you asked about him, it caught me off guard. Otherwise I wouldn't have lied. I handled his closing. That's how I got to know him. But when you asked, I lied. Regretted it instantly. I assumed you'd check. Public records show that he was a client." He shrugged. "So then you'd come after me, and you'd probably bring the sheriff with you, and then it would be too late. Now it's not too late."

Calhoun smiled. "Of course it's too late. You're cooked."

"We'll see about that." He looked around. "In case you were thinking of trying to confuse me, I know the bay pretty well myself. I know where we are. I know where Quarantine is."

Calhoun had noticed that as they moved farther from the shoreline the fog seemed to become thinner. There was a brightness overhead that suggested the afternoon sun might burn through it, and the distant islands appeared more clearly.

"I ain't going to try to confuse you," said Calhoun. "You're already pretty thoroughly confused, I'd say. Going around killing people."

Maxner shrugged. "You better stop talking now. You're starting to make me mad. Let's get up to speed."

Calhoun throttled up the motor, and then they were skimming across the bay. He glanced at Dr. Sam Surry. She was sitting there with her duct-taped wrists in her lap watching him. A little smile played on her face, as if she thought that Calhoun was in control of the situation. He didn't quite feel that way, but he gave her a quick smile and a wink anyway.

Pretty soon the low outline of Quarantine Island appeared on the horizon. Calhoun figured that Maxner intended to shoot all three of them and leave them there. He'd take Calhoun's boat back to the mainland, get off somewhere where he wouldn't be spotted, and let the tide take the boat away. Maxner knew that local people thought the island was haunted. Autumn was here and winter was fast approaching, and there wouldn't be much boat traffic in the bay. It could be months before anybody beached a boat on Quarantine Island. Their bodies might not be found until April.

As he approached Quarantine, Calhoun cut back the motor. The cove where he had landed with Paul Vecchio was studded with sharp-edged boulders, some of them just under the surface.

Maxner glanced quickly over his shoulder. His gun never stopped pointing at Dr. Surry's back. "Okay, good," he said. "We're here. Find a place to land."

Calhoun stood up, steering with the side of his leg.

"What're you doing?" said Maxner. "Sit down."

"I've got to see where the rocks are. You wouldn't want us to sink." Calhoun memorized the little cove, then sat back down.

He caught Sam Surry's eye and gave his head a tiny nod. Then he suddenly goosed the motor.

The boat shot forward, and both Dr. Surry and Otis Maxner were jerked in their seats by the little burst of speed.

Then it all seemed to happen at once.

Calhoun grabbed Dr. Surry's leg and pulled her to the bottom of the boat.

The bow rammed the underwater rock Calhoun had been aiming at and slammed to a stop.

Otis Maxner pitched backward in his seat.

Calhoun leaped over Dr. Surry and landed on top of Maxner.

So did Ralph.

Maxner's gun exploded.

Calhoun felt a searing heat on his left side, as if someone had shoved a red-hot branding iron against his ribs.

He grabbed Maxner's right wrist, the one holding the gun, in his left hand and got a grip on his upper arm with his other hand. He pushed the wrist in one direction and levered the arm in a different direction.

The crack in Maxner's shoulder sounded as loud as the gunshot.

Maxner screamed.

Ralph was growling deep in his chest. He was shaking his head back and forth, and Calhoun saw that his jaws had clamped down on Otis Maxner's crotch.

Maxner screamed again.

Calhoun gave his arm another twist, and the Colt Woodsman dropped into the bottom of the boat.

Calhoun tried to reach for the gun, but his left arm had suddenly gone numb, and it refused to move. It was hanging motionless at his side. He turned his body, got the gun in his right hand, then sat back on the middle seat.

Ralph was still worrying Maxner's crotch.

"Okay, bud," said Calhoun. "Let it go."

Ralph let go. He sat down right there, glaring at Maxner.

Maxner was lying on his back holding his right arm against his body and groaning. Calhoun figured he'd wrenched the man's shoulder out of its socket, ripped the tendons and ligaments beyond repair, cracked some bones, shredded some muscles.

He wondered where he learned to do that.

He slumped there on the seat, trying to keep the .22 pointed at Otis Maxner. He took several deep breaths. He was feeling light-headed and nauseated. He swallowed against the urge to vomit.

Dr. Surry sat beside him. "Are you all right?" she said.

Calhoun tried to shrug, but it hurt. "He shot me in the side. It's starting to hurt. My arm's gone numb."

"Can you cut this tape off me?"

He glanced at Maxner and figured he wasn't any threat. Anyway, Ralph was sitting there, waiting for the word to resume chewing on the man's testicles.

Calhoun put the gun on the seat and fished in his pocket for his fishing knife. Going into his left pocket with his right hand was awkward, plus twisting his body hurt like hell, but he got it out, opened it with his teeth, and sliced through the tape on Dr. Surry's wrists.

She peeled the pieces off, then said, "Let me take a look at you."

She opened Calhoun's jacket and shirt, baring his torso.

Calhoun closed his eyes and took some deep breaths against the pain.

Dr. Surry clicked her tongue. "It's bleeding a lot. Up to a point, that's good. Clean it out. Looks like the bullet glanced off your ribs and kept going. Also good." She laughed quickly. "This is ironic. I never go anywhere without my black bag, but looking at dead bodies all the time, I've never needed it. Now I need it and it's back in my car. I hope you have a first aid kit on this boat."

"Under the stern seat," Calhoun mumbled.

She turned, lifted the seat, and took out the big tin box. She used a wad of gauze to wipe the blood away, and then Calhoun saw how the bullet had hit him just under his left nipple and had ripped a gouge along the side of his rib cage, angling upward toward his armpit. He guessed another inch to the middle and it could have slipped between his ribs and drilled his heart.

Dr. Surry soaked another hunk of gauze with iodine. When she swabbed his wound, he didn't feel anything for a couple of seconds. Then it hurt worse than the bullet had.

She looked up at him. "Doin' okay?"

He nodded and tried to smile. He didn't dare speak.

She bandaged him up and helped him button his shirt and zip up his windbreaker. "Don't flail around too much or you'll start it bleeding again," she said.

"Not sure I'm capable of much flailing," he said. The dizziness and nausea had passed. He felt a little weak, that was all. "I got that cell phone in my pocket. See if you can fish it out for me."

She leaned close to him and patted the sides of his legs. She found the phone and slid her hand into his pocket. She gripped the phone, then paused with her hand still in his pocket. "I apologize for the, um, intimacy," she said.

He looked at her. She was grinning.

"Good thing Kate ain't here," he said.

She narrowed her eyes, then smiled and nodded and pulled out the phone. She held it up, squinted at it, and said, "Oh, this is a big help."

"What's the matter?"

"Your battery's dead."

So much for his tricky telephone call and voice mail message. The sheriff had given him a recharger for the phone. Calhoun had used it once, then stopped thinking about it.

"You're going to have to show me how to drive us back," she said.

"It ain't rocket surgery," he said. "It's just a damn boat."

"Rocket surgery." She smiled.

"You want to take a look at that man's shoulder, Doc?"

She raised a finger and pointed at him. "Will you please not call me Doc. Makes me think I'm some old geezer with a limp and a drinking problem. Everybody calls me Sam except you."

"Sorry," said Calhoun.

She looked past Calhoun to where Otis Maxner was slumped in the bow of the boat. "That man's shoulder isn't going to kill him," she said. "I don't have much interest in getting any closer to him than this."

"Fine by me. Why don't you sit back there and drive us home, then. I'm about ready to turn this man over to the sheriff."

"And get that bullet wound of yours looked at," said Sam Surry.

Calhoun turned and looked at Maxner, who was curled fetally on the bottom of the boat. He was cradling his destroyed right arm against his body and whimpering softly. "You sit tight," Calhoun said to him. "We're heading back now. In case you might think of moving around, I can tell you that Ralph here has now got a taste for your balls, like one of them man-eating tigers, and he'd love nothing more than to chew on them some more. All I got to do is tell him okay. Understand?"

Maxner opened his eyes, gave a tiny nod, then closed them again.

Ralph continued to sit there glowering.

Calhoun gave directions, and Sam Surry managed to back them away from the underwater boulders and get them headed back to the boat landing. Once he saw that she was handling it like a veteran, he allowed himself to slump on his seat and close his eyes.

He felt himself drifting, and from a long distance away came the voices of the Quarantine Island nuns, the old gray ghosts with their habits billowing in the wind, moaning and keening and wailing, and he wondered if it was his death they were mourning. He opened his eyes. The sun had set, and darkness was spreading over the bay, and the fog seemed to be thickening again.

Sam Surry was concentrating on where she was steering, and Ralph was still glaring at Otis Maxner's groin area. They apparently hadn't heard the nuns. Calhoun supposed he was a little wacky from getting shot.

When he closed his eyes again, he didn't hear the gray ghosts anymore.

After a while, Sam Surry beached the boat at the landing. When Calhoun felt the bump of the boat, he opened his eyes and sat up. Sheriff Dickman was holding the bow steady, and Lieutenant Gilsum and three or four uniformed cops were standing there.

Ralph leaped out immediately and proceeded to go exploring.

The sheriff held on to the boat while Lieutenant Gilsum helped Sam Surry get off.

"He's hurt," she said, pointing at Calhoun.

Two of the cops helped Calhoun get out of the boat. With one on each side, they steered him over to some big rocks and helped him sit down. Ralph came over and put his chin on Calhoun's knee. Calhoun patted him with his good hand.

He watched as they wrestled Otis Maxner out of the boat, half-carried him up the landing, and stuffed him into the back of a cruiser. Then the cruiser pulled out of the lot.

The sheriff and Gilsum came over and stood in front of Calhoun. "I got two messages from you on my cell phone," said the sheriff. "First one, mentioning Albert Wolinski, I checked, and sure enough, Otis Maxner handled his real estate transaction. That's when things started to make sense. Couldn't understand your second message at all, to tell you the truth. It was all muffled and far-away, and after a minute it died completely. Saw that it was from your phone again, so I called Kate, and she said you'd gone fishing. Figured I better see what was up, and giving it a second thought, I gave the lieutenant a call. Not that you needed any help that I can see. You doin' okay?"

Calhoun nodded. "Bullet grazed my ribs is all. Just a little .22. I think I might've bled quite a bit, but I'm good."

"We can talk about it later," said the sheriff, "but just so I understand, it was Otis Maxner did all the killing?"

"It was him."

"And you had that all figured out?"

Calhoun shook his head. "Nope." He tried to smile. "Not all of it. But I would've." He lowered his head between his knees. "Sorry," he said. "I don't feel so hot."

Everything was fuzzy. Images whirled in his brain, and he couldn't mobilize the energy to pin them down. He was aware of people moving around him. Somebody said, "Shock," and somebody else said, "Hospital," and then people were gripping his arms and hauling him into a vehicle.

He faded in and out. There were blurry faces—Kate and Sam Surry and the sheriff, doctors with green masks over their mouths and black solemn eyes, other faces that seemed to come from some other time in his life, children and old people speaking languages he didn't understand, all whirling around in his head. There were bright lights and antiseptic odors and murmuring voices and humming machinery.

After a while, he slept.

He woke up in gray light looking at the ceiling in his own bedroom. He couldn't swallow. It felt as if a wad of steel wool were stuck in his throat.

He tried to lift his head off the pillow, and somebody commenced hammering a tenpenny spike into his forehead.

Kate's face appeared. "Can I get you something?" she said.

He tried to smile. It hurt. "Water," he croaked.

A glass appeared in her hand. She held it to his lips with one hand, and with the other she cupped the back of his head and helped him lift up. "Just sip," she said.

He took a sip. It slid gloriously down his throat, then hit his stomach like a rock. He swallowed back the urge to vomit.

Kate lowered his head back to the pillow.

"You're here," said Calhoun.

"Don't go reading too much into it," she said. "Sam and I flipped a coin. I got tonight. She'll be here tomorrow."

"Sam," said Calhoun.

"Dr. Surry."

He nodded. Sam.

"Go to sleep, Stoney. Everything's under control."

He closed his eyes. There were thoughts he couldn't quite pin down. "Honey?" he said.

She stroked the side of his face with her soft hand. "I'm here, Stoney."

"You gonna leave me again?"

She touched his eyelids with the tips of her fingers. "Go to sleep now."

"Where's Ralph?"

"He's right here, snorin' and twitchin' on his rug."

"Did you feed him?"

"I told you. Everything's under control." She bent to him and kissed his forehead. "Relax, baby. Just relax."

Then he slept.

Calhoun insisted on getting out of bed the next morning. Kate tried to get him to swallow a pill. "For the pain," she said.

He shook his head. "The pain ain't so bad."

She didn't argue. She helped him out onto the deck. His left side throbbed from armpit to hip. Every heartbeat shot a dart of pain into his head. It felt as if he'd been run over by a bus.

It was tolerable, though, and he intended to tolerate it.

A warm sun filtered down through the big maple that arched over the house. Kate brought him a slice of dry toast. He took an experimental bite, and when he didn't vomit, he ate it all.

He dozed out there most of the day with Kate sitting across from him reading a book and Ralph sprawled on the deck beside him. She roused him a couple of times so he could swallow some antibiotic capsules.

Sometime in the afternoon Sam Surry drove her little Honda SUV into the yard. Kate went down, gave her a hug, and talked with her. Then both women came up onto the deck.

Sam gave Calhoun a smile and went into the house.

Kate sat across from Calhoun. "I'll be back tomorrow," she said, "and I'll keep coming back until you're better. But I don't want you to think anything's changed."

He nodded. She was thinking about Walter.

"One of these days things will be different," she said.

He nodded. "I know."

"Meantime," she said, "please try not to let anybody else shoot you."

"Don't worry about me, honey," he said. "I ain't going any-where."

Kate looked at him for a long moment. Then she came around the table, knelt beside him, and laid her cheek on his leg.

He reached out with his good hand and touched her hair.

When she looked up at him, he saw the glitter of tears in her eyes.

"You're a good man, Stoney Calhoun," she whispered. "I'm gonna love you forever and ever, and don't you dare forget it."

Then Calhoun felt tears burning in his eyes, too.

The sheriff came the next afternoon. Calhoun and Sam Surry were sitting on the deck sipping Cokes and watching the chickadees and finches in the feeders. The sheriff climbed up onto the deck and sat down with them.

Sam asked if he wanted a Coke, and he said he wouldn't mind. She got up, brought him Coke, then went back inside.

The sheriff asked Calhoun how he was doing. Calhoun said he wasn't complaining, and that was the end of that topic.

The sheriff told him that Otis Maxner had confessed to every-thing. He'd been required to defend sex offenders in court, and that led him to believe that his sacred calling was to rid the world of them. He'd aimed to work his way through the entire registry for the city of Portland, and then he'd branch out into the surrounding areas, and who knew where or when he'd stop? His long-term goal was to deposit a body on each of Casco Bay's Calendar Islands, all 365 of them, plus or minus. He'd cut off each man's evil dick and shove it in his mouth. Then he'd slice his throat and set him ablaze. Poetic justice. Maxner considered himself a hero.

He'd hired Albie Wolinski to help. He paid Albie a lot of money. But Albie had gotten greedy, or maybe he had a twinge of conscience. He looked up Paul Vecchio, who promised him money for his story. They met at the Keelhaul Cafe. Albie drew a map of the bay, showing Vecchio where the bodies were. Then Vecchio hired Calhoun to take him fishing—mainly so he could explore one of the islands on Albie's map and see if he was telling the truth.

Maxner got wind of Albie's treachery. He tortured him, then killed him, then followed Vecchio to Calhoun's place and killed him, too.

"That's it, then," said Calhoun.

The sheriff nodded.

"Good." Calhoun reached into his pants pocket and took out his deputy badge and cell phone. He put them on the table.

"Keep 'em," said the sheriff.

Calhoun shoved the badge and the phone at the sheriff. "I'm a fishing guide."

"And a damn good one." The sheriff pushed the badge and the phone back at Calhoun. "I'd appreciate it if you'd hang on to these, Stoney. I might want to consult with you sometime, and it would be your civic duty to comply."

Calhoun shrugged. "I'll keep the badge if you want, but you take the damn phone."

The sheriff held out his hand. "That's a deal."

They shook hands on it.

Sam Surry took out Calhoun's stitches on Saturday morning, a week and a day after he'd been sewn up. She told him he was in good shape for a man who'd been shot in the side, and in her professional opinion, he didn't need private nurses anymore.

"It's about time," said Calhoun.

"We figured you felt that way," she said.

At five o'clock the following Friday afternoon, which was the last Friday in September, Calhoun was leaning against a piling at the East End boat ramp. His boat was in the water, his fly rods were rigged, and Ralph was sitting beside him watching the sandpipers skitter around the beach on their quick winking feet.

Pretty soon a burgundy Saab pulled into the lot. It parked beside Calhoun's truck, and then Benjie Dunbar came sauntering down. He was wearing a hooded Cornell sweatshirt, a Portland Sea Dogs baseball cap, high-top basketball sneakers, and faded jeans.

He walked up to Calhoun and stuck out his hand. "Sorry I'm late, Mr. Calhoun. I had a meeting after school I couldn't get out of."

"You better call me Stoney," said Calhoun. "Only time I get called Mr. Calhoun is when people want something out of me they think I don't want to give them." He gave the boy's hand a shake. "Anyway, you ain't late enough to make any difference. Either there'll be fish or there won't. Probably won't. Why don't you hop into the boat and we'll take a look."

Benjie climbed onto the front seat. Calhoun snapped his fingers, and Ralph scrambled in and lay down on the floor.

"You sure you're all right to do this?" Benjie said.

Calhoun cast off the bow line. "Why the hell wouldn't I be?"

"Well, you got shot, didn't you?"

"I'm good to go," said Calhoun.

"What was it like? Getting shot, I mean?"

Calhoun untied the stern line and climbed into the boat. "Not worth discussing," he said. "Embarrassing, that's all. Change the damn subject."

Benjie grinned. "Sorry if it's a sensitive subject," he said. "So you telling me we're going fishing but there aren't going to be any fish?"

"As I recall," said Calhoun, "I asked you if you wanted to go fishing, not catching. You said sure. I don't recall either of us mentioning anything about catching." Repeating the fisherman's old cliché reminded him of Paul Vecchio. Vecchio had said the same thing. "The stripers've already headed on south. The bluefish generally follow along pretty soon after. But there might be some schooled-up blues still around. We'll see."

Benjie nodded and smiled. "Cool."

Calhoun shoved away from the ramp with his oar and started up the motor. He steered through the marker buoys and lobster buoys out to the bay. The motor burbled quietly. You could hear the rhythmic slap of water against the sides of the aluminum boat. "Your old man let you take his Saab, I see," he said.

Benjie half turned in his seat. "I think he's trying to make things up to us. Me and my mom. As if he did something wrong because those cops thought he killed people. Like it was his fault. If it wasn't for you . . ."

"I didn't do anything," said Calhoun. "Far as I can see, your old man's a hero. Enduring all that, what happened to your sister, then being suspected of murder. Hanging in there. Sometimes just hanging in there takes all the courage and strength a man can muster. I hope you appreciate that."

"I do," said Benjie. "He hung tough, all right. Things are good now. My folks are getting along better, and my sister's even got a boyfriend."

"What about you?" said Calhoun. "How're you doing?"

"I'm pretty glad I didn't smash your head with that tire iron."

"There never was a chance of that," said Calhoun. "I'm just glad I didn't kill you when you tried."

"Me, too," said Benjie. "So you really think all the fish are gone?"

"It's what they do this time of year," said Calhoun. "They migrate. That's half the fun of fishing. Never knowing." He picked up his binoculars. "Here," he said. "Take these. Do something useful."

Benjie turned around and took the binoculars.

"Scan the water," said Calhoun. "See if you can spot some fish for us. You know what to look for?"

"Yes, sir. I do."

When they cleared the harbor buoys, Calhoun goosed the motor. He didn't have a plan. This time of year the fish moved fast, and there was no predicting where you might find them. It was fish hunting. Watch the water for splashes, boils, and swirls, and keep an eye on the horizon for swarming gulls.

The sun was low in the west, and already the sky was darkening and the evening fog was beginning to settle over the water. It reminded Calhoun that the autumnal equinox had come and gone, meaning that there were fewer hours of sunshine than darkness in the days. The water of Casco Bay lay flat and silvery, like a sheet of aluminum foil. There wasn't another boat in sight. It was just the three of them, counting Ralph. Calhoun always counted Ralph.

After a while he cut the motor. The silence was sudden.

Benjie turned around. "Should I cast or something?"

"Nope. Just keep your eyes peeled. I thought I saw something over there." He pointed off toward the horizon.

Benjie lifted the binoculars to his eyes for a minute. Then he put them down. "It's getting kinda foggy. I don't see anything."

"Me, neither. Not now. I might've been mistaken. Just be patient. Keep looking."

They sat there drifting in the boat, not saying anything. It was a comfortable silence. Then the muffled clang of a distant bell buoy echoed in the fog, and it reminded Calhoun that they weren't that far from Quarantine Island. He listened for the moaning and wailing of the ghostly gray nuns in their billowing habits. But the nuns weren't crying on this evening. He hoped it meant that they'd found peace now that the charred bodies of those four sex criminals had been removed from the Casco Bay islands.

"Hey!" said Benjie.

"You got fish?" said Calhoun.

"Birds. Over there. Look." He pointed.

About two hundred yards away, a flock of birds, a mixture of gulls and terns, had materialized in the misty fog where a minute earlier there had been none. Now they were circling and swarming and diving at the gray water, and other birds were winging toward them from all directions. Their squawks and cries filled the air, and under them Calhoun could see the ferocious swirls and splashes of a hundred big bluefish. The blues had corralled a school of panicked baitfish, and the birds had come to scavenge the bloody pieces of leftover flesh. Right there, Calhoun thought, you had Darwin in a nutshell.

"Let's go get 'em," he said to Benjie. "Grab a rod."

Benjie slid a rod from its holder, stood up, and braced himself so he'd be ready to cast.

Ralph sat up and looked around, then climbed onto the middle seat to watch. Calhoun figured Ralph could smell all the blood and torn flesh and adrenaline in the air.

Stoney Calhoun felt his own predatory adrenaline beginning to spurt in his veins. He started the motor and sped over to join the primal chaos.